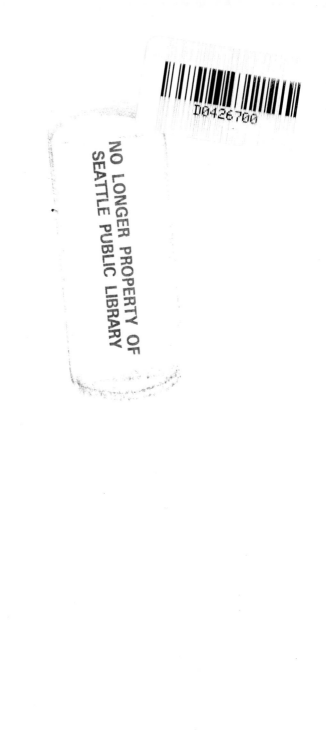

D0426700

THE BEAD COLLECTOR

Also by Sefi Atta

Everything Good Will Come (2005)

News From Home (short stories) (2009)

Swallow (2010)

A Bit of Difference (2013)

Sefi Atta: Selected Plays (2019)

THE BEAD COLLECTOR

Sefi Atta

Interlink Books

An imprint of Interlink Publishing Group, Inc.
Northampton, Massachusetts

First published in 2019 by
Interlink Books
An imprint of Interlink Publishing Group, Inc.
46 Crosby Street, Northampton, MA 01060

www.interlinkbooks.com

Library of Congress Cataloging-in-Publication Data
Names: Atta, Sefi, author.
Title: The bead collector / by Sefi Atta.
Description: Northampton MA : Interlink Books, an imprint of
Interlink
   Publishing Group Inc, 2018.
Identifiers: LCCN 2018012859 | ISBN 9781623719852
Classification: LCC PS3601.T78 B43 2018 | DDC 813/.6--dc23
LC record available at https://lccn.loc.gov/2018012859

Printed and bound in the United States of America

To order our 52-page full-color catalog, please call us at
1-800-238-LINK, e-mail us at sales@interlinkbooks.com
or visit our website www.interlinkbooks.com

"In fact, the bourgeois phase in the history of under-developed countries is a completely useless phase."
—Frantz Fanon

JANUARY

January 10, 1976

The invitation stated that the exhibition would begin at six o'clock, but by seven-thirty that evening, Tunde and I were the only Nigerian guests who had shown up. At first, I put it down to the usual disregard for punctuality in Lagos. Then I thought perhaps it was due to the rumor, which began at Christmas and spread by way of alleged confirmation, that another military coup was imminent.

Still, Tunde and I were not completely alone among foreigners. The artist, a bead painter, was Nigerian. The poor fellow was sweating away in his *dashiki* as he tried to explain postmodernism to those of us who were present. His works were hung up at one end of the hall at the Kuramo Hotel. Oyinda, our host for the evening as president of the Cultural Society of Lagos, was also Nigerian, though neither her appearance nor her demeanor would suggest that. She wore a black strapless dress that kept sliding down, so once in a while she lifted her arms in a sort of flourish. She spoke in a hoity-toity English accent, as if she had a hot potato in her mouth.

At one point in the evening, she was talking to Tunde, and I was by the table of canapés, eating an olive. She leaned over to pat Tunde's arm, and he threw his head back to laugh at what she had said. They got so loud I wasn't the only one in the hall taking notice of them. Tunde only ever laughed like that when he played with our dog, Duchess, and normally he could not be bothered with Oyinda. But he was just beginning to demonstrate how much in need of attention he was. For a moment I imagined what would happen should his neck lock in that position, which was enough to amuse me until Oyinda accidentally elbowed a waiter. A dish of tomato sauce crashed to the floor. People gasped and stepped back. The waiter apologized as Oyinda called for soda water. An expatriate appeared on the scene to advise on how to remove stains. Tunde brushed the cocktail sticks from his French suit, and Oyinda pulled what looked like a shrimp out from her cleavage.

I wasn't about to offer my assistance. I got rid of the olive pit in my mouth and stepped out of the hall into the evening air. A woman in the corridor noticed me dabbing my tears with a handkerchief. She initially looked concerned, then she realized I was laughing, not crying.

She was Frances Cooke, an American. She mistook me for a Northerner because of my surname, Lawal. She had just returned from the North, where she had visited Kaduna and Kano.

"I'm from the South," I said. "Born and raised in Lagos."

"You must be Yoruba, then."

"Yes."

"Muslim?"

"No, no. My father was an Anglican priest, actually."

"Is that the same as Episcopalian?"

"We say Church of England over here."

We walked down the corridor and sat on a bench that faced a courtyard with an ixora hedge. To our right was the hotel's swimming pool, which was closed for the day. The lamps on the brick wall surrounding us were on, and the smell of chlorine was overwhelming.

"What do you think of the exhibition?" I asked.

The artist had used far too much glue and varnish. Oyinda had advertised him as an Osogbo-trained bead painter, but I doubted his credentials.

"I'm not sure," Frances said, rubbing her bare arms, "but apparently his work needs to be stored below zero degrees."

"You're not used to the cold?"

"I'm not used to air conditioning."

"How long have you been in Nigeria?"

"Ten days."

The air conditioning in the hall had been on full blast, but I'd only ever heard foreigners complain about the heat in Nigeria. We were in the middle of harmattan, and in the mornings and evenings the air was cool enough to keep mosquitoes away.

She had a simple chin-length bob and no earrings or makeup, but she was an attractive woman and could afford to take her looks for granted. As if she were vain about appearing knowledgeable, she described her car route to the North in precise detail, complete with hand gestures. I explained that there was a minority of Christians there, as there was a minority of Muslims down south. Lawal, my marital name, was indeed Muslim, but Tunde had attended Christian missionary schools, which wasn't terribly unusual.

"He's from Kwara State in the Middle Belt region," I said. "Nigeria's womb. The rivers Niger and Benue are like Fallopian tubes on the map."

"It's funny how a country can be a motherland or a fatherland."

"Do you have any children?"

"Never been married, never planned to have any. And you?"

"A girl and boy, Rolari and Rotimi, eleven and thirteen."

Americans had a reputation for being unfriendly. They kept to themselves, unlike the Europeans, Asians and Middle Easterners we were used to. The Lebanese had been around for so long they were practically a local tribe, and the British were unavoidable. Americans didn't seem to belong, and were well known for being unable to disguise their frustrations with Nigeria. They were loud, impatient and immature, people said. It was stranger still how an entire country could be branded with negative character traits. Arrogant would be ours in Nigeria. Arrogant and corrupt.

"There's not much of a turnout tonight," she said.

"It's coup season," I said.

She may not have been aware of the shrimp incident in the hall. We were not far from there, but had our backs to the entrance.

Oyinda was usually able to draw a crowd to her Cultural Society events. The "who's who," as she described the mix of expatriates and Nigerians that normally showed up. I'd never really considered myself part of her circle, but was familiar with most of the people around. Oyinda was determined to keep our little association going. Her previous event had been a classical-music recital. On that occasion, she'd hosted some snooty pianist who had the temerity to ask that the audience not cough during his performance. He was halfway through a Mozart sonata when a rat ran across the stage. I didn't know where to look until the rat had disappeared under the curtain. Then, for the rest of the recital, I kept waiting for it to reemerge.

"What was the coup like last year?" Frances asked.

"Bloodless, thankfully."

General Murtala Muhammed was in power; General Yakubu Gowon was in exile in England. The reality was that we were expecting a counter coup. We had good reason to, after the coups of January and July of 1966 that preceded the Civil War. Last year's coup had occurred in July. Five months had passed, but there was still no sign of retaliation.

"Are things much different since the reforms?" she asked.

"Oh, yes."

"I hear a lot of people were affected."

"We all were."

I hoped she would sense my reticence. She needn't know the details. From his first address, General Muhammed had denounced General Gowon's regime. He was unknowingly speaking on behalf of the people. We were all somewhat fatigued. Gowon had been around for almost a decade and had made public his reluctance to hand over to the civilians. Inflation was out of control, and there had been several workers' strikes.

General Gowon was regarded as a stooge for the British, who seemed to suffer a lack of imagination when it came to managing their former colonies. They had supported his regime because he was a Northerner and a Christian—their assumption being that his hybrid background made him capable of uniting the country. In Lagos, we had welcomed General Muhammed's takeover and subsequent reforms, even after he retired members of the armed forces, military governors and federal commissioners. Then the second wave of dismissals began: judges, lecturers, diplomats and directors of national corporations. Our friends and us.

"They say General Muhammed has improved the civil service," Frances said.

"It depends who you ask."

"What do you think?"

"He's young. They all are."

It was my standard response. One had to be careful. Tunde was retired from the Ministry of Finance, where he had been in charge of internal budgets, but he was not one of those facing the investigative panels on corruption charges. He had made phone calls to people he knew in commerce, and Community Bank offered him a directorship. He was forty-five. General Muhammed was not yet forty, and General Gowon was barely thirty when he became head of state.

Frances pointed at the beads around my neck. "Your lapis are pretty."

"Thanks."

They were part of a set that included a bracelet and ring I had not worn. If Frances' accent hadn't given her away as an American, her disregard for Oyinda's formal dress code would have. She wore a black T-shirt, white trousers and red Hausa slippers. Her watch was chunky, with aged leather straps. She looked accustomed to traveling and was something of an enigma. Had she shown any characteristics expected of Americans, I would have excused myself.

"Were you involved in organizing the exhibition?" she asked, sitting back.

"I did the invitations. Did you get one?"

"I'm staying at the hotel. That is how I got to hear about it."

"You're a guest here?"

"In one of the chalets."

The chalets were more like suites for long-stay guests, separate from the main hotel. The Kuramo had been extended a few times over the years. The swimming pool and Golden Dragon restaurant were on this side of the lobby; the car park and crafts bazaar were on the other side, and there was a row of shops by the chalets.

"You must know our hostess fairly well," Frances said.

"Yes. She ordered her invitations from my shop, Occasions Unlimited. We're at the new shopping center at Falomo. We have postcards at a better price than you will get here. All the tourists stop by."

I knew most of my customers well enough to receive an invitation now and then, and when it came to my business, I never hesitated to advertise. Tunde would rather I didn't solicit people in that way, but the trick was to take pleasure in giving information.

"I'll bear that in mind," she said.

"And you," I asked. "What do you do?"

She was a bead collector, and was in Lagos to buy West African trade beads—millefiori and chevron. They were manufactured in the fifteenth century in Venice and brought over by Dutch merchants.

"Your chiefs wear them," she said.

"Yes, yes. I know the ones you mean."

I'd never given a thought to the history of the beads. Traditional rulers in general had been undermined over the years, by the colonials and by the civilian and military governments after independence. I was surprised their beads were not yet as devalued as they were. More so, that they would stoop so low as to hawk their beads to foreigners.

My business was dull in comparison to hers. Whenever I traveled to London, I bought greeting and invitation cards from department stores like John Lewis and Dickins & Jones and packed them in my luggage, to avoid paying import duties. The markup on my imported cards could be higher, but retailers had to have reasonable caps these days. General Muhammed's regime was clamping down on inflation.

"Queen Bee," someone called out from behind us.

It was Ade Balogun, who stood at the entrance of the hall in a white *agbada* and an embroidered navy cap tilted to one side.

"Ade boy," I said. "You're here?"

He walked down the corridor as if he were about to receive an award. That was Ade's normal gait. He had his own personal invisible crowd clapping and cheering for him wherever he went. I introduced him to Frances.

"He is responsible for the term 'African timing,'" I said.

"Slander," he warned.

We shook hands, putting on a charade. I had not seen Ade in a while and was still upset about the way he'd handled his recent separation from his wife, Moji.

"How are the children?" I asked.

"Wonderful," he said.

"And Moji?"

"She's well, she's well," he said, attempting a neutral expression.

I had not seen Moji since their separation, but I bumped into Ade occasionally. He would walk up to me and call me Queen Bee, as if he could possibly charm me, then he would hurry off somewhere. His guilt was chasing him, as far as I was concerned, and it suited me fine because Tunde couldn't stand him.

"Where's Mr. Lawal?" he asked.

"In the hall with Oyinda," I said.

"She won't forgive me for coming this late."

"Oh, I'm sure she will."

Ade was Oyinda's lawyer and had represented her in court cases involving her estate. I suspected she'd wanted to be more than his client. She wouldn't mind a Nigerian man like him— any man who could complement her cosmopolitan lifestyle.

"She's keeping Tunde occupied," I explained.

"Lucky man," Ade said, raising his eyebrows.

Oyinda and I had known each other for years, from when we were both students at Methodist Girls' High School. She went by her middle name, Harriet, back then. We traveled to England in the same year, 1952. She studied music while I got my bachelor's degree in sociology and postgraduate diploma in education. She never actually finished her degree. She dropped out to model for a while, then got married to an English chap, Alan, who died of a heart attack. They didn't have any children, and she had inherited quite a large estate from her parents, as their sole heir. Now, instead of finding something useful to do with her life, she was calling herself a patron of the arts and sharing other people's husbands.

Her need for male companionship was bordering on chronic. I'd seen her in action, attaching herself to one expatriate fellow or another and following him around until he finally gave in. She had just ended a long-term affair with a Frenchman, whom she referred to as her *inamorato*, and whose wife didn't seem to mind. Tunde called them Jean-Paul Sartre and Simone de Beauvoir. They would sit with Oyinda at parties, drink wine and chain-smoke as if they were eccentric aristocrats and the rest of us were pedestrian bourgeoisie. To me, they were the most bizarre threesome, but the rumor was that the woman was in early menopause and would rather be left alone. People excused her and her husband because they were French. Oyinda was also forgiven because she was an oddball, and a widow.

When we were students in England, she only went out with Englishmen. Some of our friends thought she was degrading herself; I thought she was playing up to a dusky-siren image that degraded us all. I actually told her that, because we were fairly close, having sailed to England together. To her credit, she never asked me to mind my own business. She just said, "But Nigerian chaps don't like me."

Her hair was natural and low cut. She had good bones— or so the photographer who introduced her to modeling in London said. To Nigerian men, she was underweight and her jaw was too square. She was too boyish-looking for their taste.

We returned to Nigeria and grew apart because her "been to" affectations began to wear me down. It was awful when Alan died, though. He had come to Lagos with her and was willing to stay. He was an architect and ran a successful practice. He was also a bit of a fuddy-duddy who always seemed to be staring at the bridge of his nose, yet he might pluck a hibiscus and plant it in her hair. Ade would never measure up to that standard.

He bowed his head at Frances. "Pleasure to meet you."

"You, too," she said.

"Queen Bee," he said, turning to me.

"Ade boy," I responded. "Tell my husband to remember we have two children waiting at home."

"I will," he said, and left.

I hoped he would deliver my message word for word. His beard was showing signs of gray. He was quite dashing. I sometimes said that to annoy Tunde, who would respond, "'Dashing' my arse." "Dashing" was the sort of word my mother would use whenever she sized up my suitors, but Ade was more like an adopted brother.

When I was a girl, I sympathized with him because he was always in trouble with his mother. They lived in a shotgun house near ours. She would stand in her doorway waiting for him with a cane if he stayed out too late with his gang of Campos Square boys. The moment she caught sight of him, she would chase him down the street, brandishing her cane. My mother was about the only mother in the neighborhood who wasn't strict in that way. Ade's was the choir mistress in my father's church. As for his father, I didn't know who he was, but from my parents' Protestant whispers managed to find out that he came from one of those conservative Catholic families that called children born out of wedlock bastards.

Ade was initially my brother Deji's friend, not mine. We got to know each other when Deji was at the University of London, studying law. Deji lived in a flat in Paddington, where I spent my weekends. I would come from Reading, and Ade, once in a while, all the way from Durham. My father was a surrogate father to him, as he was to many children who attended his church, Saint John's.

"He's an old friend," I said to Frances.

"Yes?" she said, glancing over her shoulder.

She showed no interest in him, and we began to talk about traveling. I admitted I had not been beyond cities like New York, Paris and Rome and had no desire to go anywhere provincial overseas. I needed running water, electricity, shops and full-service hotels. Museums and relics were fine, if they had guided tours. She thought I was pulling her leg. I told her no. I could barely tolerate Kaduna for more than two weeks, after which I would miss Lagos. We began to argue when she said Old Kano was beautiful.

"What is beautiful about a city of mud huts?" I asked.

She laughed. "Old Kano is beautiful!"

"I beg of you."

"You know what they say. 'What you don't have…'"

We had fun going back and forth like that over her interpretations of what she had seen of Nigeria. I insisted that

Old Kano was just another town in dire need of development, despite its history. The clay pots, calabashes and other artifacts she had come across on her road trip were simply for storing food and water. She had tried *suya* and fried plantains, which I said were the equivalent of hotdogs and fries. Mangoes, pawpaws and pineapples were regular fruit. I found apples more exotic because they were biblical and sinful. I suppose I was challenging her perception of Nigeria, and in her own way she let me know I need not patronize her.

"Okay," she asked, cheerfully, "so why does every woman I meet here ask if I'm married or have any children?"

I didn't apologize for doing that. In the absence of husbands and children, how else could women of our age begin a conversation? Perhaps, as an American, her views on marriage and motherhood were different from mine, but that was her concern.

She promised to come to my shop, and I said I looked forward to seeing her there. We must have been sitting for another five minutes when Tunde came out of the hall.

"I was wondering who had kidnapped my wife," he said.

His French suit was now free of stains. He was bordering on chubby and was also beginning to go bald but, for some strange reason, I still saw him as he was when we first met and I'd been so smitten I thought he could pass for Sidney Poitier.

In his usual formal manner, he mentioned the former United States ambassador and the present one. Frances said she didn't know either man. We shook hands before parting ways, and by the time Tunde and I reached the car park she was no longer on my mind. I was thinking about Oyinda, and waiting to hear what he had to say about their conversation. Instead, he turned around and asked, "Who was that woman?"

As I recounted my exchange with Frances, he laughed.

"What is amusing you?" I asked.

"I leave you alone for one second and you're spilling state secrets. These Americans, they come here and think they can take us for fools."

He suspected every American in Lagos of working for the CIA. They didn't necessarily have to be part of the diplomatic community.

"She wouldn't dare," I said.

"They can't help themselves."

"Why would she stay here?"

He drew a circle in the air. "She has access to everyone she needs within a five-mile radius of this place."

"Wouldn't it be more convenient for her to stay at the ambassador's residence?"

"Which Nigerians would she meet there? She is here to pick our brains, to find out what is going on so she can go back and report to her people."

"They could have rented her a flat."

"Maybe she's not staying long enough."

We were approaching his car, a Volvo that no one but he was permitted to drive. We used it at night. During the day, his office car and driver were at his disposal. I had my Volkswagen Kombi van, which our children found hilarious because it was bright orange with *Occasions Unlimited* painted on both sides.

"Why was she not mingling?" I asked. "She would have been mingling at the reception if she were a spy."

"How would you know? Have you met a spy before?"

There was a guard at the car park. Tunde ignored the man's hand signals and asked me to watch my side of the road.

The idea of Frances being a spy was, above all, embarrassing. I kept picturing her as we drove out of the hotel. Where were the clues? How did spies go about their business? She must have come to the exhibition because she was interested in beads. She had asked about the coup, but I had brought up the subject. She changed topics as soon as she realized I was not keen to volunteer more information. Americans were supposed to be nosy, yet I was the one who had started off asking personal questions. If she just happened to be here after a coup, that could be a coincidence. To me, she'd seemed harmless, though I was unlikely to befriend her, let alone divulge national secrets to her.

Tunde turned into Kingsway Road which, despite its name, was no more impressive than others. It had the same weary electricity poles that leaned over and sandy paths that passed for sidewalks. The road divided Ikoyi into two. On either side were roads named after notable men like Lord Lugard, Obafemi Awolowo, Raymond Njoku and Maitama Sule. It was dusk and we passed a block of Public Works Department houses with no lights on, which meant there had been another power cut in the neighborhood. The streetlights were also out.

"You know Muhammed is supporting Neto," Tunde said.

I was surprised. He had not mentioned General Muhammed in a while. In fact, we deliberately omitted his name from our conversations. It was difficult to do so outside, because people talked about him all the time, and with such respect. But that was the Nigerian way, to revere authority, even when we criticized our leaders, and General Muhammed had not been around long enough for the public to turn on him. In six months he had set up his anti-inflation task force, canceled the 1973 census that was so unpopular, and seemed to be making real plans for a transition to civilian rule. The common opinion was that his corruption panels had developed into witch hunts, as a few civil servants like Tunde had been unjustly retired, but they had also weeded out crooked and incompetent public officials. These days, there was hope that he might do something about the petrol shortages.

We passed a Texaco station and I thought it was best to sound indifferent, even though I was in favor of General Muhammed's support of Agostinho Neto.

"That's not enough to encourage espionage," I said.

"He snubbed Kissinger," Tunde said. "The Americans are not happy about that. They may be nervous about where he is going, especially now that he's fallen out with them over Angola."

"The Americans didn't start the war there."

"Well, they're behind most of the trouble."

"What are they looking for in Angola?"

"Their Cold War for one, oil for another."

I threw up my hand. "Always something with the Americans."

Now that they'd finally had the sense to withdraw from Vietnam, they had to find other countries on which to enforce their policy of freedom. But we were in no danger of being influenced by leftist ideologies in Nigeria. The Angolan Civil War was inevitable after the Portuguese left, anyhow. The Nigerian press was blaming it on the Cold War, as if the political parties were pawns who couldn't think for themselves. Neto's party was Marxist, and Cuba and the Soviets were backing him. The United States was behind the opposition parties. South Africa had invaded Angola with its assistance. It was the same old story of Africa, and I was sick and tired of hearing it.

My thoughts soon turned to Ade and Moji's marriage, which had thrown Ikoyi into its own civil war of sorts, with their respective friends on either side. Regardless of what was happening in the rest of the world, Lagos society was absorbed with the Baloguns' impending divorce. Their separation itself was a mess. Moji had asked me to talk Ade out of an affair he was having with her friend. I'd made the mistake of agreeing to, for the sake of their children. The next thing I knew, Ade was giving me details about Moji's affairs, though he never actually confessed to his. I eventually stopped trying to mediate, but had since learned that he'd had one mistress after another before the affair with her friend, and she'd slept with his colleagues to get revenge.

Moji was an interior designer and had clients in the military, powerful men, yet Ade had managed to throw her out of their house, and all four children were now living with him. The latest I heard was that she was drinking too much, popping Valium pills and losing her mind. There was an incident at the Yoruba Tennis Club, where she had threatened to slap him. I may not have reacted the way she had, but I wasn't the type to sit there smiling, either. I would have left Ade after his second peccadillo, at least. If he wanted our children, he could keep them. The law gave him that right—as Moji knew when she decided to sue him for custody. Why waste her time and energy? That, I still didn't understand. A sole-custody arrangement wouldn't be ideal, but she could always visit their children. Knowing Ade, he would soon get tired of taking care of them.

"Ade was late tonight," I said.

"He's always late," Tunde said.

"Oyinda didn't seem to mind."

"He's a twerp."

I smiled. He must have delivered my message verbatim.

Tunde leaned forward to get a clearer view of the road ahead. How many times had I told him to have his eyes checked? We were approaching Falomo, and the lights of Victoria Island were visible across Five Cowries Creek. There had been some talk about building a bridge in the area, but nothing had come of it.

"I ought to visit Moji," I said. "I think of her every time I see him."

She moved to Victoria Island after their separation. I could understand her withdrawal from the social scene. By now, every one of Ade's friends would be a potential betrayer, and every woman a rival. It would be naïve to consider myself above that.

"What were you and Oyinda talking about?"

"Oyinda?"

"Yes. What was she saying to you all night?"

He checked the rearview mirror. "She needs funding."

"For what?"

"She wants the bank to sponsor an exhibition."

Jealousy was such a childish emotion, and primal. It was humbling to be constantly reminded that I had neither grown up nor evolved fully.

When we arrived at the exhibition, Oyinda had asked, "Where've you two been hiding?" I'd said it was a struggle to get Tunde to leave the house, which was honest. I'd practically had to beg him to come with me. I'd slighted her effort to show sympathy about his retirement, but the truth was that General Muhammed's reforms had shaken those of us who lived in government houses in Ikoyi. Ours had been in constant need of repair and so spacious that it was tricky to explain to Tunde's elder sister why she had to return to their hometown so soon each time she visited us. In a way, I was glad we had moved into a more manageable home, though it was a little too small.

"Is that all you were talking about?" I asked.

"She wanted to have an auction," he said. "I didn't think she would have much success with one. No one buys art in that way over here."

"That was it?"

"That was it."

I was still very much in the protective mode I had slipped into after his retirement and paid special attention to my intuition, which flared up under the slightest threat. The exhibition was an overdue outing for me as well, but I'd been less hesitant than he was to reenter the social scene.

"Here we go again," he said.

There was a power cut at the shopping center, which meant that we probably had one at home. Our house was within walking distance. At home, we had works by Buraimoh and Twins Seven-Seven, who were of the Osogbo school. Tunde had commissioned a bead painting from Buraimoh. He fancied himself an art collector. He and Oyinda had that in common. I could admire works of art without needing to acquire them or rub shoulders with artists.

Our night watchman was asleep in his cement cubicle by our gate. The fellow had just started his shift. It took several honks to wake him up, then he began to fumble with the padlock for what seemed like another thirty minutes, by which time we were complaining about how lazy he was.

I was merely giving Tunde a friendly warning. He had never given me cause to suspect him of infidelity. He was the most decent man I knew, despite his occasional grumpiness.

We walked indoors arm in arm so as not to trip in the dark.

Rolari and Rotimi were waiting for us in the sitting room, which was lit by a battery-operated lantern. The house was still somewhat cool from the air conditioning. I made sure all the windows were secured and laid a towel at the foot of the fridge in case it began to leak overnight. Tunde padlocked the front and back doors, and we all went to bed before the walls heated up and mosquitoes began to surface.

"I didn't regret leaving the Ministry of Education. I only regretted not having a career."

"What career would you have wanted?"

"Oh, it's not important."

"No. If you had a chance to do it again, what career would you have chosen?"

"It's silly to talk about that now."

"Go on."

"All right. I wouldn't have minded being an ambassador."

"A diplomat?"

"I considered the idea when the Nigerian foreign service started recruiting, but they weren't recruiting women, so my best bet at the time would have been to marry one."

"Hah!"

"It's the Ministry of External Affairs now, and we still don't have any women ambassadors."

"We haven't had many in the United States. You must enjoy what you do, though."

"I do. I really do. I get to meet visitors like you, and introduce them to Lagos."

"Hey, you're a diplomat!"

"Without the immunity. I have enough experience. I'm constantly settling quarrels at home and elsewhere. And you? What career would you have chosen?"

"I wanted to be a journalist."

"Why didn't you become one?"

"I just didn't."

"You must have had opportunities to."

"I did."

"So?"

"I didn't think I was good enough."

"But you're doing what a journalist does now."

"Well, kind of."

January 11

I had a chat with Baba, our elderly gardener, that morning, as he raked the dry leaves in our backyard. Baba and I had not talked in a while. I stood on the veranda watching him as Duchess, our German Shepherd, took a nap not too far away from me, her belly pulsating. Duchess was three years old. She'd had a couple of litters in her day, but we'd never kept any of her puppies.

It was the last day of the Christmas holiday and Tunde had decided to forgo his game of golf to spend time with Rolari and Rotimi. They were going back to school in the afternoon. Jimoh, our driver, and Patience, our housegirl, had the day off, and I was glad to be rid of them. All week they had been quarreling and I was tired of playing peacemaker.

"They behave like children, those two," I said.

"It's Jimoh," Baba said. "He is the instigator."

"Patience should learn to ignore him."

"I keep telling her, but she never listens."

We spoke in Yoruba as usual. Baba worked fast for a man his age. He lived in Maroko, a town across Five Cowries Creek, and came to Ikoyi by canoe. Patience was from Calabar. She was plump and prone to tears. Jimoh was a typical Lagos boy. He drove too fast and kept his fingernails about half an inch long. He had his own room in the boys' quarters, but would somehow end up in Patience's room, complaining that her radio prevented him from sleeping and demanding that she turn down the volume. If it wasn't her radio, it was her laundry taking up space on their washing lines.

"I just want their arguments to stop," I said. "I've given them a final warning, and if they don't behave, I will have to ask them to leave."

"Don't do that, Mummy."

"I'm telling you, it's like having two extra children on my hands. I don't have time for that anymore."

"Don't sack them, Mummy. I beg of you."

Baba called me "Mummy" and Tunde "Daddy," though he was old enough to be our grandfather. He came once a fortnight and had already watered my tiger lilies and cut the lawn.

Our new garden was a riot of tiger lilies, bougainvillea, golden trumpets and hibiscus. I would have loved to spend more time there, but it was too hot during the day, even on the veranda, where Duchess had claimed the only shaded spot. Baba had tended the garden in our government house as well, and once he learned we were leaving, promised he would not approach the new residents for work. I was touched that he would show us loyalty, though I assured him it wasn't necessary. He, Jimoh and Patience were part of our household, and despite my threats I had no intention of letting go of any of them.

Someone was playing KC and The Sunshine Band on the stereo in the sitting room again. It had to be Rolari. She listened to them; Rotimi was a fan of the Wailers. Throughout the holiday they had played their records and cassettes over and over until I knew the chorus of "Get Down Tonight" and "Rastaman Chant" by heart. I couldn't wait for a Sunday afternoon of Mahalia Jackson.

"Rolari," I called out.

I had to shout several times before she heard. She appeared at the back door, wearing only a T-shirt. Then she leaned over, attempting to hide her bare legs.

"Yes, Mummy?"

"What is this?"

I imitated her. She couldn't stand still for a second without twitching. Tunde called her Shaky-Shaky, after a character in a radio drama.

"Haven't I told you not to walk around the house naked?"

She laughed. "I'm not naked!"

"Where are your jeans?"

"I've packed them."

She sounded exactly like Tunde's elder sister and resembled her, with the same pout and long hair.

"So unpack them and wear them," I said. "And turn your music down."

She returned indoors. Her father thought I was lax with both our children, but he rarely punished them. That was my duty as their mother. He would not interfere until they crossed the line with him, which they had done occasionally, like the day Rolari accidentally broke a crystal vase. She confessed she was playing Nancy Drew and was brushing it for fingerprints when it fell. He stopped her pocket money for a whole month.

"You see?" I said to Baba. "The two I have don't listen, either."

"Let them be," he said. "They're just children."

I thanked him for his work and went into the house. Rolari had turned the volume of the stereo down and was back upstairs. There was a cushion on the floor. I picked it up and put it back on the sofa. The sitting-room floor was a diagonal pattern of gray-and-black terrazzo. The room itself appeared cluttered, which was partly due to my love of knick-knacks, as Tunde called them. Apart from ebony busts and bronze figurines I'd bought in Lagos, I had ceramic and glass ornaments I'd bought on trips to Athens and Venice that now reminded me of my conversation with Frances. Her lifestyle intrigued me. I imagined how much freer I would be to run my business without a husband and children.

I could hardly call myself a businesswoman, but had always done whatever I needed to. In the earlier years of my marriage, I'd worked for the Ministry of Education. Work had always seemed to clash with motherhood, though, and it wasn't as if I could always rely on Tunde's assistance. One Friday night, which began what he later called the Kuramo Fiasco, I was nursing Rolari and having trouble putting Rotimi to sleep. He was showing the usual teething signs, pulling on his ear and crying. I didn't know what to do with him. I was hoping that Tunde might hold him, which he did for about ten minutes, before running off to Island Club to have a drink with his friends. By the time he came home, my bags were packed. Rotimi was howling, and his nappy was conveniently soiled. I left father and son in the house and drove to the Kuramo Hotel with Rolari. I didn't come home until Sunday evening. On Saturday afternoon, I had a massage at Hilda's, a salon at the hotel, as Rolari slept in her pram. Hilda was German and married to Philip Ekong, an endocrinologist. Her massages were all the rage. I called home once, to make sure Tunde had not abandoned Rotimi to his nanny.

I could not trust any of the nannies I hired. I'd heard reports about nannies letting babies cry for hours, nannies beating babies and dropping babies down the stairs. The worst was the story of a nanny who ignored a toddler as he crawled off a balcony. I well-nigh had a heart attack when I heard that one. "Well-nigh" were the exact words my mother would have used, and I'd also inherited her maternal anxiety.

For about a year after the Kuramo Fiasco we had a nanny who converted Rotimi from a left-hander to a right-hander without my knowledge because she believed it was evil to be left-handed. Rotimi was six years old before he could tie his shoelaces, and almost seven before he could write his name. He eventually became ambidextrous. I hired another nanny after her, an elderly woman, who stayed with us for years until she went and removed a rusty nail from Rolari's foot. The woman held a knife over my kerosene stove and used the hot blade to sanitize Rolari's wound.

After that I resigned from the civil service, petrified that someone might further harm our children. Tunde and I were living in the government house, though we had bought a house of our own on the southwest side of Ikoyi. Over the years I took charge of collecting the rent on our house. I was not shy, as he was, to negotiate increases.

That was when I noticed he was beginning to tire easily, and at first I assumed his workload was the cause. His weight gain wasn't unusual in his family, but he got thirsty often and would wake up several times at night to pee. Then he began to have dizzy spells and was generally unwell. He took vacations instead of sick leaves, a day here and there. He was too proud to tell anyone at work what he was going through. I finally persuaded him to see Philip Ekong, who examined him and told him he was diabetic. He didn't need insulin injections, but would have to go on a pill regimen, watch his diet and get plenty of exercise. I changed my cooking habits and he took up golf on the weekends, but his unexplained absenteeism at work had already done his reputation harm.

As soon as we learned about his retirement, I gave our tenants, a French couple, notice. They moved out and we moved in. We had a Syrian family on one side of us and on the other, the Austrian ambassador. They both had young children, but Rolari and Rotimi were past wanting to play with neighbors. They would much rather meet their school friends at the Ice Cream Pavilion at Falomo Shopping Center, which had recently been built. Through Tunde's contacts, I was able to acquire a unit there. I originally thought I might start a floral business, but on his advice, opted for a nonperishable good that would always be in demand.

That was how Occasions Unlimited began—by default, not because I had natural business savvy. Initially, I'd stocked cards, wrapping paper and postcards. The personalized invitation cards came later. Tunde joined Community Bank before I opened to the public. Running my own business was ideal, meanwhile, though he often complained it was taking up too much of my time. He was used to having me at home, but I assured him that those days were over. I still had nights when I woke up panicking over what would happen if he died. I was forced to become a businesswoman, even if I didn't consider myself one. My shop was near home. Most of my clients were within the same five-mile radius Tunde had apportioned to Frances. My life continued to revolve around the usual events in Lagos, except my social diary was now more of a work diary.

For lunch that day, we ate jollof rice, fried plantains and chicken. I made the rice fluffy, as our children preferred it, and allowed them to have soft drinks. Normally, I encouraged them to drink water. When they were younger, I used to tell them that soft drinks would rot their teeth. Now that they had hit puberty, I told them that water would clear up their spots. Only Rolari drank water, after which she declared that it was her last cold drink for the month.

At her school, Queen's College, students drank water from communal taps, and they often had shortages. King's College boys always had a regular supply of refrigerated drinking water.

"It's not fair," she said.

"What's not fair about it?" Rotimi asked.

His voice was beginning to break, but he still mumbled a lot and sounded perpetually sleepy.

"KC's boarding house is better than QC's," Rolari said.

"Because we're sharper than you," Rotimi said.

Rolari pulled a face. "KC boys behave like girls."

"QC girls don't bath."

"Maybe your girlfriend doesn't."

I raised my hand. "Enough."

"He started it!" Rolari said.

"I don't care who started what."

She pointed at him. "He's always saying our armpits smell!"

"May I be excused?" Rotimi asked.

I nodded and they both went upstairs. Then I turned to Tunde, who may have wanted them to stay.

"They're giving me a headache," I said.

He didn't say a word. Throughout the Christmas holiday they'd had silly arguments like that. I'd expected their rivalry to end in primary school, but secondary school seemed to have intensified it. Most of their friends were boarders, so they had both wanted to be. I was nervous about Rolari in particular because she was scatterbrained. I wouldn't let her board until her second year.

She soon came back downstairs to say she could not shut her suitcase after she'd opened it to get her jeans out. Tunde offered to help. I could just imagine him emptying the contents of her case, folding her navy school pinafores and rearranging her Mum roll-ons and Lux soaps. He indulged her. He would never help Rotimi, whom he called Left-Right because our son, apart from being ambidextrous, was a cadet in school. Sure enough, he had packed his suitcase with the efficiency of one, his socks, white uniforms and bed sheets in separate sections.

He, too, came downstairs, and headed straight for the stereo system. Of course he played "Rastaman Chant" again, and this time I sang along.

"Mummy," he warned.

I ignored him. I was enjoying reggae music now. The song reminded me of hymns I'd sung in my father's church.

"Man," he said and turned off the record player. "There's no privacy in this house."

"You're lucky you have a roof over your head," I said.

"We need a bigger place!"

"If we were the average Nigerian family, four of us would be sharing a hut."

He was easily exasperated, so I teased him to tame his temper. In our old government house, he and Rolari had had a sitting room upstairs, to which they were confined, but they could play their music there without interruption. They were looking forward to moving into a Community Bank house, which would have an electricity generator and a swimming pool. They were also already planning ahead for pool parties at Easter time, but I'd told them I was not having their friends running around on slippery surfaces and diving in at the shallow end.

I was glad they would spend the rest of their teens in

boarding schools, where they had rules and were relatively safe in my absence. During the Christmas holiday, I'd heard about a boy who drowned at a picnic on Tarkwa Bay. He swam too far out and an undercurrent carried him away. Two summers ago, another boy, coming home from a party, stuck his torso out of a car window and a passing lorry decapitated him. Tunde said I worried too much. Such incidents were rare, and parents couldn't always be around to watch their children. I told him that unless he had given birth to ours, I was not interested in hearing his opinions.

We dropped Rotimi off at King's College first that afternoon, and hugged him by his school gate.

"Okay, sweetheart," I said. "Do your best and God will do the rest."

He frowned, out of embarrassment, then hunched his shoulders as Tunde told him to keep away from bad company. We waited as he walked over to a group of friends, who were by the classrooms near the entrance. They shouted, raised their fists and all disappeared into the whitewashed buildings.

Rolari was next. Queen's College was farther into the mainland. On our way, we talked about a classmate who had given her trouble the previous term.

"My dear," I said, continuing in Yoruba, "anyone who makes you feel bad is not worth the effort. Avoid them at all cost. Don't waste time trying to figure out why they are like that. You can't correct them. They were born with the worst possible defect, meanness of spirit. Gravitate toward people who appreciate you and people who make you laugh. If your friendship begins with a mutual dislike for another person, it will not last. Do not expect that friends you have known for years are incapable of disappointing you, and be wary of friends you make too fast. You hear me?"

"I hear you," she said, rolling her eyes.

She, too, was becoming less tolerant of me. I didn't have to say much to get on her nerves.

We left her by the traveler's palms in the school's front yard. Her friends welcomed her, screaming and throwing their arms about.

There was a lot of renovation and construction work going on at Queen's, and the principal had staggered the beginning of the academic year by admitting senior students before juniors. The college was overcrowded, but there was no better school for girls in Lagos.

Queen's had been around since the 1920s. My mother had wanted me to go there, but my father refused on the grounds that it was secular. What he really meant was elitist and that was how I'd ended up at Methodist Girls'. I was resentful at first. To get into Queen's was a big deal in my day; now, it was more of an academic achievement, but the school still lagged behind King's in terms of facilities, perhaps because the alumni association at King's was more active. Ade Balogun was a member and amused me whenever he exchanged a *floreat* greeting with Rotimi. Queen's had less of an English public school legacy. The girls had to fetch buckets of water from the communal taps to bath. They also had to handwash and iron their uniforms and bed sheets. I thought that was a bit much, but like everyone else was proud to have a daughter there. General Muhammed's daughter was a student in Rolari's year.

On our way home, Tunde and I didn't speak until we'd passed Sabo Market, where we sometimes stopped to buy Rolari a bucket or a mosquito net. The market was closed on

Sundays, but there were street hawkers walking past the empty stalls, selling bread and oranges. A beggar stood at the street junction with his atrophied foot supported by a wooden pole.

"What about our housing situation?" I asked Tunde after a while.

We were approaching Leventis, a department store. The railway lines leading to Iddo Terminal were on the other side of us. Carter Bridge was ahead, and I could smell the night soil by Lagos Lagoon as well as petrol fumes.

"I will talk to Ibrahim," he said.

"When?"

"Soon."

"You must have some idea when."

"No."

"Why not?"

"It depends."

"On what?"

On when they had the next vacancy, he said. We'd had the same conversation a few times before. He wouldn't push for Community Bank housing because his pride was like lead under the cushion of calm he presented to the world.

"Shouldn't they give you preference as a director?" I asked.

"Why?"

"Because. You're a director."

"They can't just throw someone out because of me."

"I think you should insist. I think you should insist, as a director."

We were stuck behind a mammy wagon. The fumes from its exhaust pipe seeped in through the car vents. My temples were throbbing. I rolled my window down and heard the low hum of our engine below the traffic.

"It's not as if we're homeless," he said, raising his voice. "The house we're in is fine for now."

"Your children have been harassing me," I said. "Every day it's swimming pool this and that."

"Yes, I'm sure they will survive without one."

He would not indulge them in that way. He would lecture them about the unfortunate people around them and tell them about how he'd worked as a bellboy in Dublin when he was at Trinity College. Even I knew it was time to switch off whenever Tunde talked about his Dublin days. He would go into great detail to describe the woolen gloves he wore and the chilblains he developed.

I would have insisted on Community Bank housing. I'd even suggested speaking to Habiba, the wife of his chairman, Abubakar Ibrahim, whom I had met several times, but Tunde would not hear of it.

I rolled my window up again to block out the noises and smells.

"Stop procrastinating," I said. "Please talk to Mr. Ibrahim."

We got home in the early evening and were relieved to have electricity. The sitting room was unusually quiet now that we were alone. The television would be on if our children were at home. They no longer watched local programs like *Village Headmaster* and Art Alade's *Bar Beach Show*, having replaced them with American shows like *Hawaii Five-0* and *Star Trek*. During the Christmas holiday, I'd practically had to fight for a chance to see a Hubert Ogunde play on television.

"I've got a headache," I said.

Tunde was pragmatic, as usual. "Take an aspirin."

"It's just a headache," I said, settling on the sofa. "Maybe I should go to bed early."

He gave me a look he often gave to suggest I was being irrational.

"What?" I asked.

"We've only just got rid of the children."

"So?"

"So take an aspirin and make yourself useful tonight."

I laughed. "I'll have a glass of sherry instead."

At least he was considerate enough to amuse me beforehand. This was his usual romantic manner, to be uncommunicative for most of the day, then make an overture with a deadpan expression.

I heard crickets outside. A radio came on in the boys' quarters, and the Austrian ambassador's wife called her daughters, who must have been playing in their backyard. "Nadia? Nina?"

The Austrians were pleasant. They waved whenever they saw me as they drove in and out of their gates, unlike the Syrians, who gave a quick nod, if anything at all.

As I lay on the sofa, I thought about our former neighborhood, where we were all Nigerians and our children had attended the same primary school. After school, they had played together. We'd met up at their sports days and recitals. Barely two years ago, Rolari and her classmates were on stage, singing "Blowin' in the Wind," oblivious to its significance in the wake of the Civil War. We were at home in that neighborhood. Here, we were surrounded by so many foreigners we felt like foreigners in our own land.

Tunde brought out decanters from the sideboard. He poured himself a scotch and a sherry for me. He set up the reel-to-reel, and we listened to *Miles & Monk at Newport* before we ate dinner and went to bed. It was too soon to be bored of our routine, but I did wish that something out of the ordinary would happen now that the holiday was over and our children were back in school.

"Does traveling ever get too much?"

"Staying in one place for too long does."

"You get bored?"

"I prefer the company of strangers."

"Why is that?"

"I'm more in my element."

"In what way?"

"I'm more open, I guess."

"You call this open?"

"Don't you think I am?"

"I didn't think you were when you came to my shop. Or to my house, for that matter."

"You never gave me that impression."

"What was I supposed to say?"

"How open can you be, initially? I didn't think you were that open when I met you. You were cordial, though."

"I can be."

"Bossy as well."

"'Bold' is the word. I'm a Lagos woman. We have to be bold. In fact, if you stay here long enough, our boldness will rub off on you."

January 12

I should have remembered my wise counsel to Rolari about fast friendships when Frances came to my shop the next day. Mondays were not my busiest days, so I'd spent part of the morning window dressing, determined that Occasions Unlimited not turn out to be like some other units at the shopping center, which ended up displaying the same variety of imported goods. A few businesses, like Glendora, Quintessence and Shade's Boutique, were distinctive. Then there were a couple of pharmacies, a travel agency and, of course, my children's favorite, the Ice Cream Pavilion. The rest of the units could have anything from Marks & Spencer bras to Nido instant milk powder in their windows. My customers came in knowing exactly what they would find. Greeting cards were my biggest sellers, and the personalized invitation cards were convenient for people who would rather pay extra to order them than drive all the way to printers in the city center.

I had two employees—Festus, who was my cousin and manager, and Boniface, our security guard, who sometimes stepped in as a carrier. Festus I could trust, and often left the shop in his care to go home or run errands. He had a bachelor's degree in English from the University of Ibadan. I had taken care of his fees while he was a student there, but he couldn't find a job when he graduated, and even if he had, wouldn't have earned as much as he did working for me.

As usual, he knocked on my door a little too gently that morning and I suppressed a mild degree of frustration with him. Despite his outward show of timidity, he was guilty of ordering Boniface around and had on many occasions called him an illiterate when Boniface slammed down boxes marked *Handle With Care*.

"Excuse me, ma," he said, with his hand behind his back. "A customer wants to see you."

He had a widow's peak. Most men in our family had the same feature.

"Who is it?" I whispered.

Instead of answering my question, he gestured, as if the customer might be offended if he mentioned his or her name. I assumed, therefore, that the customer was a Nigerian, but it turned out to be Frances. I came out of my office and found her by the till, holding one of our white plastic shopping bags, inside of which were postcards.

"You're my first sale of the day," I said.

"Is that good or bad?" she asked, smiling.

"Very good," I said. "Which ones did you get?"

She had bought my most colorful postcards with photographs of the Kano durbar, the Lagos regatta and Argungu fishing festival.

"What do you think?" she asked.

"It's a nice selection," I said.

She dropped them back in the bag. She wore a sleeveless white T-shirt and a flower-patterned skirt. Her sunglasses were perched on top of her head. We were standing in the path of the air-conditioner flow, and the breeze blew right into my sleeves. It was a humid day and I was in my usual work attire, an *adire boubou*.

"You definitely have a better selection here than they have at the hotel," she said.

"No comparison."

"Theirs are pricier as well."

"Everything you buy there is overpriced. How much is it for a suite these days?"

"Sixty naira."

"Sixty? Their service had better be good."

The naira was fixed at a strong exchange rate, so one naira was worth about a dollar and sixty cents.

She removed her sunglasses. "The hotel's okay. I'm not fussy, though. My only criticism is that their coffee could be better. It's either weak or lukewarm or both. Actually, I was hoping I could get a decent cup somewhere, this morning. Do you have any idea where?"

"Coffee…"

I was a tea drinker. Tea was what we Nigerians drank in the mornings—weak tea with too much condensed milk and sugar.

"I'd love for you to join me as well, if you can spare some time," she said.

She widened her eyes expectantly, and it was a rare display of openness in a face that was usually restrained.

For a moment, I did consider the CIA issue, then I thought about Naomi. Naomi was a good friend of mine. She, too, was American, but these days it was easy to forget she was. When she'd first arrived, her accent was more pronounced. She was from Alabama and Philip Ekong had introduced us. She was a healthcare educator working for a polio-eradication program. She once told me about a dispute she'd had with a state official over her surveys. "This man," she said, "turns around and tells me he cannot show me his records because I must be collecting data for the American government. And I'm sitting there thinking, Why on earth would I want to collect data for the American government?"

Even Naomi had been accused of spying in Nigeria, yet she didn't trust the United States government, especially when it came to medical matters. She'd also told me about the Tuskegee experiment, which I'd read about without understanding how plausible it was under the circumstances.

"You know what?" I said. "I have coffee at home. I'll make you some."

Frances waved. "Oh, I didn't—"

"It's no trouble, so long as you can stomach instant coffee."

"I can. But are you sure?"

"Yes. Come with me."

I left Festus in charge. Boniface, who was sitting on a stool by the door, stood up to assist Frances, but she declined. I'd given up trying to explain that he need only do that when customers were carrying heavy shopping bags. He was also discriminatory. If a customer looked as if they were not likely to tip him, he wouldn't even get up to open the door.

We walked to the car park that led to the main road. A group of drivers loitered around the row of cars. Frances had come to the shopping center in a Peugeot with a diplomatic license plate. The driver's seat was pushed back fully and the driver himself was asleep with a white handkerchief covering his face.

"Mister man," I said, knocking on his door.

He removed the handkerchief and stretched. I pointed out my van, which was in the car park within the shopping center, under a flame-of-the-forest tree. Jimoh was sitting there with another group of drivers.

"Follow my van, please," I said.

The driver rubbed his eyes. "Madam?"

"Her van," Frances said. "She would like you to follow it, please. We're going to her house."

We were both sweating. She got into the Peugeot, and I signaled to Jimoh, who drove up to where I stood. He was chewing on a toothpick but disposed of it before I asked him to.

There was a bottleneck at the exit to the road. Jimoh had to wait for a car to reverse before he had enough space to edge out. The shopping center was not yet a year old. Some local residents had foreseen the increase in traffic and had protested against the plan, but most of the lobbying was in favor.

On the way to my house, Frances' driver swerved, as Jimoh did, to avoid potholes. I kept saying, "Take it easy," as a box of cards slid back and forth across the seat. He wasn't entirely at fault. The potholes were so wide and deep they ate into half the road. The houses in my neighborhood were hidden behind tall walls and gates. Street hawkers were stationed at every corner, their wooden stalls stocked with sweets, cigarettes and pills. They were Hausa women from the North, and their men worked as watchmen.

My day watchman wore a skullcap and carried prayer beads. During the day, he took prayer breaks and performed his ablutions in the gutter that ran beside the road. He was still more alert than my night watchman, who slept most of the time. Jimoh parked the van by the cement cubicle where the watchman was positioned, while Frances' driver parked facing my front yard. Our shoes crunched the gravel path that led to my front door.

"We could have walked from the mall," Frances said.

"Not in this heat," I said.

The short distance was deceptive. The heat in Lagos was generally dryer in the harmattan season, but this afternoon, the city might as well have been under a wool blanket.

Duchess plodded out from wherever she had been, probably the veranda. She was an outdoor dog, so she slept there during the day, and at night, in her kennel in the backyard.

Frances bent to pat her. "What's her name?"

"Duchess," I said.

We had a family joke that Duchess must have been a Nazi German Shepherd in her previous life to end up in Nigeria. Now, every time she saw foreigners, she headed straight for them, as if hoping they might rescue her.

"How are you?" I asked.

She wagged her tail. I was early. Usually I came home after lunchtime, between two and three o'clock. I asked Jimoh to call Patience and wouldn't have been surprised to learn she was somewhere else in the neighborhood. Jimoh was only too pleased to come back and tell me she was.

"That's what she does, madam," he said. "The moment we drive out of those gates, she's gone. No one sees her until you come back."

"Don't start," I said.

He stood there shaking his head as if I were making a grave mistake by not listening. I wasn't sure what irritated me more about Jimoh, his fingernails or his driving. Tunde had hired him and wouldn't hear a word about getting rid of him, yet he hardly had to deal with the fellow, except on weekends, and the occasional weekday when he was working late.

"Anything else?" I asked.

"No, madam."

"Good. Whenever she shows up, tell her I want to see her."

He swaggered off to the backyard, his bandy legs making for a comical effect. He was testing me by assuming I would be less short with him in the presence of a foreigner.

Frances smiled. "He's as bad as mine."

"He drives me crazy," I said.

Evidently, she was aware we didn't pretend we were in a classless society. It was astonishing how much we relied on help for security, transport, to keep our homes clean, take care of our children, prepare what we ate and drank, even a simple cup of coffee. Nonetheless, we complained that Lagos was a stressful city to live in, partly as a result of having to deal with them.

I left Frances in the sitting room listening to Sunny Ade and went to the kitchen to make her coffee. I boiled water and put a couple of spoonfuls of Maxwell House into a china cup. It was all I had.

When I returned, she was looking through our collection of juju music cassettes, which was next to our reel-to-reel jazz recordings on the shelf. The instrumental recordings, such as *Miles & Monk at Newport* and *Milt Jackson at the Museum of Modern Art*, were Tunde's favorites. I preferred jazz standards. Our collection included recordings of Ella Fitzgerald, Sarah Vaughan, Duke Ellington, Louis Armstrong and Frank Sinatra. I loved Sinatra's voice, whether he was swinging a song or delivering it in a straight-talking manner.

Frances held up *Ella in Hamburg*. "I can't decide whom I prefer, Ella Fitzgerald or Sarah Vaughan."

"It depends on the song," I said.

They were both superb vocalists. I had a couple of songs they'd both covered and "How High the Moon" was one. Ella scatted the standard out of the song. For me, it was like exposing chaos in the orderly appearance of domesticity.

I put the cup and saucer down on the side table closest to Frances. She was no hippie, and had probably grown up listening to jazz standards. She reached our record collection and looked at *Paul Robeson Live at Carnegie Hall, Sketches of Spain* and *El Amor Brujo*. Tunde had set them aside, hoping to find their cassette versions when next he traveled overseas. He was fond of Leontyne Price's and Miles Davis's renditions of "Will o' the Wisp."

The books underneath our records soon caught her attention. They were mostly hardback autobiographies and red leather-bound classics. We also had a few Graham Greene novels, which was why Tunde was so quick to believe in foreign espionage.

"This is wonderful," she said. "All they have at the hotel are paperback writers I've never heard of."

She was probably referring to Mills & Boon and James Hadley Chase paperbacks, which were in every bookshop in Lagos. Our children had boxes of them upstairs, yet to be unpacked.

"Feel free," I said.

She bent down. "Do you have any poetry?"

I went to the shelf and ran my forefinger past *The Heart of the Matter, The End of the Affair, The Quiet American* and *Our Man in Havana*. Wole Soyinka's *Idanre* was next. It was a signed hardback copy published by Hill and Wang in 1968.

"Here," I said. "Try this one."

The beginning of friendship was a courtship I had very much enjoyed as a girl. I was often the initiator. I would ask a girl what her favorite color was. We would then exchange notes. Rolari and her friends had slam books; hers was full of "keep on truckin'" and peace signs.

I handed Frances the only signed poetry book I had. She drank her coffee and listened to Sunny Ade's "*Esu Biri Biri*," one of the slower tracks on the cassette.

"What state are you from?" I asked.

"Virginia," she said, setting her cup down.

"That's in the South, isn't it?"

"Upper South."

"Is it cold there?"

She nodded. "At this time of the year."

I had not visited Virginia. San Francisco was the only American city I wanted to return to. Los Angeles was impossible without a hired car, and New York reminded me of Lagos—it had the same erratic yellow taxis. Everywhere I went people asked, "Where are you from?" They had no idea where Nigeria was. "Is that near Haiti?" one man asked. On the whole, I found Americans overly confident. I would have endeavored to keep my voice low had I asked the sort of questions they had.

"Will you be around next week?" I asked.

"Yes," she said.

"I have an American friend called Naomi Harris-Mensah," I said. "She's out of town right now, but I would like you to meet her when she gets back. Maybe you can have dinner with us?"

"Will it be formal?"

"None of that. It will be just the three of us, and I'll be wearing one of these. I live in them. The best part is that you can eat as much as you want."

I pulled my *boubou* to show how much space it accommodated. We were about the same height and size. In my thirties, I was always in slacks. I would have loved to get my hands on a Halston pantsuit back then. Now, I was wearing *boubous*, as my mother did in her retirement years, and my gray hairs showed.

"They look comfortable," Frances said. "I was tempted to buy one, but I'm not sure the head tie would stay put."

"I only wear mine because my hair is a mess."

"So is mine," she said, tugging on strands. "I need to get a trim."

"Try Hilda's at the hotel."

"Hilda's?"

"It's near the chalets. It's where I go. Hilda will take care of you. You know what? I'll take you there after your coffee. I haven't seen her in a while."

"You're so kind," she said. "I have friends who work at the embassy, and they tell me Americans are not welcome here."

"Who said that?"

"No one important, but they've been very helpful with transportation. I find them insular, though. I'm not used to being insular. I don't know how anyone can be insular in this day and age."

I could have told her that Nigerians were unapologetically insular. We allowed foreigners into our lives only if they didn't add stress, and abandoned them the moment they did.

"That's politics," I said. "It has nothing to do with us."

Her friends at the embassy may have talked about their strained diplomatic relations with Nigeria, but a CIA agent wouldn't have revealed that to me. A CIA agent would have a better cover than hers, surely.

"Politics never makes sense until it becomes history anyway," she said.

I wasn't sure about that, either. All I knew was that I didn't support the Kremlin or Castro, who, despite his charisma, had the same demeanor as every African dictator I'd ever seen. Nor did I care for President Ford, though I did have some sympathy for him when I heard about the assassination attempts on his life.

Again, Frances' expression was too composed, but that could have been due to her confidence. Animation might suggest something to hide. I watched out for a telltale grimace, blink, anything.

How did spies comport themselves? James Bond was my only reference. My children loved Bond films. A couple of years back, they'd made me sit through *The Man with the Golden Gun* and couldn't wait for the next release. Bond, to them, was a heroic character. To me, he was clearly meant to be comical, with his smirks and one-liners. The very idea of an Englishman who could kill any man and sleep with any woman was absurd. I had to wonder if my children were being brainwashed.

Sunny Ade's chorus, "*Mi o mo, mi o mo,*" seemed prophetic, meanwhile: "I don't know, I don't know…"

She was no CIA agent, I decided. She was just in need of company, and for an American, she was quiet.

She told me her father was in the military, her mother was a housewife and she was an only child. She got into Smith College, but didn't enjoy being in a university for women, so she left for a lesser-known college in Massachusetts. She had a bachelor's and master's degree in art history.

She asked and I told her what I knew about the history of Lagos. The Awori were the first settlers. Lagos was just a swampy island then and its original name was Eko. It was part of the Benin Empire before the Portuguese claimed it as a trading port and renamed it Lago de Curamo. It became a slave market and remained one for a number of decades. The British eventually stopped the trade with the intention of gaining control. The Aguda and Saro were later settlers. The Aguda were descendants of freed slaves from Brazil. They spoke Portuguese and lived in the Brazilian Quarter. My mother was Saro. She would say her grandparents came from Sierra Leone, but they were descendants of slaves who were liberated by the British navy and repatriated to Freetown. They spoke what they called Creole.

Lagos attracted emancipated settlers who became the elite on account of their "work experience" overseas. Any signs of foreign features were met not with alarm over what had happened to their ancestors, but with compliments on their softer hair and straighter noses. The majority of settlers came from the interior of Nigeria, as my father's family had, during migrations that began with the construction of railway lines.

When I was a girl, the city was suburban rather than urban. There were about half a million of us. We had carnivals in the Brazilian and West Indian quarters, church festivals and traditional festivals. We celebrated Christian and Muslim holidays together. Town criers brought us the news. Night soil men and sanitation inspectors kept our surroundings clean. There was no traffic and no need to lock doors. On weekends we went to the marina or had picnics on Victoria Island with our families. My parents occasionally went to the Grand Hotel and Glover Memorial Hall. Every day, I woke up to Judy Garland singing "Good Morning" from a Rediffusion box in the window of a Lebanese trader who lived down the street. He was the first person on our street to own a gramophone and played Glenn Miller records in the evenings.

We called the Lebanese *kora* because they were known to say "*ko ra*" in broken Yoruba, meaning "not buy." We called the British *oyinbo*, meaning "stranger." They lived in Ikoyi, which was known as the European Quarter.

"You were segregated from the colonials, then?" Frances asked.

"We didn't see it that way," I said. "A small bridge connected us, and since we had no business in Ikoyi, we didn't go across. Of course, after independence, we moved in and here we are today."

Lagos had about two million inhabitants now, I said, and Ikoyi was predominantly Nigerian. It was unusual to be surrounded by expatriates. She was surprised that the Austrian ambassador's residence was next door and unprotected.

"It's not as if he's the British or American ambassador," I explained.

"Does he drop by?"

"No."

I almost mentioned Tunde's preoccupation with espionage, which he extended to include European diplomats, but decided against that.

"I've taken up enough of your time," she said.

"It's been a pleasure," I said. "We should go to Hilda's now."

Hilda's salon was on the walkway Frances passed every day to get to her chalet. She had just assumed the salon wouldn't cater to her. We arrived there and found Hilda behind her till, reviewing receipts. Unlike me, Hilda didn't have a manager. She used to, but the woman stole from her. The day she found out, she sacked her and filed a police report. But the woman's relatives came to the salon to beg and Hilda then had to bribe the police to drop the case. She learned two lessons on that occasion. Now, she was in her salon most of the day, keeping an eye on her hairdressers, and welcoming customers as they walked in.

The place smelled of hairspray, and Abba's "Mamma Mia" was playing. Hilda was partial to albums by Abba, Tom Jones and Petula Clark. Her staff would sing along until she ordered them to be quiet. She was a little bully, even to us, her customers.

"What is this?" she asked, looking at my hairline. "Can't you dye your hair?"

"My dear," I said, "I've been busy."

"Why are you hiding your figure under this?" she asked, pulling my *boubou*.

I hugged her. That was her way of showing she had missed you. She tormented you. She was slim when she first arrived in Nigeria, but had gained weight over the years. She was always in *ankara* up-and-downs. Her hair looked like an Afro and she no longer bothered to press and curl it because of the humidity. Yet, she gave customers advice about dieting and criticized us for not taking care of our appearance.

"No, no, no," she said, resisting my attempt to appease her. "I don't like this. I don't like this at all, Remi. You used to be very fashionable. I liked seeing you in hot pants."

"I've never worn hot pants in my life!"

"In your slacks, then."

"I don't wear slacks anymore."

"Don't you have up-and-downs?"

"No."

"Why not? Wear up-and-downs! Show off here and there!"

She patted parts of her body. I got the impression she was trying to scare Frances.

"You have to take care of yourself," she said. "If not, your husband will find a newer model."

"*Bo*, Hilda," I said. "Attend to your new customer."

There were two other customers in her salon. One was

soaking her feet in a plastic bowl; the second was getting her hair washed. I didn't recognize either woman. On a weekend, I couldn't walk into the salon without running into someone I knew. I took a seat under a dryer that had been pushed back against the wall.

"What can I do for you?" Hilda asked Frances.

Frances breathed in, as if to brace herself. "I need a trim."

Hilda crossed her arms. "If it's a trim you want, I can do that."

She was playing the typical Lagos businesswoman, and I could understand why. The assistant who was washing hair hadn't noticed she'd spread foam down to her customer's eyebrows, and the other, who was sitting on a stool waiting to do her customer's pedicure, held her pumice stone as if it were a weapon. Someone had to control them. Perhaps, also, Hilda had not forgiven her expatriate clients for abandoning her. She had catered to most of the expatriates in Lagos before she went to England for a hysterectomy. She came back to find her former business partner, Kamal, a Lebanese man, had taken her clientele and set up a salon in Federal Palace Hotel. She stopped speaking to Kamal after that. "He can't keep his big mouth shut," she once told me. "'*Bonjour, bonjour*,' all over the place. They will soon find out. Let them go to him. From now on, I only deal with my fellow Nigerians."

For a German, Hilda sounded more Nigerian than any of us. She'd learned English, pidgin and otherwise, from her hairdressers and all manner of expatriate customers, so she could use an expression like "come a cropper" one moment and another like "*siddon* there," the next.

"You'd better not give Frances a bad impression," I warned.

"Why would I do that?" she asked, laughing.

Frances finally smiled. "I was beginning to think I was sign-ing up for beauty boot camp."

Hilda turned to me. "What?"

"Military training," I said.

She knew exactly what Frances meant. She did the same to her husband, Philip, who would sigh and say, "These Germans," as if they were of inferior intelligence.

"Don't worry," she said to Frances. "I will take care of you. I take care of all my customers. Ask Remi."

"She does," I said.

Hilda snapped her fingers. "I'm even better than that Vidal man."

"Sassoon?" Frances asked.

"Yes. I can cut a bob better than him and there is no boot camp here."

She had the temerity to look hurt. I got up and put my arm around her shoulders. She was as pale as the day she arrived.

"Why don't I see you anymore?" she said.

"My dear, I've been busy."

She smiled. "Biola, too, says she hasn't seen you since last year."

Hilda was discreet, but she had a way of dropping hints about what she knew. I was sure she was referring to the fact that Biola Kasumu and I were no longer friendly.

Of all the people who had distanced themselves after Tunde's retirement, the Kasumus had surprised me the most. Biola's husband, Muyiwa, worked for the Ministry of External Affairs. They were Rotimi's godparents and were based in Rio for a while. Now Muyiwa's posting was over, they were back in Lagos. During their previous hiatuses, I would see Biola almost every day and Rolari would play with her daughters.

"How is Biola doing?" I asked.

"She's fine," Hilda said.

"It's true I haven't seen her in a while."

"You know she can't drive. Every time she comes here it's by taxi."

"I know, I know," I said.

I didn't expect the Kasumus to offer more than the usual commiserations when Tunde was retired from the civil service. They had their own problems. The ministry had put them up at Federal Palace Hotel for several months before they got their temporary government accommodation. They had since settled in, but we had not heard from them, and I was no longer surprised. Why would they bother with us when they had nothing to gain? Why would they bother when they were busy visiting whomever they needed to in order to secure their next posting overseas?

"I'll leave you in Hilda's hands," I said to Frances.

"I'll call you," she said.

"No, I will call," I said. "We should try and get together before the dinner with Naomi."

"That would be great."

I turned to Hilda. "How's my brother Philip?"

"He's fine," she said. "How is my brother Tunde?"

"Very well."

"Greet him for me."

Philip and Hilda met in West Germany during his medical training. We were not in and out of each other's homes, so I didn't know much about her background, but she came from a small town, according to Philip, and grew up believing Africans lived in trees. Some of her family had fled to England and America during World War II. They were Jews, Philip was

Catholic and I wasn't sure what religion their children followed, but their son was in his first year at Saint Gregory's College and their daughter was in her third year at Holy Child College. Hilda learned how to oil and plait her hair. It took me a while to trust her with mine.

"*Odabo*," I said, patting her shoulder.

"*Odabo*," she said.

That evening, Tunde came home from work while I was taking a bath. Our bathroom was steamy and smelled of my Fa body wash when he walked in.

"Mr. Lawal," I said. "How are you?"

"All right," he said, unknotting his tie.

He stood by the bidet our French tenants had installed. This was his brief period of respite. Usually, he would find me in the sitting room, where he would rest for a moment, after which he'd get up and pour himself a scotch, especially if I began to talk too much. There was a long history of unauthorized budget increases and inexplicable variances in the bank's accounts. He was still sifting through the mess his predecessor had left. I could understand his need to prove to the bank, and to himself, that the regime had been wrong to retire him. I just wished he wouldn't push himself so hard.

I told him about Patience, whose uniforms were getting tighter. She would need a new set soon. Her uniforms were hanging off her when she started working for us. Back then we could barely get a whisper out of her. These days, she was hurling abuses at Jimoh through the kitchen window. She returned from wherever she'd disappeared to in the afternoon and was dragging her feet when I asked her to cut onions. Before I knew it, she was fast asleep with her head on the countertop.

"You're spoiling her," Tunde said.

"Goodness, I forgot. Can you ask her to take your food out of the oven when you get downstairs?"

He gave me his usual bemused look, so I explained that I'd invited Frances home and taken her to Hilda's, which had thrown off my day.

"The woman is opening a dossier on you as we speak," he said.

"She's not a spy, Lawal."

"I just hope she hasn't bugged our house. Did you leave her alone?"

"Only for a few minutes."

"Wonderful. We're under surveillance."

I laughed. He was insular these days and, like Frances, I was not used to being insular.

"I'm glad she has Hilda to keep her company," I said.

He stood up and bent his neck from side to side. "I'm sure they'll have fun colluding with each other."

The water in the tub was getting lukewarm, so I reached over and turned on the hot tap. Our plumbing was hopeless. The water trickled out.

"Can you believe Hilda thinks I have been avoiding Biola?" I said. "Biola must have told her that. She can't come to our house because she doesn't drive, yet she knew how to find her way to Hilda's? I ought to visit her and put the ball in her court."

"As you wish," he said, heading for the door.

"Will you come with me?"

"No. You women can sort yourselves out."

He pretended he was above my falling-out with the Kasumus, but I was sure he was just as hurt by their behavior. He was the only person I could talk to about them without fear of sounding childish.

"Don't forget to speak to Patience," I said.

"About what?"

"Your food, of course," I said.

He gave me the same puzzled look before he walked out. He wasn't putting it on, either. I could count on one hand the number of times he had stepped into a kitchen in our entire married life.

"I have better friendships with men."

"I only have friendships with women. Though, I do have one that's proving rather difficult."

"Yes?"

"It's been like this for a while and I don't know what to do about it."

"Why hold on to a friendship that doesn't work?"

"Because I can easily disappear. I disappear until things improve."

"With men you don't have the endless wrangling, though."

"I don't talk to men the same way I talk to women."

"Why not?"

"I just don't."

"Oh, I do."

"Really? What do you talk about?"

"Anything. Everything. It helps to have a common interest, like a sport."

"The last time I played any sport I was a teenager."

"What did you play?"

"Netball."

"That cuts out most men! Would you consider playing golf with your husband?"

"Absolutely not."

"You could just accompany him around the golf course."

"I talk to him only when I can get his full attention. But I can't imagine having more than a casual discussion with another man."

"Why not?"

"It might cause complications."

"Your husband is your only male friend?"

"My closest friend. He tolerates my bad behavior. With my women friends, there might be repercussions."

"See what I mean?"

"I still prefer friendships with women."

"I admire your determination."

January 14

Biola sat on a sofa eating pistachio nuts, her legs neatly tucked away. She wore a brocade *iro* and *buba* with a matching head tie that lifted her eyebrows into haughty arches. Her rhythmic popping and crunching were audible above the whirr of the air conditioner behind her. She picked the nuts out of a glass jar and discarded the empty shells in a china saucer on her side table. Her timing was remarkable.

I listened as she talked. The government house allocated to her family was unsuitable, she said. Its cemented front yard flooded during the rainy season. She couldn't wait to leave Lagos. The traffic was awful. Muyiwa's posting to Madrid had been delayed by the Ministry of External Affairs. Their daughters were in Ibadan, meanwhile, at the International School. They would have to remain there so as not to interrupt their education. She was upset about some teacher who, the previous term, would not stop punishing their eldest daughter.

"You know these teachers," she said. "They can get envious. They hear she's an ambassador's daughter and before you know it, they're targeting her."

I was bored. Left to Biola, her daughters could do no wrong. But I'd seen them ordering their houseboy around and refusing to eat *moi moi* for breakfast because that was "so Nigerian."

I was struggling for something to say. Usually, Biola and I talked about our children and husbands. Sometimes, we'd talked about other people until her gossip took a spiteful turn I couldn't abide. I didn't mind reciprocating with an amusing tidbit, but it had to be harmless.

She fell silent for a moment, so I started going on about Oyinda's exhibition to compensate for my indifference.

"I have nothing against her cultural events," I said. "Nothing whatsoever. I think we need more cultural events around here, but she invites me to an exhibition and all she can come up with is a third-rate artist? That is when I take issue, because I've paid my yearly dues as a member of that society. That's all I'm saying. It's the mediocrity, the mediocrity I can't stand."

"I don't know how you can stand Oyinda," she said, cracking a nut open.

I took a sip of tonic water and the bubbles tickled my nose. Our conversation was going nowhere. Really, I couldn't care less about Oyinda's cultural events, and I'd come to see Biola as if I were attending a funeral—and almost as reluctantly. Perhaps it was a funeral, after all, because there was nothing left of our friendship. Nothing but embarrassment.

"Ade was there in all his glory," I said, offering more bait.

"Ade Balogun. He's such a showman."

"He arrived late, as usual."

"On his own?"

"On his own."

"To be honest," she said, dropping shells on the saucer, "he's better off without that woman. When things get that bad, you should just end your marriage. They fought too much. They were disgracing themselves everywhere. There was far too much bitterness between them. I mean, don't you ever wonder how such a good-looking couple could have produced such ugly children?"

To me, the Balogun children just looked as if they lacked confidence.

"They're well behaved," I said.

"I don't know about that. I hear their son smokes marijuana."

"Really?"

"My daughters said. They said he even sneaks out of school to buy it."

"That's a shame."

I was shocked, though I downplayed my reaction. Of course, even in boarding school, children found ways to circumvent rules.

"What school is the boy in, again?" Biola asked.

"Igbobi College," I said.

"No wonder. There are too many ruffians there."

"Igbobi is not a bad school."

My brother Deji was an Igbobi man, and actually referred to himself as such. He could still remember every verse of the school song.

"It's not exactly King's," Biola said. "I hear Ade was disappointed because the boy didn't get into King's, but we can't all be intelligent."

I could ignore her occasional spitefulness before, but not anymore.

"The quota system makes it harder for Lagos entrants," I said.

She shrugged. "Some still manage to get in."

She looked so smug sitting on her sofa. It had been shipped from Rio with all the other items of furniture in the room. They were in shades of a reddish wood and so elegantly crafted they clashed with the lopsided Public Works Department windows and clumsily fitted air conditioner, which was now spluttering.

How Biola had come to the conclusion that Ade was better off without Moji and not the other way around, I did not know.

Muyiwa himself had fathered a son by another woman during one of their hiatuses in Lagos, and for years I was unaware. I was furious when I found out. Tunde defended him, telling me, "A man needs an heir," as if that was sufficient reason. He had withheld the information from me because he knew I would turn on him, which I did. I accused him of being an accomplice to Muyiwa's infidelity, to which he replied, "You should consider yourself lucky."

The Kasumus were practicing Muslims, but not in an overtly polygamous way. Muyiwa had to break the news about his son to Biola, who apparently attacked him so viciously he barely had a shred of his shirt left by the time she finished with him. She eventually forgave him, as best as a woman could under the circumstances.

I couldn't think of anything else to say to her. Our husbands wouldn't have as many unsuccessful attempts to make conversation, which probably meant we would never have been friends if they were not. I could understand her general displeasure after what Muyiwa had done, but what had I ever done to offend her?

"You hear that?" she said, as the air conditioner shuddered to a halt. "The whole place is falling apart. You would think that after serving your country overseas, someone would put you up in better accommodation than this."

The house was a typical one for External Affairs families. It had four bedrooms and a boys' quarters. Families came and went, and shipped their furniture in and out. There was no continuity, especially when it came to maintenance.

They were lucky to get one. Muyiwa was not one of the pioneer diplomats of the Nigerian foreign service who were trained by the Commonwealth Relations Office. A graduate of Fourah Bay College, Sierra Leone, he was recruited after independence. He finished his apprenticeship in Madrid, where he learned Spanish, and was later posted to Leopoldville and Abidjan. Biola didn't enjoy living in either city, but she disliked Abidjan more—the same old story about francophone Africans acting more French than the French.

There was a time when I'd wanted to be married to an ambassador, but through Biola I'd heard about the fighting and backstabbing that went on in the foreign service, and the groveling for promotions. Every foreign service officer wanted to be in cities like Madrid, Paris, Bonn, London and New York. Not all of them got opportunities to, even when they were on good terms with the External Affairs commissioner.

"How are things with your new commissioner?" I asked, desperate for a more interesting subject.

Biola picked out another pistachio. "Fine. He will be at the cocktail party we're going to this weekend. You must have heard about the promotions in the army."

"Yes."

"There's going to be trouble."

"Why?"

"Bisalla is not happy."

Bisalla was the Defense commissioner. The new government was headed by military men like him. The state governors were in the military, so was half the cabinet, including the federal commissioner for External Affairs. They were Civil War veterans, trained at Sandhurst and Aldershot.

"What is he unhappy about?" I asked.

Biola looked up briefly. "He thinks he should be on a higher rank. You know these army men. Once you upset the balance, you're in trouble. Let's pray someone doesn't decide to overthrow General Muhammed. I hope they will at least give him time to finish what he's started. Did you hear about his speech at the OAU conference in Addis?"

"No."

"Ah, he told the Americans off for interfering in African politics. He even declared his support for Agostinho Whatever –his-name-is."

I wasn't aware of the Organization of African Unity conference, or how it pertained to the Angolan Civil War, but General Muhammed was a captivating speaker. Whenever he appeared on television, I was compelled to watch. His height and Hausa accent worked in his favor.

"Angola is a disgrace," I said. "I don't know why we Africans continue to kill each other, or why we blame the Americans for what is happening there."

For a moment, Biola had a sincere expression, but what I sometimes regarded as a sincere expression, while Tunde was eating, was often caused by indigestion. She coughed and her eyes welled up.

"Are you all right?" I asked.

She patted her chest and cleared her throat. "Yes. I swallowed too fast. The Americans…are just using the Jonas man. I blame the Portuguese. They ran that country…as if it belonged to them. They didn't want to leave."

"But they've left now."

"The damage is already done," she said, dabbing her eyes with her sleeve. "They suppressed those people…and turned them against each other."

That was Biola's way. She might not know MPLA from UNITA, Agostinho Neto from Jonas Savimbi, because she could never remember names, but she remained on top of current affairs to keep up with the political discussions she had with Muyiwa. She basically repeated his views. She was shrewd rather than intelligent. It was easy to pick holes in her arguments.

"African leaders can't keep accepting help from just anyone," I said. "I've never trusted the Soviets, and to be honest, I don't trust Castro, either."

"Fidel? Why not?"

"What is his love affair with Africa about? It's not as if he loves Afro-Cubans that much. We want to be independent, but we have no business with socialism. He keeps supporting these half-baked revolutions. First, it's the Congo, and now it's Angola. He's just using us like the rest of them."

"I like Fidel."

"Why? Because of his charisma?"

"Who else are you going to trust? The Americans? Those animals in South Africa?"

"Animals have more humanity."

"You see? Fidel cares. He's one of us."

I took another sip of tonic water. Why did I bother coming to her house? What did I expect would change? We couldn't even agree on politics. I should have said she probably wouldn't be able to complain about government housing in a country like Cuba, but she might have ridiculed me by suggesting I had nothing better to do.

The Kasumus had been in the Congo after the Katanga secession. Biola's opinion on the Congo was that if we thought the British were bad, we should see how barbaric the Belgians were. "At least the British allowed Nigerians to be educated," she once said. "Those Congolese were so backward it was un-believable." She also said the Congolese were cannibals. As a Nigerian, I could understand her propensity for feeling superior to other Africans. What I could never understand was why we so often absolved ourselves of our own glaring problems. Six years had passed since our Civil War, and of course, there was the great economic divide we couldn't ignore. The country was in the hands of fewer than a hundred thousand people. You gave money to beggars, put a cousin through university, raised funds for charity, but it was never enough.

I was a trustee of an orphanage, founded by private individuals and now run by the government. I visited the children once a month. I had my favorites. There was a girl with a cheeky smile and a boy who was unusually demonstrative. The babies broke my heart, the way they cried. The director had received mounds of old clothes over Christmas, from donors. Some of the clothes were for adults, and most were of no use to the children. I suggested the director sell them to secondhand traders, and use the proceeds to pay her operating costs. She said she would consider that, after her caregivers had taken what they needed for themselves and their families. The whole situation was hopeless.

"I should get back to work," I said, checking my watch.

"So soon?" Biola asked.

"Unfortunately."

It was a quarter past three, I was out of gossip and her constant popping and crunching didn't help. We'd barely made eye contact. She was concentrating on the pistachios as if she were stringing a row of pearls.

"I thought your shop was meant to be a hobby," she said.

"Why?"

"I thought that's what you said."

"No, it's work."

She had not once been to my shop. If she did come, I doubted she would buy anything.

Biola gave up nursing when Muyiwa joined the diplomatic service. Some diplomatic wives stayed in Lagos and held on to their jobs. Despite their fancy houses overseas, their husbands were basically civil servants. She couldn't drive because she'd never learned how. Even if she could drive, Muyiwa didn't own a car in Lagos, where he used an official one.

She could not possibly be resentful about my shop. We both knew women who were lawyers, judges, accountants and doctors; high-achieving Soroptimist and Zonta International professional types who would consider me no more than a housewife. They came from families that encouraged them to pursue careers at a time when most women were being groomed for marriage. In my family, only my brothers were given the opportunity to follow careers of their choice. Deji chose to study law and our brother, Akin, medicine. I had two options, nursing or teaching. Joining the Ministry of Education was an adventure. But women I'd worked with at the ministry were now senior civil servants, and as far as successful business-women were concerned, I could, off the top of my head, name one who had several directorships and another who had made a fortune from selling gold jewelry. I needn't go that far. The reason I was sitting with Biola on a weekday, in the afternoon, watching her eat pistachio nuts, was that I was no longer in their league, so what was she so disgruntled about?

"What is happening with your housing?" she asked.

"Tunde is taking his time," I said, reaching for my bag.

"You have to push a man, you know."

I stood up feeling exhausted. Whoever said it was wise to keep enemies closer than friends hadn't considered instances when it was impossible to distinguish one from the other.

"How is Muyiwa?" I asked.

She sighed. "He comes and goes. He keeps telling me he is working on getting us out of here. Let us hope that is what he's doing."

She didn't trust him, and I didn't blame her. I would wonder about my husband's whereabouts if he had another family in Lagos. I hoped that Muyiwa would get his posting to Madrid soon. I also hoped that Biola would not feel obligated to return my visit.

"Greet him for me," I said.

I could have added "whenever he comes home," but I didn't care for her way of winning fights. It was underhanded and cowardly.

"The truth is, Frances, I'm committed to friendships rather than determined to make them work. I don't put much effort into fixing them when they're not, but loyalty is important to me."

"Listen, let me tell you something about loyalty and commitment…"

"What?"

"Gosh, I've forgotten what I was about to say! I can't even commit to a thought!"

"It must be the beer."

"Where was I? Oh. When I was in high school, I had a choice to take violin lessons, piano lessons or both. Most girls took both. If you were one of the few like me who didn't have a piano at home, you chose violin lessons. Well, my father bought me a violin, and he made me promise I wouldn't give up my lessons. But I hated my violin teacher. I couldn't stand her. She was a crusty old thing and she spat when she talked. She would yell, 'Play it with conviction,' this close to me."

"No!"

"I didn't know what to do. I couldn't just stop playing and wipe my face clean."

"Why didn't you tell your father?"

"Loyalty and commitment mattered to him."

"I'm not loyal or committed that way. I would have given up immediately."

"I wanted to, so badly, but I was stuck with the violin until I left that school. I learned a valuable lesson. From then on, I promised myself I would never commit to anything I didn't want to. I graduated *high school and got into Smith College. I didn't like it, so I left. To this day, I hear that woman's voice, 'Play it with conviction!'"*

"Do you?"

"No thanks to her."

"Your father must have been strict."

"He had his principles."

"And your mother?"

"She was what you might call a Southern belle. Good manners mattered to her. She was from South Carolina. She fussed over you and doted on you. She came from a close family. They never warmed to my father, though."

"Why not?"

"They thought she could do better for herself."

"Being in the military wasn't good enough?"

"Her father was a lawyer, so were her brothers, but it wasn't about that. There's a lot of respect for the military in the South. But he was a Yankee."

"Aren't all Americans?"

"Not within America. He was from up north."

"What state?"

"Pennsylvania."

"Interesting. My mother had a group of friends. My father called them tea-and-biscuit Africans. He had no patience for them. They were very colonial. Or should I say, they imitated colonial mannerisms. They never quite got them right. I didn't mind them, though. In fact, they were a source of amusement for me. I was too young to understand what colonialism was all about, and since I had no idea why they behaved the way they did, I just thought they were…"

"What?"

"…eccentric?"

January 15

I returned to my shop after lunch on Thursday to find out a customer had collected her invitation cards in my absence and left without paying. Festus had written down her name as Mrs. Hernandes. I knew her as Aunty Eugenia. She was exactly the sort of customer who would consider Festus too much of an underling to deal with, and he wouldn't have had the nerve to stop her. She was pleased with the cards, he said, but had refused to pay for them.

"Why?" I asked.

"She said she would like to speak to you first," he said.

Aunty Eugenia wasn't the sort to avoid paying a bill. She probably wanted a discount. I decided to call her, even though I was annoyed she had treated Festus that way. I also wished he wouldn't be so deferential to customers. He was too easily intimidated by them. During the Christmas holiday, I'd had to intervene when a customer berated him over an order. This woman changed the time of her party, after her invitations had been printed, and demanded that Festus print a new set of cards. Festus was trying to explain why she would have to place a new order, but she kept interrupting him, finally asking, "Do you know who I am?" I would normally do anything to pacify a customer, but I came out of my office and said, "Madam, you can't talk to him that way." She was exactly as I imagined, overdressed, with an accusing look in her eyes. "Are you the owner of this place?" she asked. I said, "Never you mind. All you need to know is that you can't talk to him that way." She said she could speak to Festus any way she pleased and I had no right to be rude to her. I asked her to leave. She tried to slam my shop door, not realizing it was faulty and could only be shut from the inside. Boniface was only too happy to assist her.

Festus and I were second cousins. His grandfather and mine were brothers. My grandfather converted to Christianity while his rejected it. Their family would rather have had my grandfather dead than converted, so he ran away to a Christian settlement to escape their threats. Missionaries taught him how to read and write English. The English missionary who baptized him stripped him of his family name, Durodola, and gave him the surname Thomas.

A generation later, my father attended seminary school and became an Anglican priest. He was a Thomas while Festus' father remained a Durodola. My father eventually persuaded Festus' father to convert to Christianity, and as his church services were held in Yoruba, Festus' father was able to follow them whenever he attended Saint John's. Festus' father also continued to practice polygamy, in the tradition of their forefathers. He was a cocoa farmer and Festus' mother was his last wife. He married her when he was in his late fifties and she was a mere nineteen years old. After they married, his farming business began to flounder, so his other wives blamed her for bringing bad luck to the family and ostracized her.

I'd often wondered what the Durodola side of the family would be like had Festus' grandfather converted to Christianity when mine did. In the end, I had to conclude that the only difference would be financial. On the Thomas side of the family, Christianity led to education, and education led to secular professions, which was the usual progression. My mother's Saro ancestors had almost certainly been coerced into Christianity and suffered atrocities in the New World to learn the language of their masters. But they returned to Lagos as free people and lorded it over the indigenes, until the indigenes caught up and surpassed them.

Aunty Eugenia was of Aguda descent. Her great-grandfather was an *emancipado*. Born a Franco and once married to a Hernandes, she still believed in her innate superiority. When I was a girl, her late husband's family home, Hernandes House, was one of the finest on Kakawa Street in Lagos, but it had long been demolished and was now replaced by hovels. As far as Aunty Eugenia was concerned, she came from old money, even though it was a mere two generations old and had since dwindled. She associated herself with titled women like Lady Kofo Ademola and Lady Oyinkan Abayomi, though her husband was never actually knighted; he was awarded an MBE. My mother would have said she was well-bred; my father would have called her a tea-and-biscuit African.

Her housegirl answered the phone after a couple of rings.

"Ello?"

"Hello," I said.

"Dis is Fatimoh."

"Can I speak to Mrs. Hernandes, please?"

"Dis is Fatimoh."

Aunty Eugenia grabbed the phone from her. "Give me that! How many times do I have to tell you? You ask, 'Who is speaking, please?' Honestly, use your head for once. Yes?"

"Good afternoon, ma," I said. "It's Remi Lawal here."

I pictured her with her gray wig parted in the center. I had to repeat my name several times.

"Remi," she finally said. "I didn't realize it was you. It's this new girl I have. I'm training her. She's having trouble learning telephone manners."

Her voice was low and gravelly. I was right about the bill. She wanted a discount.

"This won't do," she said. "I've known you for too long."

"Of course, ma," I said.

I gave her twenty-five percent off.

"What!" she said. "Is that all?"

"It's cost price, ma," I said.

In fact, it was slightly above cost price.

"I've known you since you were a child," she said. "Doesn't that count for something?"

I laughed. "All right, ma. I'll accept what you give."

"Don't expect me to come back to your shop to pay you," she said.

"I'll pay you a visit, then," I said.

It was all I could do, short of giving her the invitations for free.

I had more sympathy for Festus after the phone call. I'd forgotten how formidable Aunty Eugenia was. She was about to turn eighty, and her children had organized a series of festivities leading up to the day. The invitations were for a soirée she was having with her close friends. Most of her generation had not lived long. My mother had only made it to 1964.

My mother wasn't born into privilege, as Aunty Eugenia was. She was an only child and her mother died within a few days of giving birth to her. Her father was a law clerk, who with the help of his boss, an Englishman, sent her to school in England where she got a diploma in domestic science. She returned to Lagos a proper Englander, which was why Aunty Eugenia accepted her.

Aunty Eugenia was stunning in her day, my mother said. She turned down several suitors before marrying Antonio Hernandes, a Lagos lawyer. He died fairly young—gunned down by a disgruntled client on the doorstep of his law practice—and she remained close to his sister, Regina, after his death. People thought they were blood sisters, but I happened to know she was taking care of Regina because Regina was what my mother would call "slightly off."

Regina Hernandes was a spinster. My mother said she had "flittered" a lot in her youth, by which she meant Regina had been promiscuous. According to her, Regina would drive her brother's automobile around Lagos, which was unheard of for women in those days. In the rainy seasons, she would shout, "Tally-ho," just before she splashed pedestrians. She became known in the city as Tally-ho Hernandes. Street traders anticipated her appearance when the weather changed, and would warn each other as she was approaching.

In my teens, I was friendly with Aunty Eugenia's son, Bode, so I went to Hernandes House several times. It had a tennis court, a lemon orchard and stables. Indoors smelled of the camphor balls they hid behind their curtains to keep cockroaches at bay. And Brasso—there was always a servant polishing their brass.

Aunty Eugenia must have considered me a guttersnipe the first time we met. She looked me up and down, unimpressed by my Sunday dress, until Bode introduced me. "Oh, you're Felicia's daughter," she said. "Whatever happened to Felicia? Wasn't she supposed to marry Percy Olubi-Pearce?"

I hadn't the slightest idea who that was. Bode had invited me over with a group of his friends that Sunday, including Oyinda, whose parents were Anglican. Not that it mattered. The

Aguda looked to the Vatican and Anglicans to the Church of England—or, technically, to Buckingham Palace, since that was where the head of our church resided. But we didn't give much thought to the differences between (nor to the incongruities within) our religions. There were a couple of Muslims in our group who went to Christian Missionary Society Grammar School, and a Christian who had attended a primary school founded by the Ansar-ud-Deen Society because it was near home. I attended Bible-study classes regularly and was fairly well versed in its contents, but had any of my Catholic friends asked why Henry VIII split with their church, my answer would have been, "Who? What? When?" We followed our religions obliviously and obediently, and without prejudice. For *Eid ul-Fitr*, we ate fried ram together, and at Easter time we had *frejon*.

The final time I was at Hernandes House, I met Aunty Regina while we were having tea. She came out of a room she had been resting in. She was tall, wiry and wore a puce-colored off-the-shoulder dress. Her hair was pressed and curled. She entertained us to "*Ave Maria*," her voice so unsteady I feared I might wet myself from laughing. Bode took offense. He vowed never to invite me to Hernandes House again, which was just as well. He had never been to my house because he rarely even ventured to my end of town. I went back home and asked my father why wealthy families like the Hernandeses behaved strangely. My father said it was because they intermarried. He also said the Hernandeses were wealthy only because they were miserly. They wouldn't donate a ha'penny to charity if they could help it.

Later that afternoon I visited Aunty Eugenia. She now lived in Onikan, in a house with a bougainvillea garden, floral plasterwork and wrought-iron windows. Indoors, her hard-wood floors and tapestry chairs were worn out. Her sitting room looked like a secondhand shop in England. She had silver teapots and trays, china cups and plates on display. Her ceiling fan circulated a medicinal odor, which may have been camphorated oil. She wore her gray wig with a center parting, but the pupils of her eyes had faded. I had not expected that, or the cane she used. She was more fragile than I remembered. She handed me an envelope with a check inside and I curtsied to thank her.

"Let me call my girl to get you something," she said.

"It's all right, ma," I said.

"No, we must get you something. You can't come to our house and not have something to eat and drink. Fatimoh? Fatimoh?"

She hit a tin pot with her cane. It was late in the afternoon, and I could well have been in my teens again, in the presence of my mother's friends, who scrutinized me and made comments like, "She has legs like a foal," and "Her neck is like a swan's." They were constantly comparing me to animals, and they were addicted to tea. They drank tea in the mornings, afternoons and evenings. Whenever they had tea at our house, my mother would ask me to pass biscuits around, and my father would find any excuse to disappear. He couldn't bear to be around Nigerians who mimicked the colonials. He was also aware that they thought my mother would have been better off had she married a doctor or a lawyer.

Aunty Eugenia wasn't one of those who came to our house, but she remembered my mother.

"You look just like her," she said. "You could be her twin."

"Thank you, ma," I said.

"She was always well turned out, Felicia. She was supposed to marry...who was it now? Santa Maria, I forget his name."

I had long since been aware that educated young women of their day sometimes agreed to arranged marriages to maintain their social status. My mother was supposed to marry Percy Olubi-Pearce. She refused to, which caused a scandal, but her family was liberal enough not to force her. She later met my father, who was considered a good enough suitor because he was a priest.

Fatimoh came out of the kitchen. She was a slip of a girl, with threaded hair. She had opened the front door when I arrived and curtsied to greet me. Now, she stood with her hand behind her back.

"What can we offer you?" Aunty Eugenia asked.

"I wouldn't mind a tonic water."

"Fatimoh, do we have tonic water?"

"No, ma."

"We don't?"

"No, ma."

Fatimoh curtsied every time she spoke and Aunty Eugenia often referred to herself as "we."

"It's all right, ma," I said again.

"No, you must have something," she said. "What about Fanta or Coca-Cola?"

"I'm fine, really."

"You should have tea with us, then. We're about to have tea."

It was too hot for tea, but I gave in.

"Fatimoh," she said. "Make some tea as I taught you, and don't forget a side plate of custard pie. Do we have apricots left?"

"Yes, ma," Fatimoh said.

"Good. Let's have some apricots on top. And call Mama. Tell her we have a guest."

Fatimoh curtsied and returned to the kitchen. "Mama" had to be Aunty Regina. I looked forward to seeing her again.

"Yes," Aunty Eugenia said, tapping her cane on the floor. "You're just like Felicia. She was a little younger than me, of course, but I've survived everyone. I'm still here, alive and kicking. My children wanted to throw a night party with a juju band for my birthday, but I said no. There will be no juju band for me. My garden is not big enough, and I can't bear all that drumming. A simple soirée will do. My children are insisting on a thanksgiving service and lunch afterward. I might agree to that."

I asked after her son, Bode. The last time I saw him, we were students in London and I was troubled to see he had developed a stare. The whites of his eyes were visible above his pupils. People said he had inherited the Hernandes family madness. Oyinda's version was this: "Bode's just shocked at the way he's been treated over here." To us, he was tall, dark and handsome, but the English thought he resembled a gorilla. Their children followed him around, clapping, jeering and singing the chorus of the Witch Doctor song, "Ooo eee, ooh ah-ah, ting tang, walla-walla bing-bang!"

"Bode is well," Aunty Eugenia said.

"That's nice," I said.

Bode was a lawyer. He went to England before me and returned after me. It took him a while to qualify. He was, according to Ade, the most incompetent lawyer in Lagos. Ade dismissed him as lazy, rather than mad. I thought Bode just suffered from being privileged and had never learned to compete with his peers.

"How is your husband these days?" Aunty Eugenia asked, leaning forward on her cane. Perhaps she'd heard about Tunde's illness, retirement or both. I was still not accustomed to the pitying tone that sometimes accompanied questions about him, but was in the habit of deflecting them.

"He's very well," I said.

"Oh, good," she said, settling back. "You hear so much bad news…"

Fatimoh came back carrying a plastic tray with a china teapot, Peak milk and Tate & Lyle sugar. She had two side plates, with a custard pie on each. The pies looked stale, and she had topped them with the canned apricots and drizzled what looked like syrup over them. She handed me a plate and spoon. I put them on the side table with no intention of eating them.

"Did you wash your hands?" Aunty Eugenia asked her.

"Yes, ma," Fatimoh said.

Aunty Eugenia turned to me. "She was polishing the brass."

Why hadn't Fatimoh run away? I wondered. Was she a distant relative? The Hernandeses were originally Catholic, but they had a Muslim line. I remembered an Uncle Lateef who went on pilgrimage to Mecca. He would invite his whole street to celebrate *Eid ul-Fitr* with his family every year and distribute goat meat to his neighbors. Regardless, Fatimoh's parents must have brought her to Aunty Eugenia's house, and she would probably have to send them a portion of her monthly salary. To my mind, she was too young to work as a housegirl. She should have been in school, studying for her school certificate exams, instead of learning how to answer a phone and make tea.

A door creaked open and Aunty Regina waddled in.

"Ah, Sister is here," Aunty Eugenia said.

Aunty Regina was not the thin woman I recalled. She had trouble maneuvering her backside around the displays in the sitting room. Her hair was in two uneven cornrows.

"Sister, this is Remi Thomas," Aunty Eugenia said.

"Who?" Aunty Regina asked.

In contrast, Aunty Regina had a high, quivering voice.

"Remi Thomas. The one I told you about. She's Remi Lawal now."

"Good afternoon, ma," I said.

"Afternoon," Aunty Regina greeted me, without smiling. "Where is my tea?"

"It's coming, ma," Fatimoh said.

"What about my custard pie and apricots?"

"It's finished, ma."

"What!"

I didn't hesitate. I handed my plate and spoon over. Aunty Regina snatched them from me and sat down. As she gobbled the custard pie and apricots, Aunty Eugenia explained who I was.

"She's Felicia's daughter. Felicia, who attended Saint Andrew's. She married Reverend Thomas of Saint John's."

"Who?"

"Reverend Thomas. He was reverend of Saint John's."

"Saint who?"

"John's. You know, the one near the market."

"What market?"

"The one near Saint John's."

"I don't remember any such reverend."

"Of course you remember. Of course you do."

Aunty Eugenia gave up as Fatimoh handed me a cup of tea.

"Your father was a good man," she said. "He did a lot for the commoners. We called them commoners then. Now, they're 'the masses.' But he did a lot for them. Personally, I never thought they were ready for independence. It came too soon. They should have been better educated and more detribalized. That's why we had all that trouble in the interior."

What did she think our Civil War was? A native uprising? To some Lagosians, anywhere outside Lagos was the interior, and people from the interior were uncivilized, but I'd imagined Aunty Eugenia was too cultured to come to that conclusion.

She lifted her chin. "Yes, those were the days, when people were people. These days, anyone can be anyone."

Aunty Regina rounded on her. "What are you talking about? People have *always* been people! Anyone *can* be anyone!"

Aunty Eugenia sat up. "Not like nowadays, when they're so coarse with no breeding!"

Aunty Regina turned to me. "Aren't people, people? Can't anyone be anyone?"

I sipped my tea, their reasoning lost on me. Aunty Regina dragged her last bite of custard pie around the plate to soak up the syrup. She was a noisy eater. She sounded as if she were chewing on a wet sponge.

"Do you know my nephew Bode?" she asked, after a moment.

"I've known Bode for years," I said.

"Maybe he should have married you instead of that awful girl he went and chose."

"Sister," Aunty Eugenia warned.

I hadn't met Bode's wife, but I'd heard that whenever they quarreled, she went around telling everyone that Bode was impotent.

"Bode is a gentleman," Aunty Regina said. "He is like my late brother, Antonio, of blessed memory. Antonio was a gentleman. He played cricket, you know. Antonio was an excellent cricketer. How is it you never came to Hernandes House?"

"I did."

"When?"

I reminded her of how she'd sung "*Ave Maria*," and she put her plate down and clapped.

"I had a lovely voice, didn't I?"

"Yes, you did, ma," I said.

"I was a soprano."

"You certainly were, ma."

Aunty Eugenia sipped her tea with a sour expression. I couldn't tell if she was embarrassed or upset that she had been upstaged.

I got out of their house as soon as possible. My father, rest his soul, would have been rejoicing that time had relegated them. His Saint John's was the opposite of Saint Andrew's, where my mother's family had worshipped. Saint Andrew's was full of tea-and-biscuit Africans. They showed my father respect because he was a priest, but made it clear he was not one of them. He was known as The Priest of the Poor because most of his congregation was made up of market women who belonged to a union.

"Those women aren't poor!" my mother would say. "They have more money than I do!" She had to ask my father's permission for every item of clothing she bought. He would review and sanction her lists. One day, she called me aside and said, "Remi, make sure you marry a man who allows you to buy a new petticoat when you want to." She meant a slip. She still managed to look ladylike in her handmade dresses and understated traditional wear.

I sometimes attended the women's weddings and funerals with her. They tied their head ties so high they looked as if they were wearing oversized crowns. They shook their bottoms without a care while they danced. On Sundays, they would come to my father's church, sit in his wooden pews and face the pulpit with solemn expressions. They were stingy when it came to tithing and making donations. His church roof was always in need of repairs. There was a fountain in the front yard. Not once did I see water flow out of it. The women of Saint John's would argue with him over the building fund. He counseled them whenever they had marital problems, usually over money. They were vocal women, free to carry on their trades; whereas my mother, Edwardian Nigerian that she was, lived within my father's modest church income and always conceded to his views.

My father discouraged her from joining Rosebud and other such organizations for educated women like Aunty Eugenia. He said they were elitist. He became increasingly irritated with her Englander friends during the nationalist movement, and at one point even considered changing his name back to Durodola. My mother was appalled. "I did not marry a Durodola," she declared. "I married a Thomas." They had an exchange, which was rare. He said Nigerians ought to separate Christianity from colonialism, and went on about the ills of the British. "We don't know who we are because of them," he said. "I don't think the British have done badly by us," my mother said. "They brought us sanitation." "What sanitation?" my father asked. "Didn't you say your schoolmates bathed once a month when you were in England?" "Juju," my mother continued. "They put a stop to most of that fetishism."

Listening to them, it was easy to conclude that he was more proud of Yoruba culture, but she was equally as proud. She didn't so much admire the colonials as appreciate their efforts to enlighten uneducated Nigerians. My father didn't seem to mind, or perhaps he just chose to ignore the fact that most of his congregation still held on to their traditional beliefs. He was more concerned about educating them on suffrage rights. He was a member of the National Council of Nigeria and the Cameroons party. He fell ill after the general election of 1954 and died in 1956, the year I returned from England. That was the same year the Queen and Duke visited Nigeria, and the people of Saint Andrew's were beside themselves. They had British flags on display. Their choir practiced "God Save the Queen."

To the day he died, my father remained committed to the idea of separating church from colonialism. He enjoyed his reputation as a pro-African priest, in the tradition of Bishop Samuel Ajayi Crowther, Reverend Josiah Jesse Ransome-Kuti and others. He mentioned the Queen only once in his church that I remembered, when he urged his congregation not to confuse the royal visit, as other churches did, with the second coming of Christ.

"There's classism in America."

"I'm sure."

"It's just not as pronounced as it is here because we have a middle class."

"Ours barely exists, and Lagos society is blatantly elitist."

"Yes?"

"It has always been. It has no other purpose but to perpetuate what the colonials did. We moved in when they left. We moved into the neighborhood they left. They left reluctantly. We assumed their position in Nigeria, and we're not going anywhere until we're forced out."

"You could say General Muhammed is doing that."

"No. Muhammed may have driven some of us out of the civil service, but the power is still in the hands of a few in this country. We're indifferent to the masses. Self-interest comes first. We're materialistic and capitalistic to the core."

"There's no chance of a moneyless and classless Nigeria?"

"Any such system would have to be imposed on us."

"You don't think the military is capable of doing that?"

"They're part of us."

"So you doubt that communism could take root here."

"I'm saying it goes against the instincts of the Nigerian elite."

January 16

Ashake and Debayo Dada threw a party on Friday night to celebrate their eighteenth wedding anniversary, though I suspected their real reason was to show off their new swimming pool. Ashake had ordered her invitations through me and dictated the exact wording she wanted: "Chief and Mrs. Adebayo Dada request the pleasure of your company," and so on, complete with a recently invented family crest. Festus had delivered the cards to her weeks ago, and I was still waiting for her to pay me.

Ashake was Rolari's godmother and we'd known each other for years, so we weren't about to fall out over money. When we were girls, she was called Sumbo. Ashake, her praise name, meant "the pampered one." Her mother was a union leader of the women who attended my father's church and had several informal titles conferred by them. She was most popularly known as Iya, which translated to "Mother." Any Yoruba woman who held sway in her community was called Iya, but Ashake's mother was exceptional.

She'd had three husbands in succession. The first died, the second abandoned her because she had too many children, and she left the third when he ran out of money. She occupied two chairs in the front pew at Saint John's. Time to pray, and her "*amin*" had to be the most prolonged. Time to sing, and you could hear her down the street. At the peak of the women's movement, she held a press conference, during which she threatened to shut down "the whole of Lagos" if her women were forced to pay water rates. My father said perhaps she meant "a street in Lagos" and just got carried away with the media attention. But he had to concede that, while giving her arguments against the rate, Iya demonstrated she could add faster than any mathematician. Even the press had a hard time keeping up with her calculations.

Ashake and I must have been about ten years old when she walked up to me after church, as my mother was greeting hers, and said, "You're lucky to have a mother who is as gentle as a white woman." I, being equally naïve, considered that a compliment.

I later recruited Ashake as a food thief. I was in a gang with other Saint John's girls. We would sneak into Ikoyi Cemetery to steal cashews from the trees. We would hoist Ashake up because she had long arms. Her underwear was never clean and she had an odor of stale urine about her, which we ignored for the sake of solidarity. One day, a caterpillar fell on top of her head. She screamed, we dropped her and scampered off. She limped back home, where Iya beat her for disgracing her family.

I wouldn't have minded having a mother like Iya, who was the best cook I knew. She made the most delicious stews. I was always in their house, rubbing my hands and hoping that she had cooked. Outside their house was a gutter into which she rinsed her pots. I knew I was in for a treat if I saw palm oil floating in it.

Without an education, Iya managed to see her children through secondary school, and they all became successful businessmen and -women. They were proud of her reputation, including Ashake, who nonetheless claimed that the Oba of

Lagos had bestowed Iya's titles on her. Ashake often lied about her background, and I had some idea why. As the eldest daughter in her family, she had been sent to a boarding house in Lagos run by a woman who taught girls etiquette after they'd finished secondary school. If their parents didn't have the means to further their educations, she prepared them for work and marriage. She had no children of her own, so her students became her adopted daughters. Her mission was to turn them into refined young ladies. Ashake must have taken the experience to heart because shortly after she left the boarding house, she dropped her name Sumbo and started lying. She said her father was a pharmacist. He was an herbalist. She said she took a Pitman's course in London to train as a secretary. She never did. She said her husband, Debayo, graduated from Harvard with a degree in engineering. I'd only ever heard that he had attended a university in Ohio, and assumed it was one of those that issued honorary diplomas in return for a donation. Debayo was a well-known businessman, who had somehow managed to wangle directorships with several foreign companies. His business adversaries accused him of buggering his way to the top. Ashake herself was said to practice juju, which wouldn't have surprised me. Iya may have been a member of Saint John's, but she was also a regular at the local *babalawo*.

I did occasionally wonder if some of the rumors about the Dadas were embellished. They were part of the *owambe* party circuit in Lagos, which I avoided because I had no money to waste on Swiss lace, or Italian-made shoes and bags. They arrived late at these parties, apparently, sometimes two or three hours late, and stayed long enough to get themselves called to the high table, as Chief and Mrs. Dada. Live juju bands and musicians of Sunny Ade's and Ebenezer Obey's stature praised them in song. They would sit and observe other guests dance and "spray" each other with money, as if they were above such vulgarity. People either worshipped or despised them. Tunde was fascinated with them. He hailed them "the lord and lady of the manor," to their delight. Whenever they invited us to a function at their house, he would hurry me up. He couldn't be bothered with the gossip about the Dadas, but observing their excesses firsthand gave him much pleasure.

We got to their house that night, and he asked their gateman if he could park in their driveway. The gateman said guests were not allowed in.

"What about those cars?" Tunde asked, pointing at five Benzes stationed on their graveled driveway, all black. The gateman said they belonged to Master and Madam.

"Wonders will never cease," Tunde said, smiling.

I begged him not to embarrass me.

The Dadas' house was huge, with Greek-style columns. A steward in a white uniform showed us into their sitting room, which had a beige marble floor, beige damask curtains, gilt-edged mirrors and crystal chandeliers. The whole place was beige, sparkly and full of Nigerians in colorful traditional attire. There were a few expatriates around. Ashake had insisted her invitations state the dress code was cocktail wear. Tunde and I were in traditional attire. So was Debayo, who wore a white lace *agbada* with a red-and-gold cap. Ashake herself was in a full-length red satin gown that contradicted her own dress code. She was heavily made-up, but I could tell her face had lightened a shade. I'd heard that she got chemical baths in London to bleach her skin. She had voluntarily denied that to me, swearing her complexion was natural, though I remembered a time when she was darker than me.

"My very good friend," she said in Yoruba.

I hugged her, genuinely pleased to see her again. She may have kept her distance after Tunde's retirement, but I didn't take that personally. For Ashake, having an out-of-work husband would be socially calamitous.

As Tunde went off with Debayo, Ashake took my arm and led me around her sitting room, introducing me to society people, some of whom I already knew. She flashed the ruby-and-diamond ring Debayo had bought her.

"The rubies are from India," she said.

I said they were beautiful.

She tilted her head, admiring the stones. "I'm not sure where the diamonds are from."

I said it didn't matter. She should just enjoy her ring.

She was a showoff. If it wasn't her new jewelry, it was her new car. She had new furniture as well, faux Louis Quinze sofa sets, also in beige. She pointed at a blown-up photo of her family in a gilt frame on the wall.

"We took that at Christmas," she said.

"Where?" I asked.

"Jackie Phillips."

Jackie Phillips was a celebrity boxer turned photographer. His studio photos were superb, but they didn't come cheap.

The Dada boys had grown into handsome young men. They looked like Debayo in the photograph, dressed in their suits and ties. They were in English boarding schools and during the holidays were either at the polo club or at their beach house on Tarkwa Bay with friends who were similarly placed. The whole lot of them were known as *omo olowo*—children of the rich. Poor things, they were so indulged by their parents that you couldn't help but sympathize when they ended up taking drugs or getting drunk and crashing cars because no one had taught them when enough was enough. I knew this only because Ashake often bemoaned her sons' hectic social life, to other mothers' annoyance. "It's terrible," she once said to me. "They go out with all the pretty girls in town—pretty, pretty girls, from good, good homes—and end up letting them down. I tell them, 'It's not right to treat girls badly. What will people think?'"

I couldn't be resentful of her, no matter what she did or said. I wasn't embarrassed for her, either; there was no point. She didn't care what other people thought. She wasn't interested enough in anyone to see beyond herself and her family.

We had a few mutual friends, and as we passed through the house I found myself slipping into my usual polyglot party greetings: "*Ciao.*" "*E wo lese?*" "*Comme ci comme ça.*" Expatriates enjoyed a Nigerian greeting; Nigerians loved a European one. They were mostly people from the business community. Tutu, the woman who had several directorships, was there. She had qualified as a chartered accountant at a time when only Nigerian men did, and was always the lone woman in the company of men. She stood with a group of them, in a black shift dress, swirling her brandy as they smoked cigars. She was divorced from her first husband and separated from her second, who had accused her of adultery. Arin, the gold-jewelry millionaire, was there as well, resplendent in traditional regalia. So was her husband, a chief, who had fathered children by several other women he supported. He and Arin lived together, practiced juju together, but kept their finances separate.

Ashake brought up the Baloguns, who were absent.

"Those two," she said, shaking her head. "Is it true they fought at the Yoruba Tennis Club?"

"So I heard," I said.

"I invited both of them, but Ade refused to come if Moji was invited, and Moji refused to come if Ade was invited. I called Ade and asked him, 'What are you divorcing your wife for? Look at Debayo and me, married for eighteen years and we're still together. Do you think it was easy?' I called Moji, too, and told her right off. 'Go back to your husband's house and stay there for the sake of your children. See my sons. They matter more to me than any man.'"

I could imagine Ashake counseling the Baloguns about their marriage, only to end up boasting about hers. She was not taking sides. She was equally upset with both of them.

Were there any normal, happily married couples at her party? Of course there were, together for ten, fifteen, twenty years, with no major problems I'd heard about. But they were indistinguishable from the rest, who looked just as normal without captions to suggest otherwise. The husbands: drinks too much; occasionally manhandles his wife; may have im-pregnated his wife's younger sister. The wives: on Valium; not permitted to do a thing without her husband's consent; beaten on a regular basis.

"No one is perfect," Ashake was saying. "You just have to accept your husband or wife as they are."

"That's married life," I said with a sigh.

Unlike Ashake, I was quite expert at putting other women at ease. Sometimes, all it required was a fake sigh to assure them my life was no better than theirs. We parted ways and I circu-lated, encouraged by the James Last Orchestra's instrumental version of "Soley, Soley." Tunde was busy slapping Debayo's back and looking as if he couldn't contain himself.

Not that I was preoccupied with lofty ideas, but if anyone cared to know why there was a disparity of wealth in Nigeria, they just needed to observe the guests at the party, laughing and joking as they indulged in cocktails served by waiters, only to gorge themselves on food later. I behaved the same way, despite my awareness. One moment I would be making small talk, the next I would be sipping a mixed drink.

The Dadas knew how to provide a feast. Their cocktails were followed by a buffet of dressed crab, shrimp salad, avocado salad, fried rice, jollof rice, coconut rice, roast chicken, and some pasta dish I couldn't identify. That was merely part of the European continental spread. The Nigerian spread included barbecued goat, peppered snails, and *egusi* with pounded yam. I started with the dressed crab and proceeded to the shrimp salad. By the time I got to the peppered snails I was full, but the food kept coming, and so did the wines and spirits. I had some Châteauneuf-du-Pape, followed by a little Baileys Irish Cream, which I'd been meaning to try since it came out. It reminded me of Bols Advocaat: far too sweet, yet I couldn't stop drinking it.

The Nigerian guests ate and drank, unaware of the waiters. The expatriates were more polite, yet deliberately brief. We all appeared to be mixing, but on close inspection there were Nigerians who couldn't be bothered to talk to expatriates, and expatriates who would rather stick to their own kind. The Lebanese and Indians mingled with everyone. There was a Nigerian couple who only spoke to expatriates to prove—well, I didn't know what, and an English fellow who was so pleased to be in the presence of Nigerians, he shook hands with every single one of us.

After dinner, we all gathered in the sitting room with champagne flutes to toast the Dadas. Debayo declared Ashake the love of his life, and they danced to Frankie Valli's "Can't

Take My Eyes Off You." I had to admire them. They were unusually affectionate for a Nigerian couple, and united. Even when they argued, they referred to each other as "honey," "sugar," and all manner of sweet food. I'd been with them on such an occasion, the details of which failed me because they were so trivial. It was hard enough trying to keep up with their terms of endearment. She, for instance, saying, "Honey, your head is not correct," and he replying, "Sugar, I'm warning you for the very last time not to insult me."

The toast over, they launched their new swimming pool to Cliff Richard's "Congratulations." Debayo made everyone stand behind Ashake and count from ten downward, then she cut a red ribbon tied across the sliding doors, which led to the veranda.

The problem with getting caught up with bourgeois ways in Lagos was that they would inevitably bite you in the behind. The Dadas, like us, lived in an Ikoyi neighborhood that wasn't designated for government housing. Consequently it had smaller plots. But they had built such a huge house in theirs that there was hardly any room for a back garden. We walked into what used to be their sons' playground, now replaced by the swimming pool, which was so small it could pass for a paddling pool. I ignored Tunde, who nudged me and whispered, "How can anyone swim laps in that?"

We stood around the edge so we could see the bottom of the pool, where the Dadas' new family crest was depicted in blue tiles. All I could think of, when I saw the crest, were the invitations that Ashake had not paid for.

As I applauded with the other guests, I remembered her as a girl, walking past homes like Hernandes House, knowing she would never be let in. My father had thought the greatest threat to independence was not the British but the Nigerians who were waiting to step into their shoes. He was referring to the likes of Aunty Eugenia. He credited them with more longevity than in fact they had. Ashake was proof, and if people considered her an upstart, she was staying put for as long as she could. She and Debayo could buy all the chieftaincy titles and honorary degrees they wanted. The day would come when they, too, would be replaced and forgotten.

That cycle of replacement was the legacy the colonials had left and the nature of Nigeria's independence. One day you were in, the next you were out. While you were in, it was best to take advantage when you could, because there were people watching and waiting for their turn to rule—in the army and civil service, in politics and commerce, and on the social scene.

"Someone had better pay me my money," I whispered to Tunde.

"Do you love your country?"

"In what way?"

"It's a clear-cut question, Remi."

"I'm an African woman. We don't talk about love openly."

"Okay. How do you feel about being Nigerian?"

"Please don't expect me to talk about national pride."

"I don't."

"All right...I wouldn't want to live or die anywhere else."

"That's it?"

"That's it."

"Nothing more?"

"Isn't that enough?"

"Hm."

"What?"

"You have a lot to say when you criticize your country."

"Shouldn't I, as a citizen?"

"I love my country and I can say it without hesitation."

"That's good for you."

"I think you're just disillusioned."

"We've just had a military coup, Frances."

"So. You're fed up with military rule."

"The civilians were not much better and we voted for them. I feel alienated. The alienation troubles me. It worries me. I look around and people are celebrating one event after another as if nothing else matters. As if no one else matters. Where are the people who care about

Nigeria? Where are the people who can do something to change the course we're on? I don't know. Maybe the business I'm in makes me aware of the shallowness around here. But then, I depend on the same people for a living, so I have to ask myself, 'Who are you to talk? What gives you the right?'"

January 17

I was more wary of people in Lagos than I'd realized, especially now that I relied on them for an income. My customers came to my shop to buy invitation and greeting cards for christenings, birthdays, weddings, anniversaries and funerals. They called me about graduations, promotions and retirements. Add to that, holiday festivities. In that way, I was constantly involved in their lives, and our connections sometimes dated a generation back.

I had some of my mother's cordiality, as well as my father's tendency to step back and ridicule. But it was my way of trying to prevail over daily absurdities. Of course, I wasn't alone in claiming I didn't belong to the Ikoyi crowd. Yet we came together to form a web of associations that was enviable from the outside, but aspiring at best. There were always new standards to insist on and new reasons to remain pompous. There was always someone more snobbish than the next. Or perhaps I was still resentful about being temporarily abandoned after Tunde's retirement from the civil service, because it wasn't that long ago that I would have dismissed anyone with opinions like mine.

That week I said a few psalms to keep my vanity in check, but they didn't take. On Saturday morning I decided to call Frances from the shop. I needed a change of company. Why not her? She was new in town and had a different perspective. It was only polite to return her visit. If I was too old to be falling out with friends, I was certainly too old to be making new ones.

Initially, though, the receptionist at the hotel didn't recognize her name.

"Frankie?" he asked.

"Frances," I said.

"Hol' on, hol' on. Coker?"

"Cooke."

I hoped the day would come when I could make a quick phone call in Lagos.

"Nobody like dat here, please."

"She is a guest in the chalets."

"Eh?"

I could have sworn he was doing it on purpose. We went back and forth until he finally found her name and put me through to her room. She sounded as exasperated as I was, so I asked why.

"It's the laundry room," she said. "They have my clothes, and they're taking their time returning them."

"Tell them you want them now, now. No delays, otherwise you will report them to their *oga*."

"I can't do that."

"You have to threaten to get your way. That's how things work here."

"I guess so. I really do need them by the end of today. I'm traveling out of Lagos tomorrow."

"Where to?"

"Benin City."

She was going by road. Her friends at the consulate were lending her their car and driver, who would act as an interpreter. She was meeting with chiefs and would buy coral beads from them.

"You'd better get on top of what they're doing in that laundry room," I said. "Maybe you should dash someone money."

"I did dash someone money, and he lost a button on the only decent top I have!"

"Goodness. How are things otherwise?"

"The same. I saw Hilda yesterday. She says her salon has been in the hotel for years. It's all right here, really. I shouldn't complain. I don't think I could stomach another Chinese meal, though."

"Are you free later today?"

"I'm free for lunch."

"I'll take you out, then. We can go to the golf club near you."

"Sounds good to me."

We agreed on a late lunch. She wanted to make sure her laundry was done beforehand. I arranged to pick her up between two and two-thirty. Tunde was at home, and I called to tell him about our plans.

"I forbid it," he said.

I laughed so loud that Festus knocked on my office door to check I was not crying out in pain. I signaled to him that I was fine.

"Why?" I asked, after Festus shut the door.

"I've told you what I think of her. Meanwhile, what am I going to eat, while you're busy cavorting around Lagos?"

"Patience will get your food."

"I have nothing to do with Patience."

"All you have to do is ask."

"No. I don't get involved in kitchen matters."

"Come on, my friend."

"I said no. This has to stop."

"You want me around twenty-four hours at your beck and call?"

"Come home for lunch today. That's all I ask."

To do what? Stare at his face? Now that we were alone, we spent our spare time reading the newspapers or watching the news. Once in a while we listened to music. He was such a stickler for timeliness. Food at this time, bed at that time.

"Lawal," I said, "you're being unreasonable."

"Okay," he said. "Take that woman to spy on the army, then. Just don't come back to me when they charge you with treason."

We'd joined Ikoyi Club so our children could swim and play tennis. The golf club was a separate section of Ikoyi Club. It had a few military members, which was probably why it had managed to acquire acres of prime land in Ikoyi for men like him to play with their little balls.

I didn't stop at Hilda's when I arrived at the Kuramo Hotel. On Saturdays Hilda had no time to talk, even though that might not deter her. The walkway leading to the chalets was elevated about a foot above the hotel's bougainvillea gardens. I knocked on Frances' door and was stepping away from a wasp nest between two wooden beams when she opened it.

"I've got my clothes back!" she said.

"That's a relief," I said, walking into her chalet.

She wore khaki shorts and a white tank top. Her hair was a lot shorter. Indoors, the air conditioner was switched off, but the windows were open and a table fan was on high speed. I could smell oranges. Her chalet had a small sitting room with a couple of mustard-colored chairs and an oval-shaped dining table.

I sat at the table while she went to get her shoes from the bedroom. She had a black journal and a cassette player similar to the one Rolari and Rotimi had used for their *Alliance Française* tapes when they were younger. She was listening to the opera *Carmen*. Besides the journal, there were two other books on her table and *Idanre* was one of them. I held it up as she returned.

"Have you had a chance to read this?"

"Not yet. I've been reading about your First Republic."

"Azikiwe, Awolowo and the rest?"

"Yes, and your prime minister."

"Tafawa Balewa."

She smiled. "I bought the book here. Those must have been interesting times."

"They were."

At the time I didn't realize how interesting they were. We had conference after conference in Lagos and London. My brother Deji and Ade were always discussing constitutions in his flat in Paddington: the Richards Constitution, the Macpherson Constitution, the Lyttelton Constitution. They had a friend called Mark, who showed up occasionally. Mark was Welsh and had helped a few Nigerian students get flats because landlords were reluctant to rent to us. He thought that entitled him to drop in whenever he wanted, to eat my rice and chicken stews. He was such an anti-imperialist, and through him I learned about British tribalism. Prior to that, the Welsh, Irish and Scots were all English to me.

Frances sat at the table. "I can imagine how exciting it was when you got your independence."

"It was a wedding day," I said. "A wedding day for Nigeria."

The only black president we'd ever had in Africa was President Tubman, who was an American-Liberian. After the 1954 elections, Azikiwe became premier of Eastern Nigeria and Awolowo premier of Western Nigeria. The British granted the East and West self-governance in 1956. The North finally accepted it in 1959. Then Ghana became a republic, giving them President Nkrumah.

For Nigeria 1960 was more like a honeymoon year. Lagos dressed up in green and white ribbons and flags on Independence Day, October 1. We had gun salutes, RAF bombers flying over us and regattas on the lagoon. People gathered at the racecourse in the city center, under the floodlights, to send the governor general, James Robertson, off. Princess Alexandra of somewhere showed up. Harold Macmillan had visited earlier in the year. At midnight the flag went up and the crowd cheered. Church bells rang. Tunde and I were in Kakadu nightclub dancing to Victor Olaiya and Bobby Benson. Highlife music was all the rage. We raised our glasses and toasted Nigeria.

"What happened to the sense of unity?" Frances asked.

"Reality followed, I suppose."

"But there was so much hope that Nigeria would survive as a federation."

"We've never lost that."

I was being defensive. There had never been an extended period of solidarity. Even before independence, political parties had had disputes as they scrambled for territory and sought alliances.

Frances moved her hands as if she were choosing her words carefully. "The impression I get is that the British favored the North by placing it in a dominant position."

I tried to be just as calm. She wouldn't be accustomed to such a discussion ending up with raised voices. I still had vivid memories of Ade and Deji shouting at each other, and Mark, chicken drumstick in hand, stepping between them. He was worried they would come to blows. They never did. They were just showing him the usual Nigerian posturing.

Ade thought Northerners were British collaborators, and Deji thought the British had subjugated Northerners by denying them education. He was for Azikiwe's National Council of Nigeria and the Cameroons party, and Ade was a staunch supporter of Awolowo's Action Group party. Ade wasn't your typical pro-Yoruba "descendant of Oduduwa" type, but I could understand his loyalty to Awolowo. He had always needed an older man to emulate, and Awolowo, to him, was the ultimate political case study. One day, Deji called Awolowo a tribalist and Ade called Deji a buffoon. Deji walked Ade out of the flat and Ade returned a week later to say he hadn't come to apologize, he had only come to deliver the news that Charlie Parker had died.

"Actually, before independence, the East and West dominated the North," I said. "We were better educated. Our politicians were lawyers and journalists. The North had locally trained teachers. They were afraid to ask for self-governance because they thought they would be left behind. They didn't agree to self-governance until three years later."

"And after independence?" Frances asked.

The facts were in no order in my mind, so I sorted them out. "After independence, we have Tafawa Balewa, a Northerner, as prime minister, and Azikiwe, from the East, as the governor general, even though he is basically a figurehead. Now the West feels threatened, but they are not united behind Awolowo, who becomes an opposition leader. He clashes with the new Western premier, and in no time, the West is under a state of emergency."

I remembered calling my mother during the riots at the Western House of Assembly in Ibadan. Ibadan was my father's birthplace, though his family came from the town of Oyo nearby.

After he died, my mother retired to Ibadan, and my brothers would later set up their legal and medical practices there, but this was a few years before their return, so I worried about her safety. She said, "Don't mind these silly politicians. If it is not '*Penkelemess*,' it is something else. Yoruba people, that is our downfall. Disharmony. Just leave them. When they've burned down the whole House of Assembly, they will be satisfied."

In those days politics was about fistfights, kidnappings, necklacing, firebombs, sedition charges, court trials and jail sentences. The political parties changed as new alliances were formed and old alliances were dissolved. Then the politicians began to capitalize on any tensions that existed, especially after the 1963 census.

I traced patterns on the table. "So, we have trouble in the West, and now we also have an overinflated national census favoring the North. The East rejects it because it marginalizes them, but that's just a prelude to what happens a year later. The election of 1964 is a mess. Thugs take over the ballot process. There is cheating all over the place. I'm talking about women walking around with ballot papers stuffed in their wrappers and claiming they are pregnant. Crude tactics like that. The East then boycotts the election results because they are again marginalized. So, you see, every region was at some point afraid of being dominated. The irony is that each region was dominated from within, the North by the Hausa and Fulani, the West by the Yoruba and the East by the Igbo."

"Who seceded."

"Yes, but there were Igbo people in the Midwest region, which was created in the same year as the census, and that complicated issues."

"With the Civil War."

"Right, but before the war, we had a prime minister from the North, who ignored the fact that people were unhappy with the election results and who was unable to stop the chaos. By all accounts, he answered to the Sardauna of Sokoto, who was Fulani aristocracy and a Muslim leader. That was when the North became a dominant threat. A group of officers overthrew the prime minister. They killed him, killed the Sardauna and the Western premier. They were known as the January Boys, but most of them were Igbo, so people called it an Igbo coup."

"That must be the coup the book keeps referring to."

"We had two coups in 1966. There was a countercoup. A group of Northern officers later retaliated. Our new head of state was Igbo and he seemed reluctant to bring the coup plotters to trial. He imposed a unitary form of government and that was it. They killed him and the military governor of the West in the countercoup. In the North they began to slaughter Igbo people. They cut off their heads and disemboweled them."

"Awful."

"Yes. After that, everyone was galvanized into camps, and before we knew it, we were in the middle of a civil war. We had Ojukwu on one side, declaring the Republic of Biafra, and Gowon on the other, declaring twelve states in Nigeria. But not everyone in Biafra was Igbo. The minorities in that territory suffered terribly. As for the federal government, when you end up killing that many people, children and civilians included, you lose all moral ground."

"You were not sympathetic to either side."

"I was scared of war, and don't forget, we were under martial law. We were ruled by decree. No one asked civilians what we thought, on either side. Soyinka was jailed when he started talking about peace. They locked him up in solitary confinement."

"Sometimes, peace is unattainable."

"Maybe, and don't take my word for it. There might be as many versions of what happened as there are Nigerians."

I'd abbreviated the issues somewhat, and my opinion was that the political tensions preceding the war were exacerbated by the inflated census and men with inflated egos. I did not say, out of shame, that there was a tacit agreement on the war in Lagos; that we were shielded from the fighting and untouched by the news of casualties in Biafra; that we threw parties as federal troops fought for us on the battlefield. The first bomb that landed on Lagos and we were hiding under our beds and trembling.

"There must be a lot of anger and suspicion in the East," Frances said.

"Yes, but maybe in time it will dissipate."

"It takes generations. The South is yet to get over our Civil War."

We listened to the Toreador Song, and it crossed my mind yet again that Frances might be a spy, but the demise of the First Republic was public knowledge, and the details had been rehashed and disputed. We had not had another civilian government since. If Biafra had succeeded, it would be an oil-rich country. Perhaps peace was unattainable when the resources of the land were considered more valuable than people, or where the powerful stakeholders were somewhere else.

"Why do women keep trying to kill your president?" I asked.

Frances laughed. "I don't know. Here, this is for you."

She handed me a hardback copy of Sylvia Plath's *Ariel*, published by Harper & Row in 1966. It may well have been a reciprocal gesture, but I did wonder if she was trying to divert my attention.

As we left the Kuramo Hotel, she told me about Plath being an alumna of Smith College, her marriage to Ted Hughes and her suicide. Had she asked any questions about current affairs, I might have concluded she was collecting intelligence, but she didn't. In fact, the only other time we discussed politics was about a week later, and by then I didn't need much prompting to share my views.

I was as politically inclined as the next Nigerian, having been indoctrinated by my father. My mother was the opposite. She never got worked up about politics. She believed that talking about politics was a problem in itself. In other words, the problem with Nigeria was that we were always discussing the problem with Nigeria. Of her children, she would say Deji was exactly like my father, Akin was like her and I was liable to go either way. She would warn me, "Don't follow in your father's footsteps. He is a bee, always buzzing around." If I talked too much, she would make a buzzing sound. That was how I got the nickname Queen Bee, not from Ade, but from my brothers. Whenever someone called me that these days, which was rare, I saw myself as I was at ten years old, trying to hit my brothers and shouting, "I'll tell Daddy," knowing I couldn't because our father would not only conk their heads, but mine as well.

Ade Balogun was in the clubhouse when Frances and I arrived. He again called me Queen Bee and I called him Ade boy. We were not in the habit of referring to each other by nickname, but if he were trying to imply I'd taken on a matriarch's role in mediating his divorce, I was reminding him why I'd had to.

He sat at a table on the patio with what looked like a tea cloth hanging around his neck. His polo shirt was wet with sweat. His red cap and black leather gloves were on the table. Tunde said he was a fairly good player, but scolded caddies and flung his clubs whenever he messed up shots. He also wanted to be captain of the club, but would never get enough votes because he was not much of a team player.

Frances did not recognize him immediately. I reminded her that they'd met at the exhibition.

"Yes, of course," she said. "But you were so much more..."

"Dignified?" he asked.

She didn't confirm. Ade was an intelligent man when it came to the law, but his vanity often made him seem quite the opposite.

He turned to me. "You. What brings you here today? We never see you around here."

"I don't understand golf," I said.

"You should learn how to play," he said.

"It's not for me," I said.

The sun, and the walking around in funny outfits. An expatriate player in checked shorts and a visor was teeing off. He wiggled his backside, swung his club, and his ball ended up behind a row of casuarinas.

"Golf can be fun," Frances said.

"Do you play?" I asked.

"You see?" Ade said, before she could answer. "We can't get Nigerian women to join us. That's why we're outnumbered here."

He was so loud he could have been standing before a microphone, and he turned around to check that other people were listening to him.

In fact, I'd seen a few Nigerian women golfers at the club, and one or two of them were regulars. I, too, glanced at the occupants of the patio and caught sight of an English couple I knew at the far end, Dave and Bev Wood. They waved at me and I waved back. Dave worked for Barclays Bank and had played with Tunde before. I excused myself and walked over to their table.

"Hello, Bev," I said. "Hello, Jack."

Dave got up to shake my hand, and I realized what I'd just called him. Tunde often referred to the Woods as Jack Sprat and wife.

"Tundy playing today?" Dave asked.

"Sunday is his day," I said. "I'm having lunch with a friend."

"Nice frock," Bev said.

I thanked her, though her compliment didn't come across as sincere. None of her compliments did, and I could never decide if she considered Nigerian women overdressed or if she felt drab compared to us. Bev was very fish and chips. I didn't know how to explain this better than to say she was happier secluded in English circles. I'd met other Englishwomen at the club who were more open. I was quite friendly with one who had studied at the Sorbonne and the University of Lagos. She worked as a French interpreter and translator at the college of medicine. Not that she needed to do any of that to gain my approval, but she didn't have Bev's apprehensions about mixing with Nigerians.

There was some rivalry between the Nigerian and expatriate members of the club. The Nigerians resented the fact that any expatriate could join, so long as their company could afford to pay their membership dues. It was possible, for instance, for an expatriate construction worker to find himself rubbing shoulders with a Nigerian diplomat at the bar. One expatriate married his housegirl and was so besotted with her he brought her to the club, to sit with Nigerian men who were there to get away from their own wives. At first, she greeted them with curtsies and addressed them as "sir." Then she started calling them by their first names because her husband did, but they made it clear they wouldn't accept that from her, so she decided to ignore them altogether. A few expatriates did walk around as if they owned the place, but the Nigerians refused to be dominated, though they were definitely outnumbered. It was the same at the motorboat club in Lagos, less so at the polo club. At the yacht club, it was almost impossible to see a Nigerian, but at Island Club, Nigerians reigned supreme.

Ade was a member of every club in Lagos, including professional clubs like Rotary International. He didn't own a boat or a horse and had no patience for formality, but he was always ready to socialize. He was clearly enjoying his conversation with Frances, laughing loud enough to draw attention from myself and the Woods.

"Ady's having fun," Dave said.

"Friend of yours, is she?" Bev asked, blinking as if someone was throwing sand in her face, one fistful after another.

Everyone in Lagos was in need of new company. I introduced the Woods to Frances. They seemed so eager, standing there in their Bermuda shorts and echoing each other, "How d'you do," "How d'you do."

"We should have a game sometime," Ade said.

Dave agreed. "We should, really."

He smiled expectantly at Frances, who said, "That would be nice."

She seemed hesitant, and had I known how their golf game would end, I would have told her she wasn't obliged to keep her word.

"Well, that's settled then," Dave said to Ade.

"Are you here with your family?" Bev asked Frances.

Frances shook her head, her coolness now becoming embarrassing. She was too serious. You couldn't be that serious in Lagos. You had to be able to laugh at yourself and at situations.

"I only ask because there's a lot for children to do in the main club," Bev said.

"I don't have children," Frances said.

Bev laughed. "Oh! My children are there all the time in the summer holidays. I wouldn't know what to do with them otherwise."

"That's why I never had any," Frances said.

I felt that was a bit harsh, but realized what I admired about her. She didn't endear herself to people if she didn't want to. I endeared myself to people whenever I had to. I had little choice as a shop owner, but it was becoming more and more trying.

The Woods echoed each other again, "Jolly good," "Jolly good," and returned to their table as Ade marched off announcing to the entire club that he would contact Frances when she returned from her trip to Benin City.

"He's colorful," she said.

"He certainly is," I said.

Ade was just trying to prove he was not about to apologize for being Nigerian, which was unnecessary, yet he couldn't help but grandstand.

We found a table and ordered beers and sandwiches. I confessed I had not been to the golf club in such a long while that I'd forgotten it was impossible to have a quiet lunch there.

"I tell you what," she said. "I'm so grateful to be able to travel and meet new people. Where I'm from, I'm surrounded

119

by the same type of woman, with the country club member-ship, executive husband and kids in boarding schools. I've just about had it with the details of their marriages and divorces."

"I can imagine," I said.

She had no idea she was describing my life, but there was no point challenging her. Foreigners sometimes had strange expectations of how Africans lived. Reality could be a letdown. If I gave her the bare facts of my day-to-day activities in Lagos, she might find them just as mundane.

"Nigeria does have a reputation."

"The thing is, corruption happens everywhere. But what I didn't care for was how flagrant it was here. Before Muhammed's regime, it went unchecked for a while, even when it was obvious."

"Why was that?"

"The lack of shame. There was a time people in Lagos had shame. Not anymore. General Muhammed may be trying to reinstate public shaming through his announcements, but the public only ends up sympathizing with the people who are being shamed."

"Now, that is strange."

"Yes, but I'm guilty of it. Listen, I even felt sorry for President Nixon during Watergate."

"Watergate was shameful."

"For me, as a Nigerian, it was politics as usual."

January 18

Rotimi was noticeably quiet on visiting day. He sat between Tunde and me, his school uniform pressed and starched. We'd brought a few provisions for his tuck box, including his favorites, Titus sardines, Exeter corned beef and Blue Band margarine. The thought of any of those combined was enough to make me nauseous, but he made sandwiches out of them, which he ate at snacktime.

We were in his classroom and other students and parents were present, their voices interfering with ours. I asked him what was wrong, and as usual he spoke through the side of his mouth, which made it difficult to hear him. I managed to understand that he had scrubbed toilets as a punishment for punching some boy after a football game. At first, he wouldn't say why, then he admitted that they were arguing about an offside call when the boy made a rude remark about Tunde's retirement.

There were just some situations I had no control over while our children were at school. The retirements had been announced in the newspapers and on television. I thought Rotimi ought to have reported the boy, but Tunde's view was that Rotimi had reacted appropriately.

"One punch," he said, raising his fist. "One solid punch and that boy will never open his mouth to talk to you like that again."

He then recounted his legendary fight with Haruna.

Haruna was the tallest student in the missionary school Tunde had attended when he was a boy. He was also the oldest student because he kept failing his exams. He was so old he was already sporting a beard. He dared Tunde to a fight in the schoolyard, and Tunde returned home to tell his father he never wanted to go to school again. His father ordered him back, so he went to school the next day, armed with a catapult. Before Haruna could attack, Tunde took aim and struck him with a stone. Haruna fell in the schoolyard and the missionaries came running out when they heard the commotion. A nun who taught Bible-knowledge classes grabbed Tunde by his ear and dragged him to the teachers' mess, where she caned him for fighting on the school premises. Tunde didn't flinch, and Haruna never troubled anyone in the school thereafter.

I'd heard the story many times before, and the catapult was not such an ingenious idea. He'd borrowed it from David and Goliath.

"Next time," I said to Rotimi, "just report whoever it is."

Rotimi looked at me as if what I'd said was too absurd to contemplate.

"Left-Right," Tunde said. "Don't listen to your mother. She's a woman. She doesn't know what she's talking about. Next time, land him a solid uppercut he'll never forget. Men don't report. Men fight and fight to win."

"What if he loses?" I asked.

"You only lose when you don't fight."

I shook my head. Perhaps that was why peace was unattainable. The inability of men to define what it meant to win or lose.

We left Rotimi at the end of visiting hours. Rolari's visiting day was the Sunday after, but her birthday fell on the Thursday in between, so we decided that, rather than visit her, they would both come home on exeat the following weekend, and we would all go out for a family lunch.

On our way home we stopped at the Onyias', Maurice and Abigail, who were relocating to their hometown, Asaba. Abigail was already there, settling into their house, and Maurice was staying on in Lagos to oversee the movers, who would pack up what was left of their belongings. All they had in their government house on Queen's Drive were leather pouffes, surrounded by stacks of boxes that dwarfed us.

"You see life?" Maurice said.

Apart from being markedly smaller than Abigail, Maurice had dainty mannerisms. He flopped his wrist and fluttered his eyelashes as he spoke. He had been a federal judge until he was sacked and, I imagined, was used to speaking to people from a higher position. He sat on a pouffe, dressed in a red tunic with dog patterns and black trousers. On one side of him was a framed photograph of himself in a court wig and gown, and on the other was a candle in the shape of the Virgin Mary.

Tunde and I were shocked to find out that Maurice was on the list of sacked judges. He had been charged with bribery and found guilty. He later professed his innocence to the press, claiming he had nothing to his name, and invited the government to investigate his assets. But the rumor was that he had sunk all he had received over the years into his hometown house and invested the rest in a bank in Switzerland.

Still, there was no question of Tunde showing anything but loyalty to him. They'd met when Tunde was an administrative officer, fresh out of Dublin, and Maurice was working as a magistrate. Maurice was an old boy of Achimota School, Ghana, and a Cambridge man. He was as articulate and persuasive as the best of the kleptocrats.

"See how long we have been in this government," he said, giving a delicate wave. "Now they want to throw us away like…like used rags."

"I'm telling you," Tunde said.

"These military boys have no education or intellect. All they have is guns, and they think that gives them the right to lord it over us."

"They have no right whatsoever," Tunde said.

"What do I care? I've done my duty to this country."

"Absolutely."

"Nobody can tarnish my reputation."

"Nobody."

"There isn't a single one of them who would be in power today if…if they had respect for our constitution."

"Not one."

Maurice patted his chest. "And I upheld that constitution, for many years."

"You did. You did."

"They come along every time and undermine the law with their decrees."

"Every time. Every single time."

"We have a short memory in this country. A short memory is what we have. That's the trouble with us. We forget our history easily. Isn't this the same Murtala Muhammed who has the blood of my people on his hands? Now everyone is calling him a great nationalist and leader. Suddenly, he's the messiah Nigeria has been waiting for."

Maurice glanced at me as I continued to play dumb to lessen his humiliation. In fact, General Muhammed was regarded as a fearless soldier during the war. He was a hero on the federal side. Naturally, to the Biafrans, he was a mass murderer, and controversy still followed his military career. But that was the lot of soldiers. They fought our dirty wars, we washed our hands of them and left theirs bloodied.

"It's good you're going home," Tunde said.

"Ah, nothing can stop me now," Maurice said.

"You'll have peace of mind."

"You're telling me?"

"Fresh air."

"Fresh air! Who would live in this filthy, polluted city if not for work? No. It's time for me to leave Lagos now. It's long overdue, and you know, when you people start your nonsense, we head east before you start harassing us."

That was new for Maurice, to imply he was Igbo. He usually said he was from the Midwest, not quite a real Igbo.

Of course, no one considered friendships as casualties of the Civil War, but there were many. Not only did friendships die during the war, they suffered chronically as a result. I had friends from the East, one I'd known since childhood, and another who was married to a Yoruba man. Before the war, we could talk about being Nigerian. During the war, we couldn't. After the war, any conversations we had about Nigeria were like chit-chatting about debris floating on a river that harbored skeletons.

Tunde sympathized with Midwesterners like Maurice because he'd grown up in the Middle Belt region. He believed that they suffered more than other ethnic groups during the war because they were victims of both the federal and Biafran troops. In private he said he wasn't against Biafra but, if asked, would say he was for keeping Nigeria one. If his stance on the war was contradictory, mine was evasive, but everyone had their own way of dealing with the moral fallout of Biafra.

Before we met, Tunde went out briefly with Abigail's younger sister, Lydia (hideous sense of style, all bows and frills), but they broke up because Lydia wanted to go back to school in the United States to get a PhD. He said they'd quarrelled all the time because Lydia was headstrong, and not the sort of woman who would want to stay at home and raise children. She was a teacher when they met. After her doctorate, she published some poetry (feminist or something of that nature, nothing that would appeal to me). I found her a bit full of herself. She was constantly bragging about her academic achievements. Prior to the war, she'd insinuated herself into literary circles until she was within the perimeter of Achebe, Okigbo, J. P. Clark, Soyinka and other writers in the Mbari Club. The war broke out, and she returned to the United States, where she taught at a university in Pennsylvania and became part of a pro-Biafra student movement. She would write letters to Maurice urging him to leave Lagos and head east as most Igbos were doing, but Maurice would tear her letters up.

"See this woman," he once said about her. "She wants to get us killed. I've told Abigail, 'Don't listen to your sister. Ojukwu is a warmonger, and the East has never had our best interest at heart.'"

Maurice and Abigail remained in Lagos throughout the war, but I wasn't quite sure where Abigail stood on Biafra. Before the war, she would send me invitations to their children's birthday parties. Once the war began, her invitations stopped, which would have been understandable had she not continued to throw birthday parties for her children. Maurice, as far as I knew, considered Ojukwu a national traitor, rather than the leader of Biafra. Ojukwu was a King's College old boy, and Maurice had told us a story, which may or may not have been true, about how Ojukwu was so incensed by the colonial system of corporal punishment during his time at King's that he slapped a British teacher. "Ojukwu had no business joining the army," he would say. "Even in school he defied authority."

Maurice had this theory that no one in Nigeria actually disliked Igbos. They just disliked the republican spirit of Igbos from the East because it threatened established hierarchies. He believed their bid to secede ought to be studied in that light. He cheered when General Muhammed's troops liberated the Midwest from Biafra, until he heard how the troops executed Igbo civilians in Asaba. General Muhammed denied he had given the order, and Maurice recommitted himself to the idea of one Nigeria. How, I didn't know, and I couldn't imagine why Igbos from the East would come back to Lagos after the war, but they did. "No victor, no vanquished" was the refrain back then, and if it were meaningless for those on the losing side, the bloodbaths in Asaba had demonstrated just how futile winning could be.

"We have a selective memory," he said. "A selective memory and justice system in this country. Every regime wants to start afresh. There is no regard for the past or future. Only the present counts."

"Only the present," Tunde said.

Come on, I thought. It was increasingly difficult to sit there listening to their call and response. They sounded like a couple of old village chiefs.

"And," Maurice said, "those in power decide when the present begins for the rest of us. Now, we're forever at the mercy of individuals who behave as if they have the same lifespan as Nigeria."

"You think the army will ever hand over?" Tunde asked.

Maurice shook his head. "It's highly unlikely. If they do it will be short-lived. It's like giving a dog raw meat. Once they've tasted power, that's it. There will always be a cycle of military coups in this country."

"So long as there is an army," Tunde said.

"Unless," Maurice said, raising his forefinger, "the army is somehow rendered toothless. We can forget about a civilian government until that ever happens."

Maurice said a lot that afternoon, most of which was an attempt to cover up his guilt. He had served under military rule and sentenced people according to military decrees, sometimes to death. Never had he challenged a verdict until he himself was affected. He claimed he was set up by jealous colleagues, implicated people on the anticorruption panel he'd faced, called them a kangaroo court and finally blamed his predicament on the old witch-hunt.

The question of whether to show loyalty to him was on my mind as we left his house. Tunde took his time dawdling down Queen's Drive at about thirty miles per hour. He asked what I was thinking and I initially said, "Nothing," then I confessed. "You shouldn't encourage Maurice."

"In what way?" Tunde asked.

"His hands are not clean."

"What do you mean?"

"He took bribes."

"You think he doesn't know that?"

"I'm just saying, he shouldn't be pointing fingers at anyone. It's embarrassing."

We were passing the landing where canoes dropped passengers who crossed Five Cowries Creek. One was approaching the bank and the rower lifted his oars.

"My dear," Tunde said, "if this regime were to sack every public official who has done something they were not supposed to, there would be no one left to run Nigeria."

I had to agree. Maurice was merely a crooked judge, which was why he'd managed to stay under the radar for so long. Had he been a crooked permanent secretary, we would probably have had to join a long queue to say goodbye to him. There would have been a host of sycophants bidding him farewell. No one shunned corrupt civil servants anymore, especially while they were in office, and it didn't matter if they had been publicly disgraced and thoroughly gossiped about.

There was a time in Lagos when the worst a person could accuse you of was theft. I had a childhood story of my own, which I told our children, about how my days of stealing food came to an end. When I was a girl, I couldn't resist *chook-chook*. I loved *chook-chook* so much I would watch my mother prepare it. She would grate coconut meat and simmer it in coconut water and sugar until it caramelized. After the mixture cooled, she would roll it into small balls. I would eat *chook-chook* until my gums hurt.

One day, I stole a few that were intended for a church function. I wore a dress that had no pockets, so I slipped the *chook-chook* into my underwear. But they pricked so badly I had to walk with my legs apart. As I crossed the parlor where my father sat, they began to plop out, one by one. My father cried out, "Good heavens!" He thought I was defecating myself. After he recovered from shock, he lectured me for hours. I actually prayed he would beat me and get it over and done with. For weeks, all I heard from every aunt, uncle and family friend who visited our house was, "Remi, you stole the church *chook-chook*?" My mother would add, "Not only did she steal the church *chook-chook*, she hid them in her buttocks."

Rolari and Rotimi found the story amusing when they were younger. I was merely trying to show them how morals were instilled in my day. Now, we had corruption panels. The panels were meant to restore morals, but they had also succeeded in arousing pity. If some people were getting off free, then everyone should. Those in favor of shunning corrupt civil servants were in the minority and ended up looking sanctimonious. There were no social penalties anymore, except of course when an act of immorality involved a wife's infidelity. Then, everyone would remember their morals and shun her as if she'd robbed our national treasury dry.

"I really ought to visit Moji," I said, looking at Victoria Island across the creek.

"You've been saying that for months," Tunde said. "I thought I was meant to be the procrastinator."

"Where I'm from, it's the house with the white picket fence you're supposed to aspire to."

"We don't have an equivalent. But then, most Nigerian women live in huts, not houses."

"Would you say that being caught between traditional and Western cultures causes the domestic problems you've observed?"

"I'm not sure. Our cultures evolve. They change, you know, and you can hardly call the Western cultures we've adopted modern. I mean, sitting at home and playing wife would be old-fashioned to some women in Nigerian villages. If you ask them what they look for in a husband, they will give you a list of functions. If you ask an educated woman in Lagos, she might give you a list of attributes. You can walk away from a husband who doesn't fulfill his functions. You're expected to accept attributes when you get married, aren't you?"

"I think romance is a problem for American women. They go into marriage believing that marriage is romantic and end up disappointed."

"Actually, civil marriage may be the most damaging of Western traditions we've adopted."

January 20

It took me another couple of days to see Moji. I had some idea of what it was like to be abandoned in Lagos, but I wasn't interested in listening to the details of Ade's affairs. Moji hid nothing about their marriage. She was also in the habit of overcomplimenting mine. "You and Tunde are perfect for each other," she often said. She was childlike in that way and had a deceptively small frame for a woman who, according to Ade, could beat up a man twice his size.

Since their separation, she had moved into a block of flats on Victoria Island that had a swimming pool, vine-ridden tennis courts and a couple of uniformed watchmen who were so protective of the premises they wouldn't let me in until they had recorded my name and time of arrival in their logbook.

The flat was temporary accommodation until Moji could find a house. Living there was not ideal for her, she said. She needed more space. She didn't play tennis, and the swimming-pool water was slimy. She was the only Nigerian in the block. The rest were Italian men who worked for a building and civil-engineering contractor. A few of them lived with their families and one or two kept company with Nigerian women who apparently looked like prostitutes.

We were in her sitting room, and her windows and sliding door were open. Her flat smelled of her new rug, which was in primary colors. She had geometric-shaped furniture—square chairs, triangular lamps, and round and rectangular tables.

Moji's taste was avant-garde for Lagos. She and Ade had a ranch-style house with stone walls. I didn't know how she'd managed to keep it clutter free with four children. Even her kitchen was spick and span, which was unusual, because no matter how beautiful Nigerian homes were, our kitchens were usually a mess on account of the labor that went into preparing meals. Moji used modern appliances in her kitchen. She had the latest pressure cooker and coffeemaker. She would never offer a guest instant coffee. She was also ahead of fashion. In the sixties, she'd started the psychedelic trend in Lagos; now, she wore turbans and flared trousers. She had changed her makeup from what she called the Mary Quant look to the Biba look. I wasn't exactly sure about the distinctions, but she was exceptionally pretty and stylish, regardless.

After the rumors I'd heard about her, I'd expected to find her red-eyed with her hair standing on end; instead, she appeared uncharacteristically meek.

"I hope your matter with Ade has been resolved," I said.

"I'm trying," she said. "But you know Ade. He controls Lagos."

"How so?"

"He's in cahoots with every lawyer and judge in town."

"Every single one of them?"

"He will tell you himself. He has maligned me all over the place. I can't find a lawyer to represent me, and he wouldn't have known half of them if not for my father."

Moji's father was a pre-independence lawyer and founding member of the Action Group party. An avowed nationalist to his death, he held a grudge against the Colonial Office for branding him a communist supporter. He spoilt Moji—again according to Ade, who was his protégé. Ade had worked in his law firm and was being groomed for political office. I found it rather sad that he ended up marrying his boss's daughter, presumably to gain favor. When Moji first appeared on the scene, no one liked her. She was enamored with her father and demanded constant attention from Ade. She would get upset whenever he was in the company of friends she didn't know. She was not his usual type, buxom women who only wanted to take charge of his kitchen. I blamed her father, who, from all accounts, bullied her mother to submission and yet put Moji on a pedestal. Any daughter who was raised to believe she was more valued than her mother was bound to have problems with her husband.

I was sure Moji could find herself a lawyer if she was serious about hiring one. She had probably sabotaged herself by sleeping with Ade's colleagues. One of them bragged about their affair to Ade. Ade threatened to get him disbarred, so he denied everything and dropped Moji as his client. The trouble with the Baloguns was that they were over the top. Their marriage, their separation, even their drinking was in excess. Tunde and I had been to their house for a New Year's party. What didn't they knock back that night? Aperitifs, wine, digestifs, and before we left, they were talking about the Buck's Fizz they would have in the morning. For a while after that, Tunde referred to them as Tom Collins and Mai Tai. They were the sort of couple that made you think you were not glamorous enough. In fact, they could make you hate your life, if you were that way inclined. Then their fighting began, and it wasn't that people didn't get separated or divorced in Lagos, but no one had made such a public display of their marital problems as the Baloguns had. Their divorce wasn't like Oyinda's bohemian threesome that could easily be ignored because it involved an expatriate couple and oddball Nigerian widow. It was so scandalous that Tunde soon started calling them Elizabeth Taylor and Richard Burton.

"How are your children?" I asked Moji.

She shrugged. "Who knows?"

"I don't understand."

"I haven't seen them since I left the house."

"Why not?"

"Ade won't let me."

"Um…why?"

"He says I'm an unfit mother."

I was exasperated. No wonder he'd looked so guilty when I'd asked about her.

"You can't let him get away with that," I said. "You hear me? You have to pull yourself together and hire a lawyer to get visitation rights. Look, I know him. He respects strength in a woman. What is this? You're sitting here locked up while he's living it up?"

"He is?"

"Everywhere I go, I see him."

"You do?"

"Yes. Just the other day I saw him at the golf club. You have to get out of here, Moji. You can't keep hiding. You're an attractive woman. Your life is not over, and you certainly can't let Ade push you around. He's calling you unfit? Who is he to determine that you're unfit?"

I could never have predicted the trouble my outburst would later cause, but the idea that Ade would dare prevent her from seeing her children infuriated me.

"So," Moji said, nodding, "he's living it up. Why am I not surprised to hear that?"

I was surprised she was more concerned about his social life.

"Sorry. I shouldn't have said that, but I asked after you and he didn't tell me this was going on. You should have called me."

"You disappeared."

"Tunde lost his job."

"He did? When?"

"It's all right. He's working again."

"Where?"

"Community Bank."

"I would have visited you if I'd heard. I haven't been following the news. I don't even know what is happening in the country."

"I've opened a shop."

"You have?"

"At Falomo Shopping Center."

"Oh, Remi, I'm so happy for you. You've always been so enterprising."

"Not really."

"Oh, you have. Don't be so modest. What are you selling?"

"Cards. Just cards. What about your business?"

"I haven't worked in a while."

"Come on."

"I haven't had time! This divorce has taken all my energy!"

"He's taken your children, not your livelihood. Work would be the best cure at a time like this."

She nodded. "I'll try, I'll try."

"You must," I said. "You have to. You can't waste your talent. You're the best interior designer in town."

"I know, I know. It's just that I've been so upset. I don't think I will ever recover from this."

Her eyes were reddening. I hoped she wouldn't cry.

"Of course you can. Of course you will."

"You're right. You're right."

She was too obedient, but that could have been the result of drinking. I was frustrated by my inability to do what I would have done before—listen to her ramble and tell her Ade was wrong to betray her. But surely, this was not illness or death we were talking about. We had reached that stage in life. Strokes and heart attacks were taking down people our age. As if that wasn't bad enough, cancer as well.

Moji and Ade's problems were self-caused. The last time I'd seen them together, Moji had torn out pages from Ade's *Playboy* stash and distributed them all over their house—to what avail I didn't know, but she had just found out he was having the affair with her friend. "Why do you have pornography lying around?" I'd asked Ade, worried about their children. "Why are you so prudish?" he'd responded. "Are things that dull between you and your husband?"

For a moment I did think that perhaps I was a prude. Perhaps their behavior was within the spectrum one could call normal; then I went home and told Tunde what had happened and he raised his hand when I came to the *Playboy* part.

"Don't mind Ade," I now said to Moji. "He'll soon find out what he's lost."

I lifted my elbows and imitated his gait. As I expected, she laughed, then she leaned over and rubbed her arms.

"He disappointed me."

"Men do that."

"He promised my father he would take care of me."

"You have to get that out of your mind."

"I wanted to kill myself."

"Please don't say that."

"My own friend," she said. "All the time she was betraying me. She said she needed a lawyer. I put her in touch with him. She would call our house to speak to him. She would call on weekends. I told her to go to his office during the week. He took her to the Old Abbey, Chez Antoine, Quo Vadis. Everywhere he had lunch with his colleagues."

"You have to forget about her. Concentrate on getting visitation rights so you can see your children. Let him have them if he wants. He has that right."

"I can't forgive him."

"No one expects you to."

"I forgave him for all the others. But my friend?"

"She was not a friend."

"I mean, you borrow my money, you borrow my clothes, now you want to borrow my husband? There has to be limits."

She was again talking like a child, and I was reluctantly slipping back into my role as her counselor. My natural inclination was to get involved, having seen my father bring families together. But Moji wasn't as helpless as she wanted to come across. She would order her mother around, Ade said, and once called the woman a doormat to her face. She told Ade, in front of their children, that he would have been a nobody had her father not introduced him to the right people. She called him a bastard child during her *Playboy* rage.

"Look," I said. "The first step is to get out."

"I should, to show him."

"To show yourself, not him."

"But everyone is talking about me!"

"That does not mean anyone condones what he did."

She raised her hand. "Oh, don't be so insincere, Remi! Of course it does! You have the perfect husband at home, but don't pretend you don't know what things are like around here!"

I was shocked that she would turn on me, but at least she was regaining her spirit.

She was right. My own brother Deji would never defend me in a divorce case. He as much as told me that during the Kuramo Fiasco. I called to tell him where I was staying and he said, "Remi, go back to your husband's house and stop being so stubborn." I reminded him that the house belonged to the government, not my husband. He said even if the house were private property, jointly owned, with my name on the deed and I sued Tunde successfully in court, the house would still belong to Tunde because no one would bother to make sure Tunde handed it over to me, or shared the proceeds with me, should he decide to sell it. Even if Tunde beat me up every day, he said, our house and our children were Tunde's, so long as Tunde deemed, because the law didn't count.

He was only trying to cheer me up, and he wasn't telling me anything I didn't know. I'd heard of men who, during the course of a divorce, threw out their wives' belongings and forbade them from seeing their children, and women who squatted in their own homes, refusing to leave for their children's sakes. The Kuramo Fiasco was a first and last because I had no reason to leave home after that. Besides, the tensions between Tunde and me eased once I became a housewife. Or perhaps I just ignored them.

"Tunde is not perfect," I said.

"He's not like the rest."

"Neither is Ade the worst of the lot. Trust me, his guilty conscience alone is enough to finish him."

"I couldn't care less."

"Then let him go, my dear. He's not worth it."

Again, that obedient nod, as if I were an authority on marriage. She appeared to be listening, though, and I continued to encourage her, telling her to control her temper, without mentioning her drinking. I still didn't see any indication she was the alcoholic wreck people said she was, but I did wonder why she would contemplate killing herself because of Ade, or any man.

"Polygamy shouldn't exist in this day and age."

"Why not?"

"It diminishes women."

"We're diminished in civil marriages, as well."

"You can't compare the two, Remi."

"Why not?"

"Because! You share a husband in a polygamous marriage!"

"Women in civil marriages share husbands."

"That's their choice."

"If they know what their husbands are up to."

"You go into a polygamous marriage knowing."

"You have a choice to be in a polygamous marriage or not."

"I disagree."

"Who are we to judge?"

"It's just not right, Remi."

"I've seen the women, myself. I've talked to them. They don't seem unhappy to me."

"I don't believe they want to be in polygamous marriages. I'm sorry, I don't."

"Look, I chose to be in a civil marriage, and I'm telling you that some women here choose to be in polygamous marriages."

"I can't accept that. It doesn't matter how you were raised. You can't be happy to share a husband."

"I'm only telling you what I've seen, and I've seen a lot more unhappy women in civil marriages."

"That still doesn't make polygamy okay, here or anywhere. It may not be as widespread in America, but the law doesn't permit it there."

"Well, it's widespread here and the law allows it."

"That's wrong."

"I'm just saying for the sake of argument. I'm not saying I disagree with you."

"I'm sorry. I don't understand how you can say that, even for the sake of argument."

January 21

I was on the shop floor on Wednesday afternoon when Habiba Ibrahim walked in. She wore an *ankara* up-and-down, and a light-blue chiffon scarf wrapped around her head and shoulders. Her hair was partially visible and her eyes were heavily lined with kohl.

"Mrs. Ibrahim," I said. "Nice to see you."

"Ah, Mrs. Lawal," she said. "What are you doing here?"

"This is my shop."

"Really?"

She looked around as if she might find evidence to support my claim. Habiba had an air of serenity that was incongruous with Lagos. She was Abubakar Ibrahim's middle wife and attended Community Bank functions with him because, unlike his other two wives, she spoke English. Tunde usually addressed them as Alhaji and Alhaja Ibrahim because they had been on Hajj to Mecca, but I didn't think that was necessary.

"How is your husband?" I asked.

"He is well."

"And...the children?"

I wasn't sure how to refer to them because they were not all hers. Abubakar Ibrahim had about a dozen children, ranging from a teenager to a baby. Tunde liked him but found him overly conservative. Apart from being polygamous, Abubakar Ibrahim didn't drink alcohol or eat pork. He inadvertently ate some

during a business lunch at a Chinese restaurant and immediately spat it into his napkin. Tunde was mortified. I was just
intrigued by the Ibrahims' lifestyle. I couldn't imagine how
they agreed on their sleeping arrangements, for a start.

The Ibrahim wives seemed friendly enough with one
another. Habiba had come to pick up invitation cards for a
birthday party she was throwing for another wife. As I searched
for her cards behind the sales counter, I thought about Moji
crying over Ade. Was it bondage to expect a lifelong commitment from a man? Was there freedom in being able to share a
husband? If Moji was one extreme, Habiba was the other and
somewhere between them were women like me, neither crazy
nor controlled.

There were several boxes marked ready for delivery behind
the counter, but I couldn't find Habiba's cards and Festus wasn't
around.

"I'm sure they're with the printer," I said, standing up. "My
manager is out right now, but he will deliver them to you as
soon as we get them."

As I took her address, I toyed with bringing up the matter
of Community Bank housing. Habiba was pleasant and had
some influence over her husband, but Tunde would never forgive me for meddling in his work affairs. I decided he needn't
know. Then I realized the Ibrahims didn't live in a Community
Bank house, which gave me the perfect opportunity.

"I see you're in a house of your own."

"Yes," Habiba said.

"So are we."

She dipped her hand into her bag as if she was ready to pay.
I was ashamed of myself for carrying on, but the likelihood of
seeing her again was slim.

"My children are looking forward to moving into a Community Bank house. They keep asking me when it will happen. I tell them to be patient…"

I'd actually told them to stop complaining.

"Why are they keeping you waiting?" Habiba asked.

"I don't know, and I really shouldn't be telling you this because my husband has asked me not to interfere."

I hoped my expression was docile enough. Hausa women had a reputation for being submissive, though how anyone had come to that conclusion in the absence of a comprehensive study was a mystery.

"How much are the cards?" she asked.

"We can settle on delivery," I said with a smile.

"Thank you," she said.

I signaled to Boniface to open the door, and she'd disappeared from my sight before I realized she hadn't offered to speak to her husband.

In Lagos, Hausas were regarded as feudal. One successful patriarch in the family was all they needed. Abubakar Ibrahim was one of three successful brothers. His elder brother, Mahmoud, had made a name for himself as a foreign secretary until his death. His younger brother, Hassan, owned a cement business up north. Hassan was also notorious for killing his wife. She came from a prominent Kanuri family, which complicated issues. Their marriage had been arranged because Hassan had taken a while to settle down, but they never got along. Kanuris were not as conservative as Hausas. She defied Hassan in front of his family. One day, he lost his temper and ran her over with his sports car in their front yard, in broad daylight, in the presence of witnesses, and later blamed it on a nervous breakdown. No one thought he would get away with that, but their families came to an agreement with the help of an emir, and the case never reached court.

I was horrified to hear about the incident, but Tunde, after his initial shock, would nudge me and whisper, "Look," whenever we saw Hassan at social functions. He elevated the man to the status of a folk hero because he couldn't believe a Nigerian man would bother to kill his wife. Perhaps if Hassan had almost beaten her to death, that would have made more sense to him.

Festus came back later that afternoon, and I asked him about Mrs. Ibrahim's cards.

"They're here," he said.

"Why weren't they behind the counter, then?" I asked.

Boniface had mistakenly put them in the storeroom. I was annoyed that he had not mentioned that when Habiba was around, but it gave me another opportunity to speak to her about my housing concerns, in case she hadn't taken notice the first time.

Habiba's serenity bordered on apathy. She was so calm she could well be on Valium. Whenever I saw her at Community Bank functions, her facial expression never changed. I thought perhaps her disposition was due to her religion. She was a devout Muslim, and Islam, from what I'd gathered, instilled calmness in women. Tunde disagreed. He thought Habiba looked bored. "Who told you Islam instills calmness in women, anyway?" he once asked. "What about Hassan's wife?"

I was appalled that he would joke about the Hassan story, and driving to the Ibrahims' house after work, I questioned it. How did the man get away with killing his wife in broad daylight? How had he managed to silence every witness, even as the story spread to Lagos? It was inconceivable to me that a man would kill his wife publicly, even up north. Had his wife been from a prominent Lagos Muslim family, he would probably have been mobbed to death.

The Ibrahims lived off Kingsway Road, in a series of houses connected by corridors. The largest house was the main one. The rest looked newer and had probably been added over the years as their family expanded. There was a fountain in the courtyard, and several Benzes in their car park. A couple of Hausa watchmen were on duty. Their lawn was bordered by traveler's palms, and peacocks strutted around.

A man dressed in a white tunic showed me into their hallway. My footsteps echoed as I passed a fish pond and a pair of elephant tusks. I got to the main room, which had a lion's hide on the floor, complete with glass eyes and teeth.

Habiba took a while to show up, so I assumed she had been in another house. She still had the chiffon scarf wrapped around her head and shoulders, and was accompanied by a younger woman who was similarly dressed. I thought the woman was her daughter, but she turned out to be Abubakar Ibrahim's junior wife, whose name was Amina.

"*Sannu*," Amina said in Hausa.

"*Sannu*," I said.

I showed Habiba the cards, and she seemed pleased with them. She handed one to Amina who politely said, "*Nagode*."

Amina was in her early twenties and Abubakar Ibrahim was in his mid-sixties. Why would an educated Muslim man marry a woman that young? I asked myself. Why was he even considered a good Muslim? Why wasn't he just a dirty old man?

"Can I offer you something to drink?" Habiba asked.

I smiled. "No, thank you. I'm on my way home."

Amina returned the card to her and murmured, "*Yauwa*."

"The bill is attached," I said.

"Ah," Habiba said, as if I were referring to a baby.

She didn't bother to look at the bill. Another impression people in Lagos had about Hausas was that they were all rich. Yet every watchman and beggar I'd ever seen in Lagos was Hausa.

"You have a lovely home," I said.

"Thank you," Habiba said.

"It's very spacious."

"Thank you."

"I'll be glad when we move from ours."

"You're moving?"

"Remember I told you our house was too small?"

She frowned. "When?"

"In my shop," I said. "I told you we were waiting for Community Bank housing. Maybe you can remind your husband. I often have to remind mine."

We sighed in succession and made no effort to further our conversation, which was often the case between Hausa women and me, after exchanging pleasantries. I rarely got into lengthy discussions with them. I'd observed that about Yoruba and Hausa women at social functions. Yet our men talked. They talked about work and business. They'd even managed to talk themselves into becoming allies during the Civil War.

Habiba finally picked up my bill and excused herself, leaving me with Amina, who smiled at me briefly before dropping her gaze. She was so demure. Every Hausa woman I'd encountered in Lagos was—in company, at least. I knew one who had such a quick comeback that it took you a moment to decipher what she'd said, why she'd said it, and the effect it was meant to have on you, but she was still demure. I'd only ever heard of one Hausa woman whose conduct was unbecoming in public.

She apparently reserved her alcohol consumption for home, but was often spotted around town in knee-length dresses. When I asked how she got away with that, I was told she was a Christian who had converted to Islam. Then I was told she was Muslim from the start, but her husband was moderate.

How come I didn't have, not just Hausa women, any Northern women in my social circle? I wondered. Northerners were not vastly different from Southerners. Southerners were Muslim; Southern families were polygamous; Southern men married underage girls; Southern girls were deprived of their educations. I'd never subscribed to the view that the South would fare better without the North. The usual assertions that the South had oil and the North misappropriated oil wealth; that Southerners had the intellectual capacity to lead and Northerners usurped positions of authority were, as far as I was concerned, unsubstantiated. The fact was that Southerners had not had enough occasion to show how we would behave in power. It was true that Northerners on the whole were still not as educated as Southerners, and in Lagos we often said that was because they didn't value education. I had reservations about generalizations like that, but there was no doubt in my mind that Amina, who seemed unnecessarily mature sitting with her hands clasped, would be better off in a university than in the Ibrahim household.

Habiba returned with an envelope, and I stood up and thanked her.

"Thank you for coming," she said.

"*Sai anjima,*" I said to Amina in Hausa.

"*Sai anjima,*" she said.

On my way home I tried to figure out their sleeping arrangements based on what I'd seen. Did the wives come to the main house, or did Abubakar Ibrahim go to theirs? Did they spend nights or weeks with him? What happened when one of them got pregnant? What would happen if two were pregnant at the same time?

I'd grown up with children from polygamous families, Muslim and Christian, and they seemed reasonably happy. I envied them their siblings without sparing a thought for their mothers, until I was old enough to ask questions, by which time it would have been rude of me to get details. I never once heard my father condemn polygamy or suggest that it was sinful. He baptized children on the Durodola side of our family, which remained polygamous. He even baptized the children of our landlord, who had eight wives in his lifetime. He also baptized the children of a pharmacist who, already famous for owning property in London, became more famous after he married a Cockney woman as his third wife. My father attended their traditional ceremony in Lagos. He said the woman was a dancer in London. She could have been a striptease dancer for all anyone knew. He sometimes pointed out a Lagos family as an example of British polygamy. They looked Lebanese to me, but my father said they were descendants of a Scottish sailor who had married two Nigerian women and fathered several children by them. "You see?" he would say, jubilantly. "Even the white man practiced polygamy." My mother would turn up her nose and look elsewhere.

Tunde's family was polygamous—unhappily so. His late father was a town chief, and his late mother was the favored wife, so beloved that his father took her on hunting expeditions and taught her how to shoot game. His father was part of what was then called the native administration and received a monthly salary from the Colonial Office. Tunde, as the eldest son, benefited over his siblings and incurred envy from their mothers. His entire childhood was one episode after another of his father's wives accusing each other of juju. Worse, it was impossible to remember who had accused whom because most of his father's wives, in the fashion of Muslims from their part of the country, had names that ended with "tu." There was a Hannatu, a Ramatu, a This-one-tu and That-one-tu. I found it terribly confusing, as I did the men in his family, who went by their middle names, which began with Abdul—Abdul-Karim, Abdul-Rashid, Abdul-Malik. Tunde's was Abdul-Wahid, and he didn't trust any of his surviving stepmothers or half-siblings. He refused to have them in our house. Whenever he visited his hometown, he would lie that he'd just eaten if they offered him food. His elder sister was convinced his diabetes was caused by a curse someone had put on him.

When I got home, I told Tunde that Habiba came to the shop, nothing more. He wouldn't have approved of me going to her house.

"What did she want?" he asked, looking askance.

"Invitation cards."

"Why?" he said. "Muslims don't need cards."

I laughed, but it occurred to me that I didn't have a single card in my shop for a Muslim holiday or occasion. I said I ought to find out where to buy them overseas. He said I shouldn't bother. All he needed to do was send word to his hometown, and his relatives would show up in droves for any event.

When he wasn't busy making fun of his clan, he was busy defending them. He'd practically accused me of being prejudiced because of my confusion over the "tu"s and Abduls in his family. He got upset whenever people assumed he was Hausa because of his Muslim surname. "Why does everyone here think Muslims from outside Lagos are Hausa?" he would ask.

First, not everyone in Lagos thought that, and second, to a certain generation of Lagosian, it wouldn't matter where he was from. Anywhere north of the rivers Niger and Benue was Hausa territory, and anywhere east of the tributary was Igbo land, end of story.

Tunde's father himself had referred to his hometown as his country. He was suspicious of people from the next town. We liked to believe our generation was more united than theirs, but there were issues that continued to divide us as Nigerians, North from South, East from West, and one ethnic group from another. Whenever I thought about the ingenuity of the British, whose initial solution was to partition Nigeria into North, East and West, I had to wonder. Where were the considerations for intricacies like how our cultures and religions overlapped? What about the question of what to do with minorities? How did they ever expect us to function as a country when every village and town thought they qualified as one? Villages and towns were forever engaged in battles. At the slightest provocation, they grabbed their spears and cutlasses, whether anyone ignored or attempted to resolve their conflicts. If they could afford to erect borders and issue passports, they would.

For us in Ikoyi, our educations and professions united us after the colonials left. Whatever we had trained to be overseas—doctors, lawyers, nurses, pharmacists, architects, accountants, actors, artists or secretaries—our Nigerian government courted us because our country needed us. Our government was our main employer, so materialism set in as corruption increased in the civil service, or perhaps it was the other way around. Regardless, the Civil War made it impossible for us to claim that ethnic disputes were provincial in nature, and we were forced to come to terms with the fact that our bourgeois aspirations were not enough to unite us.

Tunde and I still talked about tribalism as if it were synonymous with parochialism, but before we rented out our house to the French couple, our estate agent would notify us about prospective tenants, and Tunde would reject them based on their names: this one would pound yams every day and damage the foundations of our house; that one would replace our guest toilet with a pit latrine. He wasn't entirely joking. I blamed him when we found out our French tenants had installed a bidet in our bathroom. The bidet, I said, was a symbol of what was in store if we failed to come together as a nation. He said I should go to the kitchen and make use of what was installed there.

What I was alluding to was that my upbringing in Lagos was too inclusive for me to get along with people simply because they were Yoruba, or Christian, or from Lagos. Tunde, on the other hand, was more inclined to be prejudiced, most especially against Lagosians, because he was an out-of-towner. If he read a news report about a murderer, the murderer had to be from Lagos. If he heard about thefts or any crimes, he assumed the criminals involved were from Lagos. To him, Lagosians were immoral city people, and everyone else was salt of the earth. Meanwhile, whenever I read news reports about midnight raids, hacked-off limbs, juju rituals, sexual assaults on children and other heinous acts carried out in the name of culture, nine times out of ten the people involved came from outside Lagos. I once put this to him, and his response was that I was denigrating the rest of Nigeria, which was typical of Lagosians.

"About children."

"What about them?"

"I'm just asking a question, Frances."

"Go on."

"Why didn't you want to have any?"

"They smell."

"Come on."

"You asked."

"I don't understand. The moment someone asks you a question about children—"

"They don't just ask questions, though. They make judgments."

"Who doesn't? Don't you?"

"Hm."

"Look, whether or not you want to admit it, when you say you don't want children to mothers, it comes across as an attack."

"An attack?"

"Yes. It's only polite to pretend you like children in the presence of mothers."

"I'll remember that."

"What's more, over here, you reach a certain age, you have children with or without a husband. I can understand why you might consider them a burden, but you're not encumbered by them. In fact, they free you, because once you've had them, you're allowed to get on with your life. I don't know what happens in America, but that's how it is here. Children uplift you."

"Mothers are the exalted there as well."

"As they should be."

"Try being one of the condemned few."

"It can't be that bad."

"Well, I could come up with a more acceptable answer, so no one accuses me of being condescending."

"I didn't accuse you of that."

"I don't dislike children. I just can't think of a single selfless reason to have them. Can you?"

"I'm thinking."

"I'm waiting."

January 23

Frances returned from Benin City on Thursday, and we made plans to have dinner with Naomi at the Bagatelle on Friday evening. We arrived separately. She had moved out of the Kuramo Hotel and was staying with her friends who worked at the United States embassy. They had again lent her their car and driver. Naomi showed up with Pam Ogedengbe, whom I hadn't seen in months. I enjoyed Pam's company, but we weren't close friends as such.

Naomi was married to Kwesi Mensah, a professor of morbid anatomy. He was from one of those old Ghanaian-Lagos families. I'd hardly ever seen him without his pipe in his mouth. His wife had died when their children were young, and Naomi met him when she came to Lagos in the late sixties. She was newly divorced at the time and had no children of her own.

Pam was Irish. She had curly brown hair and a missing side tooth that made her look cheeky. She came to Nigeria in the late fifties with her husband, Niyi, a history professor. She'd trained as a nurse in Dublin, but had since stopped practicing. Now, she designed necklaces made from glass beads and sold them at department stores like UTC.

At the restaurant, she sat next to me, and Frances and Naomi were across from us. She had an upcoming exhibition at a trade fair for Nigerian fashion, and I started suggesting women she could invite.

"Helen," I said.

"Helen's already coming," she said.

Helen was from Greece. She sold homemade cakes and always sent a free one over to thank me for her invitation cards. She'd had quite a few functions the year before.

A waiter handed us menus. I needed more light to read mine. The Bagatelle was owned by a Lebanese couple I knew. It was also a nightclub and an instrumental version of "South of the Border" was playing.

"It's an oral vaccine," Naomi said.

She was talking to Frances about her polio program. She had just come back from a village with no electricity or running water. She'd been from hut to hut to make sure children were immunized, and supervised the health workers who adminis-tered the vaccine. She and her crew were often chased away on such expeditions. Villagers called her white and believed she was sent by the United States government to sterilize their children. She once fled down a dirt road to escape an angry village chief. As if that wasn't bad enough, she constantly had to argue with corrupt state officials to get permission for the surveys she conducted.

Naomi and I had talked about what it was like to grow up in Alabama. Her parents were teachers. She'd wanted to be one too until she found her real calling in healthcare. She left Alabama to attend college in Chicago. Her parents weren't happy about that, but they let her go so she could get away from Jim Crow laws. The bombing of the 16th Street Baptist Church and the Selma to Montgomery marches happened while she was in Chicago. I was surprised to find out that she wasn't exposed to jazz when she was a child, not even to blues. Gospel music was what she grew up on. So, at home, her family had listened to Mahalia Jackson but not to Odetta. In high school, she discovered soul music and started following artists like Sam Cooke and Al Green. Later, at college, she gravitated toward Motown music. She had three elder brothers, one of whom was a lawyer in Alabama. The other two were doctors and lived outside the state. Her father passed away when she was at college, and her mother a year before Naomi came to Nigeria.

As usual, her hair was pulled back in a bun. While sitting, she was the same height as Pam standing. She was that tall, Pam was that small and could talk the hind leg off a donkey.

Frances was not saying much. She crossed her arms, perhaps because of the air conditioning in the restaurant. She could almost be forgotten in a group, even in one as small as ours. Naomi, on the other hand, had presence she never underplayed. I found it odd that she was considered white in Nigeria, which gave her a certain status and also excluded her. She said being tall had prepared her for not fitting in anywhere. By the time she was fourteen, she towered above her friends.

"I'll tell you who else you could invite," I said to Pam.

"Who?" Pam asked, looking up from her menu.

"Meera," I said.

"Meera?" Pam exclaimed. "She has half the crown jewels around her neck! She would never wear my cheap stuff!"

Meera's husband, Anil, owned general-merchandise shops throughout West Africa. His group was one of several foreign companies that had been around so long they were household names—Dumez, Julius Berger, Kewalram Chanrai, Leventis, Mandilas, and Cappa and D'Alberto. She and Anil had recently opened a restaurant in Lagos called the Bombay Grill.

"What about Bev Wood?" I asked Pam.

"Oh, please," Pam said. "Not her."

"Why not?"

"She annoys me. I can't stand the way she calls me Pam Ogidigiby. She's a sandwich short of a picnic, that woman."

Pam often repeated what she'd heard, not intentionally, but one had to be careful around her. She didn't exactly distance herself from expatriates in Lagos, but she made it clear she was more knowledgeable about Nigeria than they were.

Her husband, Niyi, had published a few books on the history of Lagos. Tunde said he was a socialist and pan-Africanist while they were at Trinity College. Pam made the mistake of taking care of him while he was studying. He got his PhD., they got married and came to Nigeria. Within a year the man had found himself a Nigerian woman on the side. Before we knew it, the woman was pregnant. Pam stayed with him, regardless. They already had two children and went on to have two more.

"It spreads through food, water and feces," Naomi said.

"What's all this talk about feces?" Pam asked, slapping the table.

Naomi's accent was more noticeable when she talked to Frances, but the difference between hers and Frances' was obvious to me now. Frances' was almost lacking in tone.

"We're talking about polio," Naomi said.

"I imagine there is some fear it might be exported to the States," Frances said.

"It's there anyway," Naomi said.

"Not like the time we had the iron lungs, surely," Frances said.

"No," Naomi said. "But that is one of the major problems I face here, the perception that polio is an American concern. They see our program as an imposition."

"That's too bad," Frances said.

"Yes," Naomi said. "It is a shame because I'm with an international program, but there's so much suspicion about our motives. At the federal level, we're able to talk. At the state level you have these bureaucrats who, at the end of the day, just want you to grease their palms. Then at the grassroots level you have people who really don't care where you're coming from. All they know is that you're foreign, and you're giving their children some form of immunization, which might turn out to be poison for all they know. It gets political, and now that the government has changed, we have to start making new contacts all over again."

Pam turned to me. "You know, the problem is this feud between Hilda and Kamal. I'm caught in the middle."

"How so?" I asked.

"Hilda's still upset with Kamal. She blames her customers for going to him, so there are some people I just can't invite."

"I can understand that."

"Do you think I'm being loyal to a fault?"

"I wouldn't invite them. Hilda is a good friend."

Pam nodded. "You're right."

Hilda had stood by Pam throughout her ordeals with Niyi. Perhaps similarity bred contempt, because I'd never had trouble with any of my foreign friends in Lagos. As customers, I found them more reliable than Nigerians. I could even discuss political ideas with them without being scoffed at for having nothing better to do. But then, they were outsiders. They didn't have a personal interest in making sure I toed the line.

Our waiter returned and took our orders. I ordered shrimp kebabs, Naomi and Frances ordered steaks, and Pam, grilled chicken. As we ate, our conversation drifted from traffic, to power cuts, to the cost of imports. Frances found artifacts in

Lagos pricey. I thought that was because she was new in town. Pam said she'd been around for years and people were still trying to overcharge her. She stopped sending her driver to the market when she found out he was inflating food prices. She acted out how she had confronted him.

"I said, 'Sunday, why you tell me this is one naira tomato?' He said, 'Is one naira tomato, madam.' I said, 'Sunday, but one naira tomato is bigger than this.' He said, 'Madam, I no *dey* lie. If I lie, make God punish me.'"

We'd had a problematic transition from pounds, shillings and pence to naira and kobo in Lagos, which initially increased the incidence of human sacrifices. For a while, parents warned their children not to wander around unaccompanied, so they wouldn't be kidnapped and used in money-making rituals. We'd also had to deal with the new metric system, which had increased the incidence of cheating and fraud. Pam told us another story about a woman who had sold her five yards of cloth instead of six.

"She said, 'Is sis yard, madam.' I said, 'This no be six yards.' She said, 'Is sis yard.' So I said, 'Okay, make we measure *am*.' So she gives me the tape measure, I measure the cloth and say to her, 'You see? Five!' She looks at the tape measure, looks at me and says, 'Sis!'"

Nigerian women took to Pam because she made an effort to assimilate. The fact that she stayed with Niyi despite his infidelity was proof. I was just curious to know how his socialism fit in with his philandering. Why did he break his wife's heart if he was so virtuous? And why didn't he marry a Nigerian if he was such a pan-Africanist?

Pam belonged to a group of foreign wives in Lagos called Naija Wives, which could mean she didn't entirely trust Nigerian women. Nigerian women didn't exactly respect foreign wives, especially if they were white. For years, Pam believed the woman who had a child by Niyi was his cousin. The woman would visit them and speak to him in Yoruba. Pam had no idea what was going on.

"Your trade beads," she said to Frances. "The chevron and the flowery one."

"Millefiori," Frances said.

"Sorry," Pam said. "Millefiori. Niyi says the chevron is known as the star bead and millefiori means 'a thousand flowers.' I thought, What pretty names! Then he said they were used to buy slaves, and I thought, Good grief!"

"They were?" I asked.

"Yes," Pam said. "They were used as currency. Remember he wrote that book about the slave trade in Lagos? He didn't mention the beads in it, though."

She sipped her wine noisily as I pulled a face at Naomi. We were all a bit mellow.

"I thought it was guns and alcohol they used in the trade," I said.

Naomi shrugged. "Why not beads?"

"It's incredible what you can learn from a historian," Pam mumbled. "It took me meeting Niyi to find out about Irish indentured servants in America. It's troubling, though. I mean, to think of the beads in that…"

"Historical context," Naomi said.

"Gosh, I'm nodding off here," Pam said, stifling a yawn.

"Is that why they're called trade beads?" I asked Frances.

"Yes," Frances said.

Pam stretched. "It's a bit sneaky to call them that. I can only imagine what went on to acquire them."

"You can't stay awake after eating, can you?" Naomi asked Pam.

"The blood drains right out of my brain," Pam said, patting her belly.

"No dessert for you?" Naomi asked.

"No," Pam said.

"Anyone?" Naomi asked.

"Not for me," I said.

"So," Naomi said, "I'll go without."

I was waiting for more information on the trade beads, but Frances remained quiet as if she were in danger of being judged.

"You do understand what I mean, though," Pam said to her. "You must wonder who would want to collect them. I mean, that's like collecting Holocaust memorabilia for the thrill of it."

"I wouldn't go that far," Frances said.

"Wouldn't you?"

"No."

"Still, it must be interesting to collect them. Where are you off to next?"

"Osogbo," Frances said.

Pam clapped. "Now, there's a really interesting city! They have the orisha groves and an artist called Susanne—"

"I've heard of Susanne Wenger," Frances said.

"Oh," Pam said. "But you'll have so much else to see. They have their *adire* industry and of course the Osogbo—"

"I've heard of the Osogbo artists," Frances said.

Pam turned to Naomi. "I suppose there is nothing to tell you, then. I've always wanted to travel around Nigeria, but it's difficult to find the time with children."

"I don't have children," Frances said.

Pam fell silent as an instrumental version of "Perfidia" played. Yes, similarity did breed contempt. The evidence was there in my frustration with my Nigerian friends, and in Frances' impatience with Pam. She would never have talked to me that way.

It was a mismatched evening, which could have ended on a hostile note had Pam not told us yet another story. This one was about how she was duped by a man who was masquerading as a blind beggar. She saw him the following week when he was pretending to be crippled.

"I asked him," she said. "'Weren't you the one I gave money to last week?' He said he wasn't. I said, 'Yes, you were, but you were blind then. So what's wrong with you this week?' He showed me his hand, all curled up like this, and I went whack! And guess what?"

The man's hand straightened. I couldn't believe Pam had the audacity to hit him. Her story saved the evening, though, and by then I'd pretty much dismissed her exchange with Frances, who seemed to have recovered from it.

As we left the Bagatelle, Pam entertained us further by singing "Tie a Yellow Ribbon Round the Ole Oak Tree" while doing a knees-up. Frances walked ahead of us, as if she wasn't going to be party to such buffoonery.

Our cars were parked in a lot that backed onto an office complex. Naomi and Pam left first because Naomi's car was blocking mine. Before Frances left, I asked what she did in Benin City. She said she waited around mostly. Being American didn't help. Some chiefs were suspicious, and others demanded money upfront. Being a woman also made for strange encounters. One chief referred her to his wives, another made her go through a ritual before he addressed her. He poured schnapps on the ground for libation and his oracle circled her, sounding a gong. I was just relieved they hadn't sacrificed her.

"You Americans will do anything," I said.

"I hope you don't think I'm being exploitative," she said.

"Why would I think that?"

"Pam seemed to think I was."

I didn't. She wasn't responsible for the history of the beads or the actions of greedy chiefs. In fact, she would be crediting herself with more power than she had to think she was in a position to exploit them, and might even want to check that she was buying bona fide beads from them.

We hugged and said goodbye.

As I drove off, I remembered how Niyi had once told me his most reliable sources for researching his book on Lagos were the records of the colonials and slave traders. It was possible to trace my mother's roots to Freetown if I wanted to, he said. I told him I would rather not. To be honest, I didn't want to read his book on the history of slave trading in Lagos, either. Growing up, I never heard the word "slave" mentioned, except when children said to one another, "I'm not your slave." It was easy to reach adulthood and think the only reasonable response to the trade was to pretend it had never happened. The Saro people I knew talked about their history in terms of family trees: who gave birth to whom, who married whom and who died. All I was told about my maternal great-grandmother from Freetown was that she was called Sarah and changed her name to Aina, given to Yoruba girls born with their umbilical cord wrapped around their neck. To acknowledge that my mother's ancestors were once traded as commodities would mean admitting they were considered inferior, and I could either shrug off that part of history or be burdened by its depravity. I refused to acknowledge the colonials for the same reason. I was fully aware of the downside to being colonized, even for those of us who redefined ourselves as cosmopolitan. For some, it was the difference between being conscious and unconscious of breathing. For me, it was the slight inconvenience of switching languages when no number of English synonyms would suffice. Still, I preferred to think of the colonials as silly so-and-sos who had come over for a while, gone back to wherever they came from, and never really affected us.

"To be honest, Frances, I was no good at being a housewife and I found housework such a thankless task. You raise children, you support your husband. They might love you and thank you for your efforts, but they really don't appreciate the sheer drudgery of your work. You put food on the table, they eat and they're hungry again. You clean up their mess and they make more mess. Day after day. You begin to think, What is the point?

"Sincerely, at this stage in my life, I can't even say I'm doing something for myself by running a business. It's more than that. I don't want to reach the age my mother was when she died and look back on my life with nothing but my children's achievements to show for it. For my mother, that may have been all right. Her generation was the first to subscribe to the view that a woman should consider herself privileged to depend on her husband's income. That idea is foreign to us here.

"Most Nigerian women take care of their homes and go to work. They have to. My duties as a wife and mother have not changed because I own a shop. My focus on what is important has. The moment I started working for myself, I had a better understanding of what I ought to be doing at home. I wasn't just running a home. I was meant to be running a successful one. The responsibility to face your husband and speak your mind—'I agree with such-and-such.' 'I don't agree with such-and-such.' The responsibility to guide your children—'This is the way to go,' 'This is not the way to go,' or 'Go wherever you want.' These are the duties in which I take the most pride. I'm not the best mother, I'm not the best wife, but I can make that small contribution as a Nigerian woman.

I don't care what anyone says. You can't build a nation from a head of state's house, but you can begin to build one in yours."

"The ideal situation, of course, would be to have a Nigerian president instead of a head of state."

"No."

"No?"

"I just want a good leader. Or should I say a leader with good intentions. I don't even have to look up to him."

"Or her."

"Her? Even the United States hasn't managed that."

"We'll get there eventually. You know, leaders may have the best intentions, but power—"

"I beg you, this is Nigeria. If your intentions aren't good, there is nothing anyone can do to stop you from becoming corrupt."

"Intentions change. That's where the system of government comes into play."

"Yes, yes, we had one and a group of army officers decided they didn't like it."

"Nigeria is a young country. It will take time for the army to accept an elected government."

"Maybe that's the problem. We're a young country of old nations. We had our own customary laws. We had our own systems of government—royal, feudal and otherwise."

"They won't work on a national level."

"Maybe not. But I'm not about to defend any government with a bad leader."

"It's not about your leader. It's about your rights."

"Ah well, if my rights will give rise to a bad leader, then I'm not about to defend them, either."

"I'm too American for this conversation."

"Don't kill me!"

174

"I'm not kidding."
"Neither am I."

January 24

Rolari and Rotimi came home on Saturday, as planned, and we went back and forth over where to have lunch for Rolari's birthday. We finally agreed on Café de Chine at Federal Palace Hotel.

Rolari was twelve, so I gave her a mother-to-daughter talk, which she didn't quite appreciate, then I handed her the platform mules she'd asked for. They were only about two inches high, but she couldn't walk properly in them. She tripped once or twice, and Rotimi laughed at her and from then on called her Boogie Shoes whenever they passed each other. I asked him several times to stop doing that, but he wouldn't listen until she began to sulk.

Saturday was my busiest day, and I'd opened the shop before they'd come home, and brought back my bookkeeping records. The financial year ended in March so I needed to review them. I would have liked to stop at the shop during the day, but I wanted to spend as much time as I could with my children. I'd missed them, even though I was no longer used to dealing with their antics.

At Café de Chine, Rotimi ordered two large chapmans to drink, one after another, and piled his plate as if he had not seen food in years.

"One helping at a time," I said.

Tunde said he could pile his plate as high as he wanted to, so long as he finished his food, which of course he couldn't. After gobbling most of what he'd taken, he struggled to eat what was left. Now, Rolari was the one laughing and he was sulking.

He decided to retaliate on our way home in the car. I didn't know how, only that Rolari kept saying, "Stop."

"What's the matter?" I asked, turning around.

"He's breathing on me," she said.

"Why are you breathing on her?" I asked Rotimi.

He was looking out of the window. They brought back memories of Christmas: she, accusing him of something, and he feigning innocence.

I turned back just as their father swerved to avoid a blown-up tire on the street. We were driving past Bonny Cantonment. He almost ran into a taxi that had stopped to pick up a passenger. The taxi driver spread his fingers and cursed as Tunde steered us back on course.

"Didn't you see him?" I asked.

"How could I with all that noise going on behind?" he said.

"You should get your eyes checked," I said.

He hissed. "The man is lucky I didn't ram his taxi."

Rolari and Rotimi, who had been shocked into solidarity, now laughed, relieved that someone else was getting the blame.

"It's not funny," I said.

"Relax," Tunde said.

"Yeah," Rolari said. "Stay cool, calm and connected."

"Collected," her brother said. "Dunce."

"You have no table manners," she said.

"You can't walk straight," he said.

I turned around and gave them another warning look.

We got home and they headed straight for the stereo. "That's the Way (I Like It)" came on and Rolari did a dance called the wicky-wacky, rocking back and forth.

The song seemed to be taunting me. Tunde went upstairs with a copy of *Time* he'd bought at the hotel, and I went to the dining room to review my bookkeeping records. I could easily have given them to him to sort out, but he would only criticize me for not paying attention to them on a monthly basis. I'd avoided that task because I was too scared to find out if I was making a loss. He had warned me to be prepared for that in my first year, and I'd asked him not to jinx me.

As if checking numbers that proved him right wasn't bad enough, I also had his children's loud music to contend with. After a while, I asked Rotimi to turn down the volume of the stereo, and he slouched around as if I were the nuisance. Then Rolari got on the phone to call a classmate who was at home for the day, and spoke in school slang. I'd managed to pick up a few words and phrases listening to her and her brother over the years. "Spoots" were cool clothes and "chewing rock" was having a lousy time. Her classmate was apparently chewing rock at home. She then slipped into a type of pig Latin, so I wouldn't be able to understand her, asking, "Are-za you-zu serious?" as Rotimi snorted at intervals because he couldn't be bothered to blow his nose.

When I'd heard enough, I said to her, "Get off the phone," and to him, "Do something about that sniffle."

He turned off the stereo and went upstairs in a huff. She followed him in protest. I thought they were going to their bedrooms. One of them, I didn't know which, reported me to Tunde, who came down in crumpled shorts to plead on their behalf.

"Let them listen to their music," he said. "How long are they around for? All they want is to have a good time before they go back to school."

Suddenly I was the tyrant. He'd once threatened to ban them from playing their music because KC and The Sunshine Band's lyrics were explicit, and the Wailers encouraged the use of bad grammar and marijuana. I'd defended their music, reminding him of records we'd bought them, of films like *Dumbo* and *Gigi*, without sparing a thought for what they'd learned from wholesome songs like "When I See an Elephant Fly" and "The Night They Invented Champagne." Because of *Dumbo*, Rotimi wanted to be a jive-talking crow, and because of *Gigi*, Rolari wanted to be a French courtesan.

I said I never stopped them from playing their music, and they could continue to so long as they kept the volume low. He returned upstairs to read, they went back to the stereo and "I Shot the Sheriff" came on. The song tested the limits of my patience. I didn't know how I would survive their teenage years. I wanted to be an easygoing, fun-loving mother, but my children continually reminded me that I wasn't.

They got into an argument over the stereo. Rotimi played the Wailers for too long, and Rolari's tolerance lasted until "Get Up, Stand Up."

"Wait," Rotimi said, nodding. "Let me finish."

He deliberately shut his eyes to annoy her.

"You're so selfish," she said.

"Wait," he said.

"I hate the Wailers!"

"Wait, just wait…"

"Hurry up!"

I told them to get themselves into the dining room, and they looked as if they had reason to doubt my sanity.

"What is wrong with you?" I said. "I'm sitting here trying to work and you're arguing like babies."

"Babies don't argue," Rotimi said.

"Stop acting like children, then."

"We are," Rolari said.

I pointed. "When I was your age, I didn't argue with my brothers."

"You said you did."

"When?"

She twitched. "Bzz!"

"I was ten. You are twelve and you're almost fourteen. At your age, my brothers weren't lounging around listening to the Wailers on a Saturday."

"Why does everyone hate the Wailers?" Rotimi asked, spreading his arms.

"I don't care about the Wailers," I said. "I want you to stop arguing with your sister. You should stick together and support each other."

"Yes, Master Po," he said.

"What?" I asked.

"That's how he talks to Grasshopper," Rolari said.

I had no idea what they were going on about. Rotimi explained that I sounded like Master Po, a character in a television series called *Kung Fu*.

"Keep the noise down," I said. "This is your final warning."

Later that afternoon, we dropped them off at school and I went back to the shopping center to close the shop. I came home and gathered Tunde's used shirts together for the washerman on Sunday. I was taking them downstairs when he walked out of the guest bathroom carrying the copy of *Time*. Instead of assisting me or stepping aside, this man stood in my way and smiled suggestively.

"Why are you looking at me like that?" I asked.

I could walk around our house naked, and he wouldn't notice. The moment I started to do a domestic chore, I was irresistible.

"Can't I look at you?" he asked.

"I'm not in the mood," I said, edging past him.

He slapped my backside as I tried to lift his shirts so I wouldn't tread on them.

"Will you leave me alone?" I shouted.

"Lazy," he said in Yoruba.

"Tell me, Remi—and please stop me if you feel I'm being intrusive. I've been in Nigeria for about a month now, and I still don't have a sense of your national identity."

"By 'national identity' you mean…?"

"Your identification with Nigeria, as a citizen."

"Mine in particular?"

"Nigeria's as a whole."

"You've been in Ikoyi for the most part, Frances."

"Yes, but the political and commercial elite are based there."

"Not entirely. There's Victoria Island, and other places."

"Ikoyi is an important place to start."

"Not if you're interested in ideas. You might want to try the mainland for that. The mainland is full of intellectuals."

"And Ikoyi?"

"Ikoyi is full of people who have ideas about themselves."

"That's funny."

"Actually, Nigeria is well represented in Ikoyi, but you'll have to look beyond elite circles."

"I see."

"Is it even possible for a country like Nigeria to have a national identity?"

"I think so."

"Despite our differences?"

"I believe so."

"And America? What would yours be?"

"Our belief in freedom."

"Would freedom for people in a state like New York be the same for people in a state like—let's say—Alabama?"

"Well, not everyone agrees, but we're constantly debating the idea. The idea of freedom unites us as Americans. We're preoccupied with it."

"The idea of unity preoccupies us here in Nigeria."

"Yes?"

"Who knows, Frances. I've never seriously considered this before. But I suppose every country is bound to keep revisiting the foundation on which it was formed, to make progress, if progress is at all possible."

"Progress is always possible."

"You think?"

"Of course! The trick is to figure out how to make it happen."

"Only from within, though."

"What?"

"I mean, from an African standpoint, outside interference—no matter how well-intentioned—has never worked for us."

"Sometimes there's a duty to intervene."

"But look at our history, our recent history, even. Before independence, we had the colonials to contend with. Now, we're between East and West. Foreign intervention has been disastrous for the African continent, however you look at it. You have to admit."

"Sure, sure."

"Actually, you could tell me more about that."

"Foreign intervention?"

"Where America stands on Nigeria. But if you're interested in the people of Ikoyi, I can tell you something about them."

January 25

On Sunday morning, Tunde went to play golf and I stayed at home and listened to Mahalia Jackson. I rarely went to church these days, except for occasions and holidays. I'd spent my entire childhood in church anyway, and had only ever enjoyed singing hymns. My father's sermons were far too long, and listening to them I believed that God disapproved of wealth. As I grew older and saw how he denied my mother her little indulgences, I began to imagine a camel could pass through the eye of a needle after all. I found his sermons more and more puritanical. He believed that greed was the worst cardinal sin. For my mother it was wrath. Though, after I was caught stealing *chook-chook*, I was inclined to believe she thought gluttony was worse. For me, sloth was the worst cardinal sin. Sloth sounded awful and served no purpose.

Frances called that morning. She asked if I would come with her to Palm Island later in the afternoon. Her friends from the embassy lived in a block of flats by Lagos Lagoon. Their block had a jetty, and they knew someone who had a beach hut and a speedboat. I immediately said yes. The washerman was doing laundry, Jimoh and Patience had the day off and Tunde wouldn't be back until lunchtime.

"You bring Plath," she said. "I'll bring Soyinka."

"I'll bring drinks as well," I said.

We agreed to meet after lunch. I'd abandoned Tunde once before, and once was enough.

He returned from his golf game, and I told him about our plans. We were in the sitting room, and our lunch was laid out on the dining table. We were having *eba*, *ewedu* and a fish stew I'd just prepared. He looked as if I'd announced Frances was having lunch with us.

"Have you met her friends?" he asked.

"I'll meet them today," I said.

He removed his visor and slung his towel over his shoulder. "I'm not sure about this."

"Listen," I said. "I don't have any inside information about General Muhammed, and even if I did, there is nothing she can make me say or do. She would have to drown me first."

It wasn't as if anything that interesting could happen.

"Just be careful," he said.

"I'll come home early," I said, to placate him.

Frances' friends, Greg and Denise Miller, lived on Victoria Island, a few minutes' drive from the yacht club. After lunch, I drove my van there. From the outside, I could tell expatriates occupied the place. The walls were whitewashed and the gutter that ran parallel to the road was fairly clean. A uniformed guard peered into my window to get a closer look at me. The sunglasses and *adire* one piece I wore hardly said "big madam."

I removed my sunglasses. "Open this gate, my friend. I'm in a hurry."

Nigerian staff and their expatriate employers. This one was not about to be intimidated.

"You're here to see…?" he asked.

"The Millers."

He paused, as if assessing whether I were good enough for them, then he returned to the gates and opened them.

The Millers lived on the third floor. Their block didn't have a swimming pool or tennis courts, but walking up the stairs, I got a view of the jetty and Lagos Lagoon. There was a playground with a slide, a see-saw and swings in the backyard. I rang their bell and a dog barked indoors. Their houseboy opened the door dressed in a white uniform.

"Afternoon, madam," he said.

"Good afternoon. Is the dog secure?"

"Yes, madam."

The air conditioner was on. I smelled hamburgers. Frances was in the sitting room with a man who had to be Greg Miller. She was in her khaki shorts and white tank. He was in navy trousers and a navy-and-white striped T-shirt. They both stood up and Greg was about a foot taller than her. His gray hair matched his steel-rimmed glasses.

"Let me see," he said. "I can always tell from features. You must be from the Yoruba tribe."

A tribe, as I understood it, was a horde of relatives.

"I am," I said. "And you?"

"German-Texan, aren't you, Greg?" Frances asked.

His face turned red, though his smile didn't wane.

"Yes," he said. "Sylvester, please tell madam I'm going outside."

"Yes, sir," the houseboy said.

I imagined Denise Miller was less likely to pretend she wasn't insular. She was in the bedroom with their dog, which didn't seem keen on strangers either. It was still barking. I couldn't well look around to ascertain her taste, but on their dining table was a white plastic doily with a display of condiments like Heinz ketchup, French's mustard and Hellmann's mayonnaise. A Pat Boone album leant on a speaker of their stereo system.

Greg Miller had a boat boy called Zacchaeus. He asked Zacchaeus to put my cooler of drinks in the back of the boat. It was a hot afternoon, but once the boat was in motion, the wind and spray of salt water cooled me down. I had to squint to see ahead and shout to be heard. My sleeves flapped in the wind and I bounced on the seat, quite painfully.

As the shoreline disappeared there were fewer bottles, corks and oil leaks on the lagoon. We passed other luxury flats on the waterfront; cranes on the mainland; ships at the port; wrecks farther out; and occasionally, a buoy or a rusty drum bobbing in the waves. I pointed out Tin Can Island. Frances was curious about the fishing villages built on water, their huts raised on stilts. She asked about their makeshift white flags. I told her the flags signified that the villagers belonged to the Celestial Church of Christ.

We approached Palm Island from a gentle stretch of water and slowed down through a crowd of hyacinths. The water was shallow, and a few children were swimming in their underwear. There were several canoes on the beach. A group of women dressed in wrappers beat their washing clean. An elderly man rowed his canoe out as two young men shouted to Zacchaeus, who cut the engine and steered toward the concrete landing, where they stood. Other speedboats were docked there. The young men helped us out, and Zacchaeus carried my cooler.

The islanders had wooden huts with thatched roofs. The palm trees provided shade. The sand was far too hot, so I kept my slippers on. So did Frances, as Zacchaeus walked barefoot ahead of us, my cooler on top of his head. Children followed us and pestered us for our bags. All they wanted was money. I gave them a few coins, and they ran off cheering. As I expected,

Frances paid no attention to them. We stepped over broken tree branches, coconut husks and oyster shells.

"The currents on the other side of the island are dangerous," I said.

"I don't intend to swim," she said. "I might wade, though."

"I wouldn't even wade there."

The islanders knew how treacherous the sea was. Every so often, bodies showed up on their shores and were immediately buried. The islanders would then make offerings to appease their water deity. Expatriates didn't seem to care. They swam anywhere.

The palm trees gave way to casuarinas and banana trees, and we came to a clearing with several circular huts for weekenders, some with corrugated-iron roofs. Ours had a bamboo fence and a veranda overlooking the sea. The waves breaking on the shore sounded like applause. There were two ships on the horizon where the sea was greener. A circus of birds chirped and dove above us.

"It's heavenly here," Frances said.

I breathed in deeply and tasted salt. Lagos was congested, but it was hard to tell just how much until I was away from the city. Zacchaeus put my cooler on the sandy veranda floor, and Frances and I sat on the wicker chairs. She took out Soyinka's *Idanre* from her bag, and I took out *Ariel* from mine and smoothed the cover.

"This Plath woman was brave to take her life," I said.

"You think?"

"Shouldn't it count as an act of bravery if you take your life?"

"Desperation, I would say. My mother took her life."

She was looking toward the sea, and I was shocked by the manner in which she revealed that. Perhaps, as an American, she was less histrionic about death.

"I'm sorry to hear that," I said.

"We should take a walk," she said.

It took me years to come to terms with my father's death. He was the most active man I knew before he fell ill. My mother died in her sleep. She'd had a heart problem, and my brother Akin had tended her. His death was the only sudden death in my family. He was killed in a car crash on his way from Lagos to Ibadan in 1966. He had just got engaged and we were looking forward to their wedding. Deji drove all the way from Ibadan to Lagos to break the news to me, rather than tell me by phone. I took one look at him and slammed the door in his face. It could have been worse. I'd seen women physically assault bearers of bad news.

Frances and I walked along the beach as Zacchaeus returned to the boat. The sea rolled over our bare feet and receded. With every step I took, the waves clapped. We passed other expatriates in their beach huts. They were tanning and playing ball games. Once in a while a passerby greeted us, unable to disguise their curiosity. Apart from the islanders, I was the only Nigerian in sight.

The islanders were not actually Nigerian. They came from as far up the coast as Cotonou and Lomé, and spoke a language I didn't understand. Frances thought there was segregation on the island because expatriates kept to one side of it. I said that was due to the islanders' knowledge of the sea. Nigerians who could afford to wouldn't buy a thatched hut on a remote and dangerous beach. They bought houses on Tarkwa Bay. Bar Beach was the place for the general public on a Sunday afternoon, and they went there in their church clothes.

"People here are so proper," Frances said. "It reminds me of Connecticut in the fifties."

"It's a façade," I said.

Ikoyi was Peyton Place, I said. The people she'd met could have been hiding affairs, alcoholism and Valium habits for all their propriety. Civil marriages could be a front for polygamy. Couples stayed together because women were afraid of the stigma of divorce. Drug use was becoming more rampant among teenagers.

"We're not prepared for this decade," I said. "We talk about the political effects of colonialism, hardly ever about its social effects, on families in particular. If parents are confused, you can imagine how children feel. I watch my children and listen to them, but there are no guarantees. They hide as much from you as you hide from them."

Frances shook her head. "I would be a terrible mother."

"What makes you say that?"

"I'm not patient with children."

"Nor with mothers who talk about their children."

"I don't understand."

"The other night at the Bagatelle, you almost bit Pam's head off."

She smiled. "That's an exaggeration."

"Pam didn't deserve that."

"I could have done without the Holocaust comparison."

"She just talks. She doesn't mean any harm."

"It doesn't matter, anyhow," Frances said. "I don't get along with women in general."

"How come?"

"I never have. There always seems to be underlying competition."

If a woman said that about other women, I had to wonder if the problem was with her.

"Perhaps your issue is with mothers," I said.

"Maybe," she said. "I always seem to be justifying myself to them."

"You don't have to justify yourself to me. Only yesterday, I gladly sent my children off to school."

"On a Saturday?"

"They're in boarding schools."

"Why?"

"You're against that?"

"I went to one after my mother died. There's so much snobbery in those institutions."

"It's different here. The federal government funds their schools and they have students from all over the country. The idea is to raise a new generation of Nigerians more united than ours."

"But they're away from home for most of the year."

"They wanted to go. They like being with their friends. They prefer it to being at home. It makes them more independent."

"Sounds like you're justifying yourself to me."

"Of course."

"Why have children only to send them away?"

"Have them and you will know."

A couple ahead were waving at us. The woman wore a black bathing suit and the man navy shorts. They were the Woods. I was not surprised to see them.

"It's Bev and Dave," I said, waving back. "You met them at the golf club."

"I remember," Frances said, coolly.

They were elated to see her. Dave couldn't stop grinning and Bev, as was her wont, blinked as if someone were periodically throwing sand in her face.

"Having fun?" Dave asked.

"Yes," Frances said.

"This is the best-kept secret in Lagos," Bev said, breathlessly.

"Beats Bognor Beach any day," Dave said, glancing at me.

He watched his feet as Bev interrogated Frances.

"I thought you were going to Benin City?"

"I did."

"Do you know people there?"

"It was a business trip."

"Really? What business?"

Frances told her about her research on the trade beads, as Dave now watched her, his face flushed.

"Where are you heading for next?" Bev persisted.

"Osogbo," Frances said.

Bev turned to Dave. "Isn't that where that woman lives, the German one who married the local drummer?"

"Actually, she's Austrian," Dave said, rising on his toes. "She was born in Graz. She was initially married to Ulli Beier, who founded the Mbari Club for Nigerian writers, but she's become something of a local dignitary in O…"

"Osogbo," I said.

He turned to me. "She was initiated as some sort of juju priestess there, wasn't she?"

"A priestess of the Oshun shrines," I said.

Silly so-and-sos, I thought. To them, Yoruba religion was juju and no one in Nigeria wrote stories before Ulli Beier. Osogbo and its entire history would not exist but for Susanne Wenger. Of course they would dismiss the Osogbo school as "naïve" art.

Dave remembered his golf game with Ade and promised to arrange one after Frances returned from Osogbo. As we said goodbye, he and Bev echoed each other.

"Right you are."

"Right you are."

"They're so nosy," Frances said, when we were at a safe distance.

The Woods were also outdated. She asked how I knew them, and I told her that Dave worked for Barclays and Tunde was with Community Bank, finally mentioning his retirement from the civil service.

We had felt let down, I said, but General Gowon's leadership had maintained the status quo, while General Muhammed's was a step away from looking to the West for patronage. Africa, on the whole, needed leaders who had Muhammed's independent vision, but Gowon had diplomacy in his favor, which could be useful for international relations, and reorganizing the civil service. The civil service didn't function the way the military did and responded to Muhammed's policies on the basis of fear. Muhammed was a controversial head of state, despised or admired depending on where Nigerians stood on his record in the Civil War. He had called on Nigerians to be disciplined. Discipline was what we needed to rebuild Nigeria, but why couldn't we function without someone telling us how? Why did we need a messiah to lead us? Hadn't Nkrumah's demise taught us anything about the fallibility of African leaders?

I shared my views without feeling like a traitor. Showing that sort of loyalty to a country was insincere. The spirit of nationalism was invoked as a deliberate effort to rebuild Nigeria, and I preferred to interpret nationalism as a call to take responsibility for my actions.

"In this place," I said, "you very quickly find out who your friends are when you're out of a government position. But it's a blessing when people reveal themselves to you, and the best part is that it woke me up. For years I didn't have the courage to go into business. Now, I've taken the step."

"You might eventually renew your friendships."

"If resentment doesn't get in the way."

She laughed. "I suppose that was what I was referring to about the women I know. It's almost as if they belong to a twentieth-century culture of domesticity. To them, I'm unconventional. But moving around was normal for me."

"Where did you live?"

"California, Colorado, Montana, Washington DC. Not overseas, though. We moved practically every other year. My mother was terribly lonely. She didn't find it easy to make new friends. Then she got depressed. But when you're raised in a home like that, the last thing you want to do is get married."

I told her I never thought I had a choice, but I wasn't afraid of marriage. My father used to say he was in God's army, and my mother believed it was her duty, a woman's duty, to stay at home and raise children. The culture of domesticity in Ikoyi was a Western import, I said. I found my mother's lifelong dedication to my father admirable, but had not realized how much my occasional presence at his family mediations had influenced me. I was impressed by the financial independence of the women of Saint John's. Running a business gave me a sense of autonomy I'd never had working for the government. Marriage had slowed me down only in the short term; I still believed I was free to pursue my ambitions.

"What do you do for companionship?" I asked.

"Um…"

"You know."

"Oh, that? My best lovers have known when it is time to leave."

"My husband is the only lover I've ever had."

"No!"

"I was a priest's daughter!"

"Where I'm from they have the worst reputations!"

"Here, too, but I took eternal damnation to heart."

"Don't you ever feel trapped?"

"Not at all," I said. "I've never understood why sleeping around is liberating. Anyone can do that. I'm not even sure that equality with men is all it's made out to be, to be honest. All it means for me is that I have to work harder than my husband to be on par with him."

She may not have believed me, and her answer about her lovers had sounded rehearsed, but I'd told Rolari as much. Sex was sacrosanct and not to be given away freely. Then I said she was in charge of her body, which was somewhat contradictory. In fact, it would have been progressive to tell her to save herself for marriage. Young women who got pregnant could end up being disowned by their families and shunned by society, with little chance of having a career. So, women elsewhere could espouse ideas about sexual freedom, but they were not applicable in Nigeria. As for equality with men, it seemed incomplete to fight for women to be on par with men and not the other way around. If men couldn't look after children, who else but women would be left with that duty?

On the whole, I found Frances' views limited. Where did American women who didn't have her opportunities fit in? What would the vast majority of Nigerian women do without men with whom they could pool resources? Still, she was more than a change. She was a promise—that it was possible for a woman to choose to be single and childless without looking like a sorry case. I didn't know one Nigerian woman like her.

I knew one who had a child by someone else's husband and started using Mrs. with her maiden name, which was ingenious, but we still pitied her.

"It gets lonely sometimes," Frances said.

"Even with husbands," I said.

We headed back to the hut, and I continued to share my views with her, glad that she was astute enough to have dispensed with hyperbolic foreign expectations of African life. Without mentioning names, I gave examples of families I knew—the Baloguns, the Kasumus, the Ibrahims, the Onyias and the Dadas. If she wanted a profile of Ikoyi people, then she would get one. I almost asked why the United States demonized leftist ideology and elevated democracy to the status of a religion, but decided against it. She wasn't what I would call a friend yet, but we were past showing each other false courtesies.

"You should come to Osogbo with me," she said.

"I don't travel around Nigeria for fun," I said.

The last time I'd traveled within Nigeria for pleasure was in the late sixties. I had nice memories of family holidays at Hamdala Hotel in Kaduna, Kainji Lake National Park in New Bussa and a little guest house on a hill in Akure.

"Aren't you curious about the orisha groves?" she asked.

"They are religious edifices not tourist attractions," I said.

"You must have visited churches overseas."

"I have."

I had been to the Vatican, I'd even been to Lourdes, where I'd sprinkled holy water on my head. I was curious about the orisha groves but not enough to visit them. They were like Stonehenge to a Londoner. My father, for all his tolerance of Yoruba beliefs, would never have visited them. To him, they would be symbols of idolatry; sacrilegious, rather than religious. But I did wonder why it took an Austrian woman to restore them and an American woman to point out their significance to me.

Frances began to read Soyinka's "Death in the Dawn" out loud. "Traveller, you must set out | At dawn. And wipe your feet upon | The dog-nose wetness of earth…"

"I'm not setting out anywhere," I said.

It was all right for her to go traipsing around the country. She had no one to answer to.

"Is it me or are people here suspicious of me?"

"Should we be?"

"Are you?"

"You know your people. You cause trouble everywhere you go."

"You've been quite welcoming for someone who's suspicious."

"You arrived at the right time."

"Coup season?"

"No. I'm no longer a government official's wife."

January 29

Ade called from his law firm on Broad Street, that week.

"I hear you've been fraternizing with the CIA," he said.

"What makes you think that?" I asked.

I was in my office, but had time to talk; it was almost closing time.

"Haven't you heard?" he said. "Lagos is teeming with them since Muhammed's OAU speech."

"How do people know these things?"

"The same way we know there's going to be a coup."

I trusted Frances a lot more after our beach outing, but not entirely.

"What are the CIA doing here, then?" I asked. "Twiddling their thumbs until a coup happens?"

"They're probably arranging it," he said. "How is my friend Deji? I keep inviting him over to Lagos, but he keeps postponing."

"You know how much my brother dislikes this place."

I hadn't seen Deji in a while and planned to visit him and his family in Ibadan at Easter time. I would never allow him to stay with Ade if he came to Lagos. Ade would take him to every club in town and introduce him to every woman he knew, anything to ensure Deji's marriage ended up as miserable as his.

I asked how he'd heard about my trip to Palm Island with Frances, and he said Dave Wood had told him about it.

"So your friend Frances is in Osogbo?" he asked.

"So she says."

"Don't you believe her?"

"I didn't say that."

He laughed. "You think she's with the CIA?"

"I think we overrate our importance by assuming every American here is."

"I need her phone number, please."

"What for?"

"To arrange this game with the Woods. They've been harassing me about it."

"Aren't you against fraternizing with the CIA?" I asked.

"I will tell the CIA anything and everything they need to know," he said. "Let them come and neutralize whatever elements they're not in favor of."

I'd accused Ade of a lot, but never of being unpatriotic. His practice had flourished during the First Republic. It seemed as if every time I opened a newspaper he was there, giving the victory sign over a political case he had won. Now, he was waiting for the end of military rule, so he could get into politics himself. The mere mention of the word "military" could set him off.

"At least they've spared us a coup this January," I said.

"Don't speak too soon," he said. "We may have one any day now."

"I don't pray for that to happen."

My opinion was that General Muhammed hadn't had enough time to implement his reforms. His was that Muhammed's reforms would be the downfall of the civil service—because if civil servants didn't know how long they would be in office, the incidence of corruption would only increase.

"Besides," he said, "I've had enough of these army boys. They keep throwing their weight around and trying to take over everywhere. They even want to take over the golf club. You should see the trouble one brigadier is giving me because I want to be captain."

"What is he doing?"

"Everything to make sure I lose."

The brigadier had maligned Ade to the Nigerian members of the golf club. Ade was upset because he felt the Nigerian members ought to be more united in their bid to vote in a Nigerian captain; otherwise, the next captain would be an ex-patriate. The whole matter seemed rather schoolgirlish to me.

"What hurts me most is that Moji is carrying on with the stupid fellow," he said. "I couldn't get her to come to the club with me. She said she wasn't interested in golf. Now, she keeps showing up there all dressed up and telling me she is decorating his house."

"That's partly my fault."

"How so?"

"I told her she should get out more and get back to work."

"Why would you do that?"

"Do you intend to support her financially?"

"Remi, the moment I divorce that woman, she will be cut off."

"Ade—"

"Please don't defend her. You don't know what she's like. The woman is a disgrace."

"Why aren't you allowing her to see your children?"

"Because she didn't raise them. She ruined them. You should see my fourteen-year-old. She wears more makeup than a forty-year-old. My son is behaving like a...a lout. The youngest one doesn't even know how to make her bed. I'm sending all of them to boarding school in England next year, and if I have my way, their mother will never see them again."

I pitied their judge; they would wear him or her out with their recriminations. Moji didn't spoil their children; she used them. She gave them anything they wanted to win them over—money, the freedom to do as they pleased—and now Ade was using them.

"You think that's fair?" I asked.

"Look, Remi, you know how much I love my children, and understand what they have been through, but I can't let them become juvenile delinquents."

I would never tell Ade I'd heard his son smoked marijuana, but perhaps he'd already found out. He said the boy had been suspended from school the week before. He and his friends had sneaked out of their boarding house to go to Fela's nightclub, Shrine. His housemaster caught them coming back, caned them and called Ade the next morning. Ade was furious.

"I sat him down and tried to talk some sense into his head when we got home. I said, 'You gave up piano lessons. You can't even remember where you put your guitar and you're sneaking out of school to see Fela, who graduated from Trinity College of Music. You'd better think straight and face your studies.' Instead of my son learning his lesson, he was smoking in his room the next day. I caught him red-handed. I told him I would flog him with a horsewhip if I ever caught him doing that again."

"You won't flog him with a horsewhip."

"Why not? It won't kill him. My mother caned me throughout my youth and look where I am today. I have her to thank for that. Mollycoddling our children will only backfire on us. They're African, not European. If we don't discipline them, of what use will they be to themselves?"

I was astonished whenever people who were otherwise reasonable and intelligent used some hackneyed idea of African culture or tradition as an excuse for their appalling behavior. But Ade was just grandstanding as usual. He was not capable of flogging his son with a horsewhip.

"I know you're upset," I said, "but you must show your children kindness at a time like this, and you're not doing that by alienating them from their mother."

"Remi, let us not waste time talking about that woman. She's out of my life. I have a client with a huge estate I'm attending to right now."

Ade annoyed me terribly, whenever he gave me unsolicited information about his affairs.

"Leave Oyinda alone," I said, assuming he was referring to her.

"Oyinda?" he said. "I haven't seen her since her art exhibition, and from what I saw, she was more interested in your husband than in me."

He was mischievous to bring that up, but that was typical of Ade, to imply he was no different from other men.

He continued to pester me for Frances' number, so I gave him the Millers', which she had given me, and warned him to behave himself.

"The Miller man works for the US embassy," I said. "Our relations with them are already shaky, so please don't do anything that might end in a diplomatic disaster."

He laughed. "Don't worry about that. Greet Mr. Lawal for me."

Tunde played golf only on Sundays, so he might have missed the ongoing drama between the Baloguns. He got home well after I did that evening. I was busy preparing dinner and I stepped out of the kitchen to say hello to him in the sitting room.

"Have you seen Moji at the club lately?" I asked.

"No," he said. "Why?"

"Ade called. He said he's running for captain."

"He's wasting his time. No one will vote for him."

"He said he's running against some brigadier Moji is involved with."

Tunde sat in his chair. "I don't want to hear anything about the Baloguns."

His grumpiness amused me. He was used to having his dinner ready and waiting for him when he arrived, but today I was running late.

On a whim, I asked, "Have you heard from Oyinda?"

"Why would I have heard from her?"

"I'm just asking. Ade and I were talking about her. He said he hadn't seen her since her art exhibition, and since you two are such art enthusiasts…"

He gave me the look. "I thought you were meant to be busy in that shop of yours."

I laughed and returned to the kitchen. I was only making sure we hadn't caught what Ade and Moji had, and what had afflicted most marriages in Lagos. There was a lull in our marriage since I started my business that I couldn't ignore. Men went back to the rudiments of tradition for lesser crimes—late meals, a lax attitude to disciplining children, a refusal to obey, all of which I was guilty of. No woman wanted to be that tragic wife, oblivious, vulnerable and finally undone.

"Well, this has been informative."

"For me as well."

"Really?"

"What we've talked about wouldn't come up in a conversation with another Nigerian."

"I suppose not. Do you think there will be another coup this year?"

"I'm not sure. January has almost come to an end and we haven't had one."

"You have the rest of the year."

"We'll have to see how next month goes. Will you still be around?"

"In February?"

"Yes."

"You bet."

January 31

Oyinda was at the trade fair for Nigerian fashion on Saturday. It was held at the national museum, in a part of Onikan that was the closest we had to an arts and culture district in Lagos. Outside the museum was Ben Enwonwu's statue, "Rising Sun." Indoors, there were collections of Benin bronzes, Igbo-Ukwu pots, and Ife and Nok terracottas. Next to the museum was a craft center, and across the street was J. K. Randle Memorial Hall. The hall was one of two public venues on the island where people could see theatrical productions. The other was Glover Memorial Hall, which had been in existence before I was born. Not far from Glover Memorial were the Nigerian Arts Council, the French Cultural Center and the Goethe Institute. A Bulgarian construction company was in the process of building a national theater on the mainland. A real theater in Lagos was long overdue.

On the tarred section of the museum's grounds, rows of chairs were arranged under canopies with a catwalk in between. A few expatriates were already seated. There wasn't a Nigerian in sight, and I assumed that was because they were late. I was barely on time. The trade fair was to end with a fashion show sponsored by the French consulate. The designer, Efuru, had trained in Paris and her fashion line, *L'Ananas*, was for caftans made with *adire* and *ankara* cloths. Her brochure said she was a child of Biafra, and described *ankara* as Dutch wax print and *adire* as tie-dyed ancient symbols. The latter description must have been conjured up for the benefit of expatriates. The *adire* she'd used was dyed by a co-op of women in Ibadan, and the *ankara* was manufactured by a Chinese-owned textile mill in Kaduna.

Efuru could pass for a model. Her hair was threaded, and her eyes were boldly penciled. She wore one of her caftans. A middle-aged Frenchman guided her around, his errant hands on her back.

Vive la France, I thought, walking past them.

I headed for the exhibition stalls, which were on a stretch of lawn between a mango tree and an almond tree. Pam's glass-bead necklaces were on display in hers. She wore an indigo *adire* dress. Helen was with her, in a white shift dress and gold choker.

"My favorite customer," Helen said, as we hugged each other.

"I've told everyone about your cakes," I said. "So you'd better tell everyone about my cards."

She laughed. "We should go into partnership—Cakes and Cards."

"That would be perfect. I need someone to absorb my loss."

Her skin was almost as dark as mine, and she'd lost a few pounds. Her husband, Stergios, owned a shipping company in Lagos. They had been to Athens with their children over the Christmas holiday. Before she left, she'd complained that her bakery business was wreaking havoc on her weight. Helen was the only woman I knew in Lagos who used imported diet shakes and bars correctly. The Nigerian women I knew had them for snacks between meals.

She took over the stall so Pam and I could talk.

"Have I missed the fashion show?" I asked.

"It hasn't started yet," Pam said.

"Why not?"

"We're waiting for the Minister of Communications."

We joked about African timekeeping. Pam said Hilda had been to the fair earlier, but had to return to her salon, and Naomi was up north.

"When will she be back in Lagos?" I asked.

"Sooner than she thought," Pam said. "Her polio program has practically come to a standstill."

So had the history department at the University of Lagos where Pam's husband, Niyi, worked. I didn't see my friends in academia as often as I would have liked because they lived on the mainland. I'd once thought they were more level-headed than Ikoyi people, but had come to find out about the bickering that went on in their circles. Academics were vicious to one another, and their rivalries never seemed to end. Kwesi Mensah and Philip Ekong were well-regarded at the College of Medicine. Niyi Ogedengbe, on the other hand, wasn't popular, having hindered the progress of several of his colleagues.

I told Pam I would be back to buy a necklace or two and wandered around. There were stalls for jewelry made by Nigerian silversmiths and bronzesmiths; stalls for *aso oke*, Akwete, Okene, Nupe and other hand woven textiles. The idea of having textiles on display at a trade fair was unusual. If I needed to buy fabric of any sort, I simply went to Jankara Market. Besides, apart from handwoven cloth, such as *aso oke*, most of what we used to make traditional wear was not indigenous to Nigeria. Lace came from Switzerland and Austria. God only knew where silk head ties came from. Even the *adire* my *boubous* were made from came from somewhere else, and so did their dyes. It was rare to find *adire* dyed, as it originally was, with indigo.

Most of the expatriates around were French, but there were a few francophone West Africans and Lebanese who spoke a more *occidentale* French, and seemed to have perfected French mannerisms. Watching them, I was glad the British had colonized Nigeria. The fact that we didn't quite live up to British expectations was a good indication that they'd failed where the French had succeeded.

Hilda's nemesis, Kamal, was there. So were several of his customers, who all had his signature bob. He was a chubby fellow, with striking hazel eyes.

"*Bonsoir, madame,*" he said.

"*Bonsoir,*" I said and nodded.

Kamal was always courteous, but I had to let him know I was in Hilda's camp.

I stopped to say hello to Yasmine, who was Lebanese as well, but not one of his customers. She wore a loose chignon and diamond earrings.

"Remi, my sweet," she said.

"Congratulations," I said, apologetically.

She kissed me on both cheeks. Her husband, Emile, had just been made a chief. Emile was born in Nigeria and his father, who was still alive, spoke fluent Yoruba. I hadn't been able to attend his ceremony. He and Yasmine were known for wining and dining influential Nigerians to gain favor, but they did it with such charm it was hard to hold their behavior against them. They also made a point of dissociating themselves from a couple of Lebanese brothers who had been exposed for making dubious deals with government officials, though I had a sense that had more to do with rivalry than righteous indignation.

"Why didn't you come?" Yasmine asked.

"I'm terribly sorry. You know I have a new shop."

She shimmied. "I heard. We must make libation."

Even a casual celebration for Yasmine and Emile would involve champagne. Despite their reputation for merrymaking, I was sure the civil war in Lebanon was heartbreaking for them. They were Catholic. Kamal was Muslim and, from what I'd gathered, a confirmed bachelor.

I returned to the fashion-show location to find a group of Nigerian women dressed in flared pants and wrap skirts. They sat with their legs crossed, studying their brochures.

"Is *L'Ananas* banana?" one of them asked.

"It's pineapple," another said.

"I thought that was *pamplemousse*."

"No, that's grapefruit."

Nigerians of their stature admired glamor and sophistication, and they would consider French people glamorous and sophisticated, whether or not the French people around us actually were. Most of them wore casual T-shirts, khaki trousers or shorts, and a few had even brought their children along.

Meera walked up to me, adjusting her *sari*. She, too, had a Kamal bob.

"Remi," she said. "When did you arrive?"

"About half an hour ago. I was at the exhibition stalls."

"I was there, too. We must have missed each other."

"I gather I've missed nothing here."

"We're waiting for the Minister of Communications."

We sat next to one another. The seats were already half full.

"So this Efuru lives in Paris?" I asked.

Meera nodded. "They flew her in."

"Did you see Pam's collection?"

"Yes, it's lovely."

Meera was always tactful. She would never be impressed by Pam's necklaces. She wore double-strand pearls and matching earrings.

We fanned ourselves with our brochures as we talked about the opening of the Bombay Grill, which I'd also missed. She and Anil were Punjabi Hindus and quite the opposite of the low-key Indian teachers my children encountered in school.

Fela's "Palaver" began to play, and a woman stepped onto the catwalk. For a moment, I thought the fashion show was beginning until I realized the woman was Moji Balogun, who proceeded to strut down the catwalk in a caftan.

"She arrived like that," Meera said, making drinking gestures.

"I know her," I said.

"You do?" Meera asked.

I nodded as Moji posed with her hand on her hip. People were staring at her. She was clearly enjoying the attention because she smiled and pivoted.

"Oh dear," Meera said. "This is most unusual."

I was about to say it was embarrassing, but gasped as Moji staggered. Two Frenchmen rushed to her rescue and escorted her to a chair. I decided to go over and speak to her. Someone had to.

"Remi!" she exclaimed. "I didn't know you were here! I've been meaning to call you! Sit here, sit here…"

She pushed a brochure off a chair. She smelled of gin and her speech was slurred.

"How are you?" I asked.

"Wonderful," she said, holding my hand. "I took your advice. Yes, I did. One morning, I just got up and said to myself, 'Moji, get going.' So I did."

She could barely keep her eyes open and wouldn't let go of my hand. I sat awkwardly as she talked in her usual naïve manner.

"I told myself, 'Moji, you have to move on. Life is what you make it. This is a new beginning for you. You have the world at your feet. You just have to seize the day. Men will be men. A woman has to do what a woman has to do. The worst is over and you're none the worse for wear.'"

"I'm glad you're up and about," I said.

"I am, I am."

"I spoke to Ade," I said, after a moment.

She hissed. "Please don't mention that man's name to me. When I'm finished with him, he will not be able to hold his head up in Lagos."

"What happened?"

"I saw him at the golf club and I said to him, 'I want to see my children.' He said I could forget about ever seeing them again."

"He can't say that."

"You don't know him. He threatened to send them to boarding school in England. I told him that if he tries any such thing, I will deal with him. I know people in the army. I will do anything and everything I can to bring him down."

I resigned myself to the fact that I couldn't help the Baloguns. Brokering peace in Angola would be easier.

"I like your outfit," I said.

"It's *L'Ananas*," she said, lifting her chin. "By Efuru."

Biola showed up with a host of other tardy Nigerians. She was dressed in a lace *iro* and *buba*. I made the mistake of getting up to greet her, partly in an attempt to escape Moji, who continued to hold my hand and spout platitudes, but within seconds of my doing so, a woman took my seat and Moji didn't see fit to stop her, so I was stuck with Biola. We stood by a canopy pole that seemed a solitary shake away from toppling over.

"Why hasn't this thing started?" Biola asked, above the noise.

"We're waiting for the Minister of Communications."

"These people…"

"How did the cocktail party with your commissioner go?"

She shrugged. "You know how government functions can be."

I was thankful Tunde had spared me from attending some government functions when he was in the civil service. I walked into them and my back straightened. I talked to people I didn't care about and was astonished by the inanities that came out of my mouth. To top it all, we were sometimes subjected to police bands playing songs like "*Guantanamera*" and "Strangers in the Night" too loudly.

"Any inside information we should be aware of?" I asked.

"We might have more states soon."

The last time the government had created new states we'd had a civil war. Biola thought a military coup was inevitable.

"It's a matter of time. That's why we've had no light."

I'd never understood the connection between new states, power cuts and coups, but I accepted it as I did the Holy Trinity. My acceptance was as final as the certainty that our government would continue to fail us, and all we could do as Nigerians was manage the system.

"You're sweating," Biola said, handing me a tissue that smelled of Chanel No. 5.

I dabbed my face. "How have you been?"

"You have tissue stuck on your lashes."

Never a compliment from her, even when we were friendlier.

I was furious with myself for getting up to greet her, and fell silent as she began to make rude comments. About the French: "They love African culture, but they hate Africans." About their diplomats: "They send them to Nigeria to punish them, you know," and about Efuru: "If she is a child of Biafra, what is she doing in Lagos?"

I hoped there was a difference between Biola and me. Was making fun of people the same as putting them down? Perhaps the former just begged a willingness to admit cynicism. Perhaps we had more in common than I was prepared to admit.

The Minister of Communications never showed up. He sent a representative who apologized for her lateness, blaming Lagos traffic, and gave a long speech, which she couldn't even read properly. The French cultural attaché then introduced Efuru, in French, without a translator.

Efuru's collection was playful. She had caftans with one sleeve, thigh-high slits and low backs. After her show, the audience applauded her. She posed with the government representative for the press, and then for group photos with her models. Biola, who had watched them as if they were a parade of prostitutes, asked, "Is that it?"

"It looks like it," I said.

"I'd better get going."

"So soon?" I asked, relieved.

"I have to. I sacked my houseboy."

"Why?"

"He was stealing food from me."

"That's a shame."

We hugged and said goodbye. I went in search of Pam, but instead bumped into Oyinda, who was being tugged by a Frenchman.

"I've been trying to catch your eye!" she said. "I spoke to your husband! I asked him to fund my next exhibition! Remind him that I'm in desperate need of funding!"

I wasn't sure if she was referring to their conversation at her Cultural Society event or a subsequent one, but before I could ask, the Frenchman had dragged her away.

Pam and Helen were packing up at her stall when I caught up with them. Pam was excited about the interest in her bead necklaces and had sold most of them. I was unlikely to wear any, but I bought a couple to give away as presents. After we said goodbye I looked for Moji, who was nowhere in sight, and it was just as well. I'd had enough for the day.

Driving out of the museum was hellish. The car park was full of French cars mostly, Renaults, Citroëns and Peugeots, but there were a few Volkswagens and BMWs, and the odd Benz and Volvo. I'd come to the trade fair in my van, to advertise Occasions Unlimited, but each time I tried to reverse, someone strolled past as if they were on rue du Faubourg Saint-Honoré. I waited for a chance, wondering why it took foreigners to discover, nurture and promote Nigerian talent. But for the French and their claim to superiority in the field of humanities, I would never have heard about Efuru. No one would be talking about *L'Ananas*. They would probably be calling her a bloody Biafran. Everyone who needed to make a name for him- or herself in Nigeria came to Lagos. Efuru would know that, if she had any sense. That was the lot of Igbos who had ambition, having to curry favor from the very people who had sought to destroy them. She probably hated the whole lot of us.

I finally got a chance to reverse, while taking directions from a driver who shouted, "*Oya, oya, oya*, madam," to hurry me along. He stood in the way of other drivers, and I was so grateful I waved at him as they pressed on their horns and cursed him. At the entrance of the museum, I caught sight of him in my rearview mirror. He refused to budge as the other drivers emerged from their cars and gesticulated, and their masters and madams rolled their windows down to find out what the hullabaloo was about.

I was no cynic. A cynic wouldn't take pleasure in that sight. A cynic would never be amused by Lagos, or love the place as much.

FEBRUARY

February 1

My mother saw conflict as a manifestation of evil—or, more accurately, a potential for evil to arise. She avoided arguments for that reason, and encouraged me to do the same. My father, on the other hand, believed that arguments were inevitable and necessary for advancement, which was how I sometimes saw them. Conflict, he once said, was a confluence of oil and water, which could never be possible without spin and heat. Evil was quite separate and more likely to thrive in still and quiet places.

Frances called on Sunday morning to say she was back from Osogbo. Tunde and I were in bed reading the newspapers when I answered the phone, which was on my bedside table. He was in his pajamas, and I was in my housecoat and about to go downstairs for breakfast. Patience was in the kitchen, making pancakes from a mixture I'd prepared earlier on.

"Did I wake you?" Frances asked.

"No, no," I said.

Tunde and I had been up for a while. Neither of us could sleep after six in the morning because our bedroom window faced the sunrise and our curtains were translucent.

She said Ade Balogun had called her the night before. He had invited her to play golf with himself and the Woods the following Saturday. He had also offered to lend her a set of clubs he'd bought for his wife, who had never used them. She asked if it was okay to accept his invitation.

"Of course," I said. "But I must tell you, he and his wife are going through a divorce."

"They are?"

"Yes. In fact, I was against him contacting you because of that."

"Would it be seen as improper?"

"No, but I just think you should know beforehand."

"Oh, good. It's only a round of golf, but you never know. It's funny that he talks about the lack of enthusiasm from Nigerian women, yet he seems to think golf is a man's game. But I'm always up for a sports challenge. Will you join us?"

"I'm not interested in golf."

"I mean for a drink, afterward."

I knew Tunde was listening, even though the newspaper he was supposedly reading hid his face. He was playing golf later in the morning, and after lunch, we were going to visit Rolari.

"Next Saturday may not be good for me," I said.

"I'm leaving Lagos soon, though," she said.

"Are you going home?"

"No, to Ghana, then I'm going home. I would really like you to join us. It would be nice to have you around."

I wondered why she would accept Ade's invitation to play against the Woods. Between their nosiness and his chauvinism, her golf game might not be such a pleasant experience. I agreed to meet her for drinks anyway, and after I replaced the phone told Tunde, who then spread his newspaper across his legs and began to interrogate me.

"Where is she staying?"

"With her friends."

"Which friends?"

"The Millers."

"What is she going to Ghana for?"

"I don't know."

"Didn't you ask?"

"Does it matter?" I said, irritably.

He raised his hand. "You've given the woman enough information! What more does she want?"

His insistence that she was a spy was now just ridiculous.

"Tunde," I said.

"What? I don't know why she's inviting you to the club, that's all. You take her there once and now she's inviting you, as if she is the member. That's the trouble with these Americans. You give them an inch, they take…ten miles. How long has she known Ade, anyway?"

He was being insincere. Perhaps he didn't want me going to the golf club and infiltrating his territory. He had always been overprotective about the place.

"Ade invited her. She wasn't even keen, at first."

"Why must you have drinks with them?"

"Why can't *you* join us?"

He folded the newspaper. "Sunday is my day for golf and I have no time for Ade. I'm not sure why you have time for him, if you're so busy."

His petulance was beginning to bore me. I turned the focus on him.

"Have you spoken to Oyinda recently?"

"Why would I have spoken to Oyinda?"

"I saw her yesterday and she said she spoke to you."

"What has that got to do with what we're talking about?"

"I'm just saying. You have your associations and I have mine."

"Oh, so I'm associated with Oyinda now?"

"She said you talked about her art exhibition."

"Someone calls me at work to ask me for funding, and suddenly I'm associated with them."

"The point is, I don't tell you who you can or cannot talk to. I don't even know who you're talking to on a daily basis."

"My dear, you either focus on what we're talking about or we can forget this discussion. I'm not interested in irrelevant digressions."

He could so easily become condescending. He wanted me to go back to being a housewife. That was the issue. He was against Frances, Ade or anyone who interfered with my precious time at home. I wasn't sure if I was angry at him or myself that he'd come to the conclusion I was that kind of woman.

I stood up. "You can't control where I go and who I see. I will walk away before I put up with a marriage like that."

"Oh, here we go. Kuramo Fiasco, Round 2."

"Try me, if you think I'm joking," I said, snapping my fingers. "You knew who I was when you married me. The best thing you can do as a man is let me be. If you can't manage that, then carry your trouble and go."

"I thought you were the one threatening to leave," he said.

"It's not a threat anymore. I'm running my own business now."

He laughed. "How? By gallivanting around Lagos?"

"Who has time to gallivant?"

"By socializing with friends?"

"They're my clients!"

"I see. Now, they're clients."

I pointed. "Another thing. I'm going to the club, whether you like it or not."

He shrugged. "As you wish. You said it yourself. I never married a woman who would obey my every word."

Annoying man. He had his game of golf that morning, and we were barely on speaking terms when we visited Rolari in school. She may have noticed, even though we made attempts to smile at each other and greet other parents.

The building reconstructions at Queen's meant that certain sections of the yard, normally accessible, were now out of bounds. Students had to take classes in the chapel and quadrangle. A temporary kitchen had been set up. We sat in the Quiet Zone near the principal's office. Rolari was in her Sunday uniform, a navy gingham dress with a butterfly collar.

"I forgot to say 'Rabbit, rabbit,'" she said.

"Don't worry, my dear," I said.

She and her boarder friends had superstitious rituals. This one was to chant "Rabbit, rabbit, come to me," at midnight before the beginning of every month to prevent bad luck. I thought it was their way of managing their anxieties. Their boarding school was strictly hierarchical. Rolari had two more years to go before she became a senior, and seniors, meanwhile, could send her on errands. They called that "fagging." Some seniors went as far as to fag juniors to fetch buckets of water and wash clothes.

Rolari seemed happy enough with her boarding-school life, but she told us she'd participated in a coup against a class bully that week. She and a few classmates got together and informed the bully that she had been overthrown. Staging a coup was new for them. Their usual system of justice was to summon offenders to their class storeroom for mock tribunals. This time, the bully was so upset to be compared to a dictator she broke down and cried, so Rolari called the coup off.

"Why did you do that?" Tunde asked.

"We dealt with her, Daddy. She said she was sorry."

"You should never have forgiven her."

"She's piped down now."

"For how long?" he asked. "She can mistake your pity for weakness and start giving you trouble again. You have to follow through to crush the opposition."

Master Po, I thought. He despised bullies, yet, in his own way, he could be one. He went on giving advice that seemed more conducive to military men planning a strategy. If I had a tendency to be inconsistent with discipline, his guidance was often way off course. Yet he seemed to think he was entitled to have the last word in the family. Rolari, too, was taken aback by his stance on the matter, though she didn't object.

"You don't give people like that a chance," he said. "Not for a moment. If it were the other way around, she wouldn't be so forgiving. So follow through and there will be no question of a next time. You hear me?"

"I hear you," she said.

She was more lenient with her father. Advice like that would have earned me an eye roll.

February 2

That week we had frequent power cuts in our neighborhood. They started in the early evenings and ended well after midnight. At work, the noise from other shops' electricity generators was incessant, and I didn't use one in my shop, so I had to keep my office windows open.

On Monday evening, I came home to find Patience in tears. I asked why she was crying, and she said Jimoh had attacked her before he'd left to pick up Tunde from work. He looked forward to the odd days when Tunde was working late and he was allowed to drive the Volvo. On this occasion, the privilege had apparently gone to his head because, according to Patience, he'd grabbed her by her sleeve and her uniform got ripped as she tried to free herself. She showed me the split seam, which she'd reattached with a safety pin.

"Why would he do that to you, for heaven's sake?" I asked.

"He say I use juju, madam," she said, wiping her tears with the back of her hand. "He say I rub potion for my skin, so you can like me."

I'd assumed their hostility toward each other was due to the fact that they shared the boys' quarters. I had no idea it had anything to do with gaining favor with me.

"Why would he even think such a thing?" I asked.

"I no know, madam."

Whenever I passed her, she had a distinct powdery scent.

She was Catholic, and Lent was around the corner, but that might not stop her from buying a potion if she were that way inclined.

The thought alarmed me. "Why were you people talking about juju, anyway?"

"No be me, madam."

"Are you using a potion on your skin?"

"*Na* common pomade, ma."

She shifted from one foot to the other and I remembered Tunde saying she had an untrustworthy face. At the time, I thought she was just uneasy around him. He was her *oga*, after all, and hardly ever said a word to her. Her attempts to ingratiate herself with him always came across as forced.

"It had better be," I said. "Because if I find out otherwise, you will leave this house and take your juju with you."

"I no do juju, madam!"

She continued to plead her innocence, but I couldn't be sure she wasn't putting on an act. Today, it was a potion on her skin; tomorrow, it could be a potion in our food. Next, it might be poison.

Tunde believed that juju worked. "Through the skin or through the stomach," he would say. He didn't buy the idea that juju could be transmitted supernaturally. I had no evidence that juju of any kind worked, but had witnessed strange cases involving my father's parishioners. I once saw a thief in a trance, sweeping a house he had robbed. The owners of the house claimed they had left juju in their house to make thieves do that. I also saw Ashake's father heal a boy who had meningitis—not with his herbs, but with a broomstick. He stroked the boy's bent neck with the broomstick, and the next morning the boy's neck straightened. Everyone thought the boy had been healed, but in time I reasoned that he may not have had meningitis in the first place. He may just have had a stiff neck, which got better overnight. The sweeping thief remained a mystery, unless the whole incident was staged to prevent potential thefts.

I asked Patience to bring me her pomade, so I could inspect it, and she did. It was a brand imported from India and sold on the streets. I opened the lid in her presence and sniffed the powdery scent. I believed her, though I didn't show it.

"I don't want to hear any talk about juju again," I said.

"Yes, ma," she said.

I was furious with Jimoh. When he returned home with Tunde, I launched into a tirade against him as Tunde walked through the door.

"Your driver attacked Patience today," I said. "He accused her of practicing juju and tore her uniform. I don't know what is going on in his head, but tell him that if he tries that again, I will not only get rid of him, I will have him arrested for assault."

Tunde didn't even bother to look at me. He put his briefcase down and sat in his chair.

"Jimoh says she's been buying potions," he said. "If that is the case, then she's the one who has to go."

"Have you heard her side of the story?"

"Have you given me a chance?"

I didn't answer, but called Patience while he rubbed his eyes as if the sight of me wore him out. Patience practically crept into the sitting room.

"Yes, madam?"

"Please tell *Oga* what happened with Jimoh today."

He didn't look at her, either, which made her more nervous. She stammered and her voice broke at the very end.

"I no do juju, *sah*."

Tunde finally looked at her, rather like a judge. "Since you've been employed here, it's been one thing after another. Jimoh insulted you. Jimoh came to your room to accost you. Jimoh did this to you. Jimoh did that to you. Today, Jimoh attacked you. But Jimoh has been with us longer than you, has he not?"

"Yes, *sah*."

"At first I thought I would let all this pass. Perhaps in time you two would learn to co-operate with each other. That didn't happen, and today he's telling me about this potion of yours. Now, I don't know about madam here, but for me this is very troubling. I can't have such things going on in my house, so, whether or not it is true, you have to leave."

She cried out, "Heh, *Oga!*"

He raised his hand. "You have until the end of the month. We will give you a reference and severance pay."

She knelt down and began to cry. "*Oga*, I beg, I beg…"

"Excuse us," I said to her.

She staggered to the kitchen. Her tears had wet the floor.

"You can't sack her," I said.

"The girl is a nuisance."

"What about your driver, who assaulted her?"

"I'll have a word with him."

"A word?"

"What else would you have me do to him?"

He was so unyielding. I wanted him to stop taking his frustrations out on other people and admit he would rather have me at home.

"Tunde," I said. "Patience will not leave this house unless I say so. I hired her and I pay her."

"That's fine," he said. "But someone has to be around to watch her. You can't just leave her alone all day to do as she pleases. You're only asking for trouble."

I considered bringing up his retirement and the insecurity that had caused me, but that would be hurtful. Then I considered bringing up my mother, who'd spent her entire married life dependent on my father, but he would only say that was irrelevant.

"How many years did I do that?" I asked. "How many years did I stay at home without once complaining?"

"You complained, Remi. You complained, nonstop."

"So? I did it anyway! And now, I'm doing something for myself! What is wrong with that?"

"Someone has to be around. That's all I'm saying. If there's no one here, this is the end result. Juju in your house."

He was impossible. I returned to the kitchen, where Patience was still crying.

"It's enough," I said. "You can stay."

"I no do juju, madam. *Na* Jimoh *wey* cause *am*."

"Where is the foolish fellow, anyway?"

"In the backyard."

"Wait here. I'm going to deal with him."

As I walked across the veranda, Duchess got up and followed me. Jimoh was sitting on the septic tank at the far end of the yard. The moment he caught sight of me, he prostrated himself on the grass.

"Evening, madam."

"Good evening, Jimoh. Why did you attack Patience?"

He stood up, glancing nervously at the kitchen door.

"She flies by day, ma," he answered in Yoruba.

"What is that supposed to mean?"

"She's a witch. That's what I was trying to warn you about before. She disappears once you're gone. She came back and tried to use her juju on me, so I pushed her away like this, and she leapt toward me like this…"

He looked like a contortionist as he demonstrated what happened. I wondered if what had transpired between them was the result of a relationship gone sour. That wasn't entirely implausible.

"Have you ever seen her fly?"

"No, ma."

"So what makes you think she can do that?"

He watched the ground, unable to provide an explanation.

"You dare not lift a finger to her again," I said. "I must not hear any talk about juju, either. Look at me. Look at my eyes. I will walk you out of here if you touch her or talk about juju in this house again."

"Yes, ma."

He prostrated himself again and apologized as Duchess growled at him.

He terrorized Duchess as well, according to Patience. He threw stones at her kennel whenever she fell asleep there and laughed at her as she scampered out.

I sent him to Obalende Market to buy batteries for our lamps. He didn't return for hours, and that night we had another power cut, which lasted until daybreak. The one night we had electricity during the week was the night the government announced the new states. We had nineteen states now, and Western state had been divided into three, which worried me. Ibadan was the capital of Western state and still the hub of political hotheads. If the people of Ibadan got upset over the division of their state, they would take to the streets and start rioting. I called my brother Deji, who said that hadn't happened, so perhaps the people of Ibadan recognized their limits with General Muhammed. Abuja, meanwhile, was the new federal capital territory, which effectively demoted Lagos, and soon revived the rumor about a military coup. The recurring power cuts were seen as an indication that one was around the corner. Underneath that, of course, was a growing national anxiety, but I was so distracted by the fallings-out and goings-on at home that I soon stopped paying attention to what was happening in the country.

February 4

On Wednesday morning I got a phone call from Rotimi's housemaster after Tunde had left for work. He said Rotimi had been in the sickbay overnight with malaria and was not keeping his medicine down. I decided to bring him home in case he took a turn for the worse.

Boarders usually didn't come home unless their malaria got so bad they needed to be hospitalized, and Rotimi was particularly proud of his capacity to overcome bouts of malaria. He attended classes and played in football games regardless. He swore that sweating out his fever under a blanket was the best cure. In the evenings, when his headaches intensified, he simply took a couple of Panadol and went to bed early.

This time around, he could barely get out of bed, but he'd packed his overnight bag with his usual efficiency. I took the bag from him when I noticed his arm trembling, but he insisted on carrying it. I refused to hand it over, thinking he only did that for the benefit of his friends who had come to the sickbay to see him off. As we all walked down the corridor, he huddled over for fear that he might start vomiting again. It was tricky to gauge how much care to give him. With Rolari it was easy. She demanded care, and since her father was always willing to oblige, I felt it was necessary for me to hold back a little. When she was a day student, she was quite capable of telling me she wanted such-and-such a meal waiting for her when she got home from school, no excuses. Her cheekiness was another matter, but her dependency was flattering. Rotimi's self-sufficiency could come across as a rejection.

On our way home, I asked him, "Did you ask your house-master to call me?"

"No," he said.

"Didn't you want to come home?"

"I didn't want to miss school."

"What's happening in school?"

"I don't want to fall behind. I'll have to catch up later."

His class was competitive in a way that Rolari's wasn't. In Rolari's class there was an order that was accepted. A certain girl came first and another second, two girls vied for third and fourth positions, and everyone else followed. In Rotimi's class, the highest mark was up for grabs. Any of the top students could achieve it, and Rotimi was one of them. His friends called him Nighthawk because he was in the habit of studying by flashlight at night.

"You need to rest," I said.

"I've rested enough," he said.

"You need to eat, then."

"I don't feel like eating."

"Just try."

"I'll only vomit again."

I rubbed his back. "I'll make you some *ogi* when we get home."

He pressed his temples, unable to shake his head.

At home, he again tried to take his bag from me, even as he struggled up the stairs holding on to the banister. He changed into his pajamas, and I drew his curtains open. He said his eyes hurt, so I drew the curtains shut. He didn't want the air conditioner on, though his room was too hot. I went to the guest room to get an oscillating fan and put it on his bedside table. He was already in bed when I returned, so I plugged in the fan and felt his forehead. It was burning.

I pointed at his pajama top. "You have to take that off."

"Why?"

"So I can sponge you to bring your temperature down."

I had not done that in years. He turned his face away.

"I can sponge myself."

"Are you sure?"

"Yes."

"Make sure you lie in your underwear for a while. No covering up, now."

"Mummy," he said. "Go to work."

"Did I say I wanted to go to work?"

I had to. My accountants were coming in to look at my bookkeeping records. I would rather pay for the extra service than have Tunde lecture me.

"Go to work, Mummy," he said. "Stop worrying."

I patted his shoulder. "I'll make you some *ogi*."

He sponged himself while I made his *ogi*. He wanted it with sugar, but no milk. He was back in his pajamas when I walked in with a tray. I watched him eat and left him lying in bed afterward.

When I got to work, I called Tunde, who was surprised I'd brought Rotimi home. Tunde suggested I take him to the doctor, but I said it wasn't necessary. He just needed to rest.

I was touched by Rotimi's maturity. At his age, I accepted that my mother did whatever she was meant to as a mother. It wasn't my place to give her options or tell her to stop worrying. I remembered how she'd looked after me whenever I was sick as a child. The incidence of malaria in Lagos wasn't high because sanitation inspectors went from house to house to make sure no one kept tins of water, in which mosquito larvae could grow. My mother may have believed a woman's place was at home, but she often had outside engagements as a priest's wife. However, if my brothers or I had malaria, she would cancel her engagements to nurse us until we were well, which sometimes annoyed my father. He would say God would take care of us while she was away, and she would say it was the other way around. Mothers took care of children while God was away.

She was adamant when it came to our health. She would make *ogi* for us to eat until our stomachs settled and stay at home until our fevers broke. That may have been the result of her tendency to panic. Malaria may have been less widespread when I was a child, but children did die easily from it, and information about the disease was scanty at best. A common cure used in my neighborhood was *agbo*, a quinine tea. *Agbo* was what Tunde took for malaria when he was a child. He drank it and bathed in it. "Get *agbo*," he said, whenever our children had malaria. I would tell him I'd grown up in a civilized family and we'd taken chloroquine tablets.

I called Rotimi once that afternoon to check on him. There was no point waking him up. Once was apparently too much for him, because the phone rang and rang before he answered it. I asked how he was feeling and he said he was sleeping.

"Yes, but how are you *feeling*?" I asked.

"Sleepy," he said.

"Okay, sweetheart," I said. "Go back to bed."

I was still at work when Tunde went home early, convinced that Rotimi had a bad case of malaria. He found Rotimi in his room, covered not just in his bed sheet but in a blanket he had taken from the guest room. Sometime during the afternoon, Rotimi had decided to sweat out his fever and hadn't bothered to call me.

I returned from the shop and walked into his room. His bed sheet was visibly damp and he was curled up in nothing but his underwear. Tunde seemed to be checking his spine for his temperature. The blanket had been discarded on the floor.

"What happened?" I asked, in alarm.

"His temperature is high," Tunde said.

Patience came in with an aluminum bowl I recognized. I used it for raw meat. No matter how many times she washed it, it had a lingering smell of blood. She had poured cold water from the fridge into it and dropped ice cubes in to make it even colder.

"What is that for?" I asked her.

"*Oga* said I should get ice water," she said.

"Why?"

"To bring down his temperature," Tunde said.

Rotimi was still curled up. I turned his fan to the fastest speed and checked his forehead. He was not dangerously feverish.

"Have you been vomiting?" I asked.

"No," he mumbled.

"Good. We have to get your temperature down."

"What about *agbo*?" Tunde asked.

"*Agbo* doesn't work."

"Madam," Patience said, handing me the bowl.

"That won't work either. Please get me cold tap water."

She left and so did Tunde, who seemed to have taken offense that I'd interfered with his medical intervention.

Patience came back with the same bowl. I asked her to return it to the kitchen and went to our bathroom to fill a clean plastic bowl with water. Rotimi was too weak to protest as I sponged him. I did his chest, back, arms and legs.

"We'll have to change your sheets," I said.

"Thank you," he said, as he lay back.

"Why did you wrap yourself up like that?"

"I do it in school."

"Please don't do that again, my dear."

"It's just sweat."

I shook my head. "People die from dehydration. What if that had happened to you? That would be the end of me."

He sighed. "Mummy, if I die, it would be the end of me, not you."

That was the sort of mother I was. Not the sort who deputized for God. Not even the sort who could trust that God would protect my child. I couldn't separate his mortality from mine, yet I'd given my work priority. I was ashamed that I failed to meet my mother's standards.

I monitored Rotimi overnight. The next morning he was able to come downstairs. He still didn't have an appetite because his mouth tasted bitter, but it was a sign he was getting better. At night, I allowed him to watch television. Tunde said that was a sign he was ready to go back to school. I didn't think he should hurry back, in case his malaria recurred. I would have preferred he wait until Sunday, but he agreed with Tunde; he wanted to go back on Friday evening.

"I've fallen behind," he said. "I need to catch up."

"What is all this falling behind and catching up about?" I asked.

There was too much pressure at King's. It wasn't as if he

242

were in university. I was about to insist that he stay home until Sunday, but Tunde weighed in, as if I were encouraging him to throw his entire academic future away.

"Stop fussing," he said. "Let the boy catch up if he needs to."

February 7

Ade was in a foul mood at the golf club on Saturday. We sat in the clubhouse overlooking the patio, and he looked sullen, drinking his beer, as the Woods prattled on about their game. He and Frances had won, but Frances had played better. The Woods echoed each other about her marvelous shot on the ninth hole, her birdie on the eleventh and her final putt.

"Sorry," Dave said. "I'm getting a bit carried away here."

He was sweaty and Ade was drenched, despite the ceiling fan above us. Bev had taken off her cap, which had molded her hair into the shape of a bowl. They all looked as if they had been doing manual labor under the sun.

"That was fun," Bev said, composing herself. "We really ought to do this again, Ady."

"Yes," Ade said, without interest.

He was upset that Frances had outshone him. Frances, meanwhile, shrugged off the Woods' praises, even as her false modesty encouraged them to praise her even more. Her handicap was twenty-three and Ade claimed his was eleven. He mulled over the game between scribbles. He apparently preferred to wait until he finished playing before filling out his scorecard. I doubted he would ever have a game with the Woods again, especially after Dave teased him about Moji's clubs. That was another reason for his sour disposition. For some reason, he'd promised Frances the clubs if she finished with a score below par, which she had. She didn't think it was necessary for him to keep his side of the bargain, but he did.

"I really don't need them," she said, cheerfully.

"No," Ade said. "You earned them, so you keep them."

"But I can't travel with them. Honestly, they're more of an inconvenience."

"They're yours. Do as you please with them."

She turned to me. "I suppose I could give them to the Millers."

I had not seen this side of her. All she needed to do next was poke out her tongue. As the Woods continued to congratulate her, Ade looked as if he were ready to strangle both of them. Bev then questioned his scorecard, insisting he'd taken more shots than he recorded. He raised his arm slightly, trying to shield the card from her, as she leaned over to check.

"Sure about that, Ady?"

"I'm sure."

"I could have sworn you hit a seven."

"No, it was a five."

"Sure, Ady?"

"I'm absolutely sure."

"Hm. That's funny."

He signed his scorecard, by which time his jaw was as tight as a tire clamp. It gave me some satisfaction to see him humiliated.

"Ade boy," I said, "I might be tempted to take up golf lessons."

He glanced at me. "Really?"

"Well," I said, "only if Frances would be kind enough to lend me her new clubs."

Frances reached for my hand as if she were genuinely encouraging me. "What a great idea! I'd be happy to give them to you!"

Ade stood up abruptly and said he had to turn in his

scorecard. Dave waited until he was out of earshot and then whispered, "He didn't take that very well, did he?"

"I can't imagine why not," Frances said. "It was a good game for him as well."

"It must have been better than we thought," Bev said, "or his scorekeeping is way off."

She sat like a neat package of indignation as the rest of us reveled in our newfound camaraderie. We were united in our separate desires to put Ade in his place: I, because of his handling of his divorce, Frances, presumably because of his chauvinistic attitude, and Dave, because he was the sort of fellow who enjoyed ganging up behind someone's back.

Ade returned and ordered the next round of beers, though he remained in a bad mood. Frances then decided to give me a pep talk about golf being a mind sport, knowing full well I wasn't serious about taking it up.

"Everyone says that," Ade interrupted, "but overall, golf tests your physical ability."

"I'm not sure about that," she said. "You may have a powerful drive, but putting is not your strength."

"You need control to putt," he admitted. "But physical ability counts, otherwise men and women would have the same handicaps."

"Mind control is also important," she said. "I would never have been able to outperform you otherwise."

No wonder she never got married, I thought, as Ade pretended to stifle a yawn.

The afternoon deteriorated further when, as we were finishing our drinks, Moji showed up at the club. I was first to see her. She walked across the patio with a man who had to be her new brigadier friend. They attracted attention because she was overdressed in white flares and a red kimono. He ushered her to a table with much ceremony. The patio was full of expatriates and waiters served them, accepting tips with bows. There were a few other Nigerians in the clubhouse and the sliding doors were open, so we had a clear view of what was happening outside, though people there were less inclined to be interested in what was going on indoors. Moji, having perused her surroundings, caught sight of us. She was obviously looking for Ade, who by now was aware of her arrival. The Woods and Frances were oblivious. Dave was going on about a utility club called the Baffler, the details of which were lost on me.

Moji sauntered over, arms outstretched, and spoke with a coloratura trill that instantly made me nervous.

"Remi, my darling! How lovely to see you here!"

The Woods couldn't contain their enthusiasm. Bev, in particular, was blinking away as I introduced them. Dave got up to shake her hand. Frances seemed bemused by her grandiosity. Ade remained seated, refusing to acknowledge her.

"Ade, *se ko si*?" she asked.

"I'm just a little tired," he said.

"How are the children?"

"Very well."

"When can I see them?"

Ade looked at her pointedly. "Not anytime soon."

He wasn't about to let Moji ambush him over visitation rights, but Moji wasn't ready to give up.

"Why not?" she asked.

Ade drank his beer slowly and wiped the foam from his upper lip.

"I'm talking to you, Ade," she said.

"Calm down," I said to her in Yoruba. "You can always

discuss this later."

"I can't get a moment with him," she responded, in English.

"*Ni suuru*," I said.

"No," she insisted. "I've been patient long enough. Ade, I asked you a question."

"You heard Remi," he said, putting his glass down. "We can talk about this later."

"Why not here?"

I was beginning to have doubts about coming. My presence may well have encouraged Moji. Frances and the Woods seemed preoccupied with the beer bottles. Again Ade didn't answer and Moji appeared to be on the verge of leaving when she noticed the black leather Wilson golf bag.

"Aren't these my clubs?" she asked.

"They are," Ade said.

"What are they doing here?"

"I gave them away," he said, after a pause.

"But they're mine, not yours," Moji said.

Where was her brigadier? He had escorted her in. Why couldn't he escort her out? Everyone in the clubhouse watched as the Baloguns began to argue.

"You've never used them before!"

"What right do you have to give them away?"

"I bought them for you!"

"I asked you a question! What right do you have to give my clubs away?"

"Moji, please, go back outside. We were having a nice time here before you came along."

"You'd better tell me who you gave them to."

"He gave them to me," I said.

She eyed me. "Oh, don't treat me like a child, Remi. You

know I hate that. So who did he give them to? This fat one here, or this one who is looking at me as if I owe her money. Will you turn your face away? And you, what are you standing up for?"

Dave Wood immediately sat down. He'd stood up to intervene.

"Moji," I said, "they're just clubs."

"No, Remi, they're *my* clubs, and he's taken everything else away from me. Now, I want to know who he gave them to, and he'd better tell me, or else…"

She wanted to embarrass him, perhaps more than she wanted a chance to see her children.

"He gave them to me," Frances said.

Americans and their heroism, I thought. Why did they always walk right into conflicts with no consideration for how their interference might make matters worse?

"Was I talking to you?" Moji asked, narrowing her eyes.

"You asked—"

Moji slapped her. "Shut up! Who asked you to open your mouth? You're not in your country! You're on Nigerian soil!"

I heard a collective gasp. People came in from the patio to find out what the commotion was about. The waiters stood still. Moji's brigadier maintained a safe distance. Frances held her cheek. Ade didn't make a move to defend her, which told me he was right about Moji. I had no idea how out of hand she had become. I took my cue from him. So did Dave, who must have realized this was not an occasion for British chivalry. He remained seated as Bev's eyes flickered like defective traffic lights.

Then Frances stood up and I thought she was about to walk away, but she slapped Moji back—hard—and instead of immediately running off, glared at Moji with a reddened face.

"Oh, no," I whispered.

Moji grabbed her hair and pulled. Frances began to struggle. Now, there was an outcry from everyone, including myself, and we hurried to Frances' aid, freeing her from Moji's grip as Moji dived and bit her in the breast.

Frances bent over. Ade carried Moji away as she kicked and screamed like a toddler, "I want to see my children! I want to see my children!"

The crowd broke around them as the commotion escalated. An expatriate was calling for a doctor. How they managed to be so practical at times like this, I had no idea. We Nigerians didn't know what to do with ourselves. One man in a red Slazenger visor leaned over and offered Frances a table napkin. Dave Wood shepherded Frances and Bev, who was sobbing, "We shouldn't have come." I wasn't sure if she was referring to the club or Nigeria. The crowd trailed them through the back door by the bar and formed a bottleneck. I took the long way through the sliding doors and hurried across the patio, catching up with the Woods in the car park, by which time Ade had bundled Moji into his Benz and was reversing out.

Frances was still huddled over, her hair covering her face. The crowd now included security guards and caddies. Dave Wood shooed them away, seemingly overwhelmed by the sight of so many Nigerians. A few expatriates had formed a protective circle around him, his wife and Frances. I stepped forward to assist him but he appeared terrified.

"Stand back," he shouted. "We have enough help here."

I did as I was told. Far be it from me to overstep my boundaries. I was still trying to absorb what had happened, anyway. Moji's brigadier was nearby, his posture altogether too stiff considering the chaos around him. He coolly elbowed an animated security guard out of his way and headed for his Land Rover.

I would remember him months later when Tunde said he should have known there was going to be a coup when he noticed the military men had disappeared from the club: the only ones likely to be around were not involved in plotting to overthrow General Muhammed.

The Millers' driver pressed on his horn as he drove out. People were peering through the windows of the Peugeot to catch a glimpse of Frances. The Woods' car followed with a convoy of expatriates. A few of them remained, with an equal number of Nigerians. It was clear the Nigerians were appalled by what Moji had done. They were shaking their heads and dusting their hands in disgust.

"She's mad," the man with the red Slazenger visor said. "She has to be, to bite a diplomat's breast."

He may have assumed Frances was a diplomat because of the Peugeot's license plate. I agreed that Moji needed help, which made me have some sympathy for her, momentarily. Then I worried about Frances. Moji must have injured her. I remembered Tunde's warning and could only imagine what he would have to say when he found out. I could no longer claim the Baloguns were at fault. Without my involvement, Ade would not have met Frances and Frances would not have met the Woods. The Woods would not have invited her and Ade to play golf, and Moji would certainly not have shown up.

I returned to the clubhouse and retrieved her golf bag— before any caddy took the opportunity to steal her clubs. They were grubby with mud and grass. There were a couple of woods, several irons and a putter. I put them in the back of my van, with the intention of returning them to her, knowing she'd never really wanted them in the first place.

February 8

I didn't say a word to Tunde about what had happened. He was bound to find out on Sunday morning anyway, when he played golf, and after our recent clashes, I could use some respite. I did call the Millers several times from the privacy of our bedroom, to ask after Frances, but no one answered their phone, so I gave up temporarily. As for the Baloguns, I swore to myself that I was finished with them for good.

Sunday was Baba's day to tend the garden and he arrived before Tunde got back from the club. As usual, we talked as he raked the lawn. He wasn't sorry to hear that Patience had been in trouble.

"I warned that girl," he said.

"So did I."

"What if Daddy had sacked her?"

"I managed to persuade him to let her stay."

I lied only because Baba wouldn't approve of my more direct approach to handling the matter.

"Next time Daddy might not give her a chance," he said. "If he sacks her, I will find you someone else. Someone more mature."

"I would prefer that."

I still had no intention of letting Patience go. She and Jimoh had the morning off and she had gone to church.

I thanked Baba for his work and returned to the house. In the sitting room, I called the Millers yet again. Their phone rang as I looked through the window and watched him gather the dry leaves and pile them in his basket. A car horn made me jump and I hung up the phone, thinking it was Tunde, but it wasn't.

He came home before lunch and didn't look in the least bit perturbed. We exchanged hellos before he went upstairs to take a bath, and I wasn't sure if I ought to be relieved or not. The food was ready and Patience was setting the table when he returned downstairs, by which time I could no longer feign innocence. He must have heard about the fight. This had to be an attempt on his part to prolong my guilt.

"How was your game?" I asked.

"I didn't have one," he said.

"Oh? What were you doing, then?"

"Practicing."

"How did your practice go?"

"So-so."

He slipped on his sandals, which were at the foot of the bookcase, and walked to his chair. Patience came through the kitchen door with a tray of serving dishes. We were having pounded yam and okra stew.

"Anything new happening at the club?" I asked, watching her.

"You tell me," he said.

I was glad Patience was in and out of the dining room. So long as she was around, Tunde and I could have a peaceful conversation. I switched to Yoruba so she couldn't understand what we were saying.

"Why didn't you say something?" I asked.

"I was waiting for you to."

"You said you didn't want to hear anything about the Baloguns."

"This would qualify as an exception."

I nodded. "Yes, yes, it's a shame. I had thought the rumors about Moji were exaggerated. What I saw has changed my mind. The woman is out of control, but that doesn't excuse her behavior. She knew exactly what she was doing."

While I was busy thinking she was threatened by other women, she posed the bigger threat. Other people recognized it and that was why they'd banished her.

"How could you get yourself involved in such a mess?" Tunde asked, as Patience carried the empty tray back to the kitchen.

"What do you mean?"

"How could you get caught up in a fight like that?"

"I just happened to be sitting there."

"You knew Moji would be there."

"No."

"Didn't you say something about her going to the club more often?"

"I said she was involved with a brigadier there."

"So there was a chance she would be there."

I hesitated. "Yes."

"Yet you went to meet Ade."

"I didn't go there to meet him."

He gave me the look. "You knew he was playing a game with the American woman."

"Frances."

"Whatever her name is."

"The Woods were there as well."

"Exactly. Nothing escapes those two and they've told everyone about the fight. Everyone is talking about it, and guess what? Your name keeps coming up. 'Mrs. Lawal, Mrs.

Lawal,' everywhere I turn, and I'm thinking, How long have I been coming to this place? I come and go quietly. My wife comes here once or twice, and before I know it…"

One day, and the rumors were out of control. Patience returned with a bottle of cold water.

"I wouldn't bother about idle gossip," I said in English.

"Who is idle?" Tunde asked. "The gossips or the two women who were fighting?"

"Moji was the one fighting."

"She has disgraced us all. The expatriates are talking about her as if she is a market woman."

I'd seen market women fight. They tore each other's clothes and sat on top of one another. Biting a breast was the ultimate victory. But where were the expatriates themselves coming from? Dave Wood was a bank clerk in England. In Nigeria, he was a senior manager. God only knew what Bev did for a living before, but she was "madam" now. I wasn't the one averse to foreigners, but suddenly I was impatient with the whole lot of them at the club, wearing their silly shorts and caps, and trying to impose their daft values on Nigerians.

"They say she bit the woman in the breast," Tunde said. "Over what? That nincompoop, Ade?"

"She's either an adulteress or a spy," I said.

"The Woods said he cheats at golf."

"So what?"

I would cheat at golf with all the unnecessary competitiveness that went on. It was almost like the Battle of the Sexes tennis match, the offensive between Ade and Frances.

Tunde sat up, looking as adamant as Bev Wood. "It goes to his character if he cheats at golf."

"According to whom?"

"Are you defending him?"

"I'm just saying that cheating at golf has nothing to do with what happened."

Tunde shook his head. "The man is a twerp, and I'm not sure why you have to be right in the middle of his divorce—"

"Moji asked for my help."

"My dear, for someone who wanted to help…"

"Madam," Patience interrupted.

"Yes," I said.

"Food is on the table."

"Thank you."

She returned to the kitchen, looking embarrassed.

"You were there," Tunde said.

"I never denied that."

"Yet you kept quiet for an entire day."

"Yes, I did."

He pointed at me. "From now on, I would prefer that you keep away from Ade."

He would *prefer*? I never wanted to see Ade again in my life.

"Why him?"

"His reputation is not doing you any favors."

"And Moji's?"

"Hers would be intact if she hadn't married him."

"I don't see why it's all right for me to keep company with her and not with him. I don't have much to do with him, anyway. I don't see him any more than I see my other old friends like…Oyinda."

"Oyinda is a woman."

"With a reputation, but I would never suggest you keep away from her."

He aimed his thumb backward. "Oh, we're back to that

again? We're back to my association with her?"

"You said she called you at work."

"In fact she called me several times. Did I complain when that twerp called you at the shop? If you don't know by now, I leave work matters at work. I was sitting quietly in this house when you told me I wasn't sociable. Now that I'm being sociable, it's a problem. Next time, go to your cultural event on your own. I'm not the Lagos socialite here."

I laughed at the absurdity of our exchange.

"What is amusing you?" he asked.

"She called you several times? Look at that! You'll be the laughing stock of Lagos! It will be the scandal of our lifetime— worse than any scandal about a woman biting another woman's breast!"

"Are you all right?"

"Men. Your need for attention is insatiable. Please don't disgrace me. Find someone more attractive than Oyinda, I beg of you."

"You think I'm…?"

"Poor woman. She is so desperate. Shall we eat?"

He once said he would never show he was jealous, even if he was. I told him I was incapable of jealousy, and he actually believed me. He had never been pleased about my friendship with Ade. Oyinda, on the other hand, was a surprise. I didn't actually believe she would have the temerity. As for Tunde, if he were enjoying her attention, he would end up running away from her when I was through with mocking him.

Later that afternoon, we visited Rotimi in school and he could tell we were on edge as he walked up to us.

"What happened?" he asked.

"Nothing, my dear," I said. "How are you feeling?"

"Much better."

I patted his shoulder so as not to embarrass him in front of his friends. Tunde rubbed his head. Despite his newfound machismo, Rotimi was sensitive. Even as a child, he knew whenever I was not speaking to his father, and would get us to make up, sometimes going as far as to stand in between us and join our hands together. His sister didn't believe in neutrality. She would adjudicate by rounding on whoever she thought was at fault and say, "Naughty boy," or "Naughty girl."

Of course, Mummy was usually the naughty one.

February 9

Tunde may have been right about my involvement with the Baloguns, but he couldn't tell me how to make amends. I was still worried about Frances, and the Millers were obviously avoiding phone calls, so on Monday morning I decided to go to their flat to check on her.

A different watchman was on duty when I got there, and perhaps because I was dressed formally this time, he was courteous and let me in without making a fuss. The car park was fairly empty. I assumed that was because most of the tenants had gone to work. I didn't see the Peugeot that Frances normally used, which could mean she wasn't in.

I'd barely knocked on the Millers' door when their dog started barking. I'd forgotten about the unfriendly animal. Why expatriates kept dogs indoors was beyond me, and no matter what their dogs did, they would insist they were harmless. Above the barking, I heard voices indoors.

"Sylvester, go and see who it is!"

"Yes, madam!"

"Who is dat, please?" Sylvester asked.

"Mrs. Lawal," I said.

"Who?"

The dog was so loud I had to raise my voice. "Mrs. Lawal!"

"It's a stranger, madam!" Sylvester said.

"Well, tell the stranger I'm not in!" Denise Miller ordered.

I knocked again. "Mrs. Miller?"

"Whaddaya want?"

Her voice was so guttural I immediately straightened up. Whatever I thought of her husband, at least he'd sounded polished.

"I'm looking for Frances Cooke!"

"Geddaway from my door!"

I tucked my chin in. Who was she to talk to me in that way?

"Listen!" I said. "All I want to know is if she's all right! You hear me? If you can't help me, that's fine, but don't tell me to get away from anywhere!"

"Aw, shaddap! I'm sick of all of you!"

"Who do you think you're talking to, Mrs. Miller?"

"Ged off my properdy!"

"You're in my country!"

"I don't wanna be in your lousy country! Ged off my properdy or I'll set my dog on you!"

I didn't wait to find out if she was serious or not. I hurried down the stairs and to my van, fearful that at any moment her dog would come charging after me.

Where was I, for heaven's sake? Pretoria?

February 10

February was turning out to be a challenging month for friendships in general. Ashake Dada—the lady of the manor—and I got into an argument when I phoned to ask when she would pay for the invitations she'd ordered for her wedding anniversary. It was a polite argument, but an argument nonetheless, and no one argued as politely as Ashake.

"My very good friend," she said in Yoruba.

I was sitting behind my office desk. My window overlooked the car park of the shopping center and a flame-of-the-forest tree. My accountants had advised that I should make more effort to chase up on past-due accounts. Festus would be no good at that, so it was up to me alone. I'd had some practice with late-paying tenants in the past, but they were not friends as such.

"Quite an age," I said, also in Yoruba. "I was just looking through my records and it occurred to me that you might have forgotten about the cards you ordered."

"What cards?"

"The cards Festus delivered to you for your anniversary."

"Festus?"

"My nephew, who works at my shop."

I called him a nephew because he was young enough to be one.

"Oh, him!" she said. "I've been so busy I forget everything. You know I traveled overseas?"

"Where to?"

"London. I must have told you we have the new place in Chelsea."

"No."

I only knew the Dadas had a house in Brighton, somewhere near the beach.

"Look at me," she said. "I thought I told you about it. We had to get a little *pied-à-terre* in Chelsea because of the boys. They go there for exeats. They want to be near their friends. I have to show my face now and then, so our porter won't think we've abandoned the place. I've only just returned and I'll be off again in a few weeks. Maybe this time I'll fly over to Zurich for a weekend and do some shopping on Bahnhofstrasse. I go shopping in Knightsbridge these days and I see Nigerians everywhere, especially in that Harrods."

She'd never learned the art of a subtle brag. She also managed to make *pied-à-terre* and Bahnhofstrasse sound like Yoruba words. For a moment, I considered reminding her of the caterpillar that fell on her head, to bring her back down to earth.

"While you're here in Lagos," I said, "can I send Festus over?"

"Why not?"

"When will it be convenient?"

She laughed. "Anytime you want, since you're in such a hurry."

"Today? Tomorrow?"

"Tomorrow would be fine," she said.

"What time? Late morning? Let's say around this time?"

"How much do I owe you again?"

I told her, wishing I had the guts to increase the price. That would jog her memory.

"Is that all?"

"That's all."

"I hope I'm not going to be harassed over a small bill like that."

"Of course not, since you should have no trouble paying it."

"My very good friend," she said. "Don't wear yourself out with all this work you're doing."

"I'll try not to."

I wrinkled my nose after I hung up the phone. Next time, I would make her pay for her order upfront.

Ashake herself had a boutique at Federal Palace Hotel. It was easy to forget because she was hardly ever there. She had two shopgirls and stocked imported clothes, mostly in her size, and ended up wearing them because no one else bought them.

About half an hour later, my phone rang and it was Ade Balogun.

"Remi?"

"Yes, Ade?"

My tone immediately subdued his.

"Uh, how are you?"

"Very well."

"I was, uh, wondering if you were on your lunch break."

"I'm not. What can I do for you?"

"I called to find out how you are doing. And to say I am sorry. Moji should never have done that. It was partly my fault, though. I should have stopped things from getting that far."

"At which point?"

"Pardon?"

"At which point should you have stopped things from going further?"

He paused for a moment. "I said I was sorry."

"Have you heard from Frances?" I asked.

"Why?"

"I've not been able to reach her."

I had no intention of telling him what had happened to me at the Millers'.

"I see," he said. "Here I was assuming you had contacted her already."

"Have you?"

"Yes. I called her to apologize, then Moji got on the phone and started cursing her."

"Why would Moji do that?"

"Do what?"

"Start cursing Frances."

"I don't know. She agreed to apologize, then she got on the phone and accused the woman of spying."

"Spying on whom?"

"I don't know," he repeated. "All I said was that Frances had asked suspicious questions, but Moji went crazy as usual and called her all sorts of names."

No wonder the Millers didn't answer their phone. No wonder Denise Miller had threatened to set her dog on me.

"Listen, Ade," I said, switching to Yoruba.

"What?"

"Let me tell you this, as a friend, since nobody else is likely to. You and your wife have brought nothing but shame on your heads, and anyone who associates with either of you will have the same fate visited on them."

"There's no reason for you to talk to me like that, Remi."

"This is not a life-or-death matter we're dealing with!"

"That shows how much you know about divorce."

"Everyone is talking about you! Don't you realize?"

"Who cares? Didn't they talk when your husband lost his job?"

"Don't you dare bring my husband into this discussion. Why did you say such a thing about Frances?"

"The woman was prying!"

"During a golf game?"

"Not then. We met before that, during the week."

This shocked me more than his calling her to apologize.

"Where?"

"At Federal Palace Hotel."

"What did she say?"

"She asked my opinion on the government and other things. I thought she might be looking for Nigerian recruits. I told Moji, but I didn't expect her to get on the phone and start threatening to have her arrested."

"Heavens," I said.

"What?"

"Ade, I'm saying this out of kindness. We have known each other a long time. There are issues you have not addressed, issues you have not come to terms with…"

I wondered if I'd gone too far. Apart from the rumor that he was a bastard child, his grandmother, a beautiful Saro woman, had owned a drinking parlor frequented by foreign sailors. The polite version of the story was that she'd sung to entertain them, as his mother played the piano.

Now, he too switched to Yoruba. "I didn't ask for your kindness, Remi. I only called to apologize. Yes, we've known each other a long time, and I take you as my sister, but I never once asked you to interfere."

"Your wife asked me to and you were only too happy for me to do so, until you saw I wasn't going to take your side."

He laughed. "Married men have affairs! That's just the way it is! I'm an African man! I'm not cut out for monogamy!"

"Ade, none of that nonsense, please. It's not our culture or tradition to beat each other or break each other's hearts. Even if it is permissible for men to have multiple women at one time, you have a mind of your own, and pride. How would you like it if Moji did that to you?"

"She does!"

"Stop it. She only did it in retaliation."

"She still did it! What is all this hypocrisy about? It's not as if I brought another woman to our marital home, or had children outside! What more did she want? I respected our home. I never beat her. In fact, she beat me! All I did was defend myself!"

"Ade, I'm sorry, but you have to own up to what you did."

He sighed. "Remi, you can be such a prude and it's not an attractive quality in a woman. Since we're revealing things to each other, here are the facts. I have a room at Federal Palace Hotel. I go there once in a while. I take women, we play black-jack at the casino and sometimes we spend the night. Single women, married women. Frances and I had dinner at Bacchus, after which we went gambling."

"Did you spend the night with her?"

"That has nothing to do with you."

"Listen, I couldn't care less about your love life, but I have to know who I'm dealing with."

I really wasn't concerned about him. He'd had a string of relationships with English girls as a student, though he had no intention of marrying any of them. He seduced them with his jazz-musician act. He was a talented pianist, but not much of a saxophonist. Yet they went gaga whenever he played his saxophone, perhaps because he was the closest they could get to Birdland.

Frances, on the other hand, would go down in my estimation. I thought she was intelligent enough to see through him. I was never impressed by Ade, even when he was younger. Now, he was middle-aged, and nothing was sadder than a middle-aged hedonist.

"It's not important whether I spent the night with her," he said. "It has nothing to do with my marriage, either. I am a man."

"You're still a boy."

"What difference does it make, when you prefer emasculated men?"

"Goodbye."

"Not all of us are under lock and key like your husband."

"I said goodbye, and let this be the last time you mention my husband. You're not in his league."

I hung up and pushed the phone aside. Who cared about his affairs? I was just angry that he'd handled them so childishly. He could have been more discreet. He could have married a woman who wouldn't care so long as he was discreet. Plenty of women would be prepared to do that. He could even have been polygamous, and he could afford to be.

"Silly man," I muttered.

I was still fuming when I got home that evening. I changed out of my clothes and went down to the kitchen to prepare dinner as Patience set the table. Tunde returned from work, and we were fairly cordial to each other. I was more likely to hold on to grudges than he was. I asked about his day and he asked about mine. I told him about my conversation with Ashake but didn't mention Ade's phone call. There was no use stirring up more trouble. My gossip about Ashake was more a peace offering. He may not have wanted to hear about the Baloguns, but he was always game to hear the latest about the Dadas.

After dinner, he had his scotch and I my sherry. He read the latest copy of *Time*. He barely resembled Sidney Poitier anymore, but he was graying in an attractive way. I couldn't remember when last we had been intimate. A week? Ten days? I was too tired of late, and if he sensed that, he left me alone. He might call me lazy occasionally, which I was. I'd been lazy from the day I opened my shop. I was also tired of his recent pessimism, and his enduring predictability. I could tell exactly when he would get up and padlock the front door. Tonight, I could do without hearing that final click.

"Well," I said, standing up, "I'm off to bed."

"So soon?" he asked.

"I'm tired."

"Goodnight, my dear."

"Goodnight and God bless," I said, patting his shoulder.

We had another power cut that night, and I was still awake when he came to bed. Strangely, so was Duchess, who barked until the early hours of the morning.

February 13

As usual that Friday, I left home after Tunde, between seven-thirty and seven-forty-five in the morning. Fridays were not busy for me until the late afternoon. Festus and Boniface were already in the shop when I arrived, and I asked them to tidy up the storeroom. Each time I walked past, Boniface was doing all the work as Festus stood around giving orders. I wasn't surprised. Festus was overqualified for the job and probably bored with his daily routine. I later talked to him about an idea I had to make gift hampers to sell to businesses and he agreed it could be profitable.

At about nine-thirty, he came to my office to say Patience and Jimoh were on the shop floor, and I knew something had to be wrong. Jimoh wasn't supposed to come for me until lunchtime, and Patience had no reason to come to the shop at all. I walked out of my office, and she was wringing her hands. I just assumed they had come to tell me she was pregnant because she was in her new uniform, which was loose fitting.

"What happened?" I asked.

Jimoh crouched by the postcard stand and began to cry. I turned to Patience, who stammered through the details. She was listening to Radio Nigeria when an announcement came on. It was a soldier. She couldn't remember his name. He said General Muhammed had been killed, and everyone should remain calm and stay by their radios. She called Jimoh, by which time the announcement had ended and Radio Nigeria played martial music from then on.

Patience hummed the tune for me. Jimoh stopped crying for a moment to tell me a fellow driver had confirmed that there had been a coup and a curfew had been imposed. All borders, air and sea ports were now closed.

As he was talking, Boniface walked into the shop and announced, "Madam, them done kill Murtala!"

He looked at me as if I had the power to do something about it. My first thought was that General Muhammed was the only head of state that Nigerians called by his given name. My next was to call Tunde, but back in my office I tried and his phone line was engaged. I decided to close the shop for the day. Festus and Boniface lived on the mainland, and getting home by public transport would be a problem, especially if there was a curfew. I could only imagine the pandemonium at the bus stops.

Jimoh started to cry again, and I asked him to pull himself together.

"Madam," he said, "it's as if…as if my own father has died."

"Come on," I said. "Can't you see Patience, here?"

She smiled to show she was taking the news well. Any opportunity to show him up.

That didn't stop him from crying. Yet, on our way home, he managed to kill a cat because he was driving too fast. The cat ran across the road and I heard a sickening thump.

After I recovered from shock, I asked him, "Didn't you see it?"

"My mind was on Murtala, madam," he said.

"Well, take your mind off Murtala," I said. "We don't want anymore deaths today."

272

Through the rear window, I caught a glimpse of the cat lying on the road. It was probably a stray. The sight of it saddened me further.

Duchess was sleeping when Jimoh pulled into the drive. Could she have sensed there was going to be a coup? She didn't bark during the coup that had brought General Muhammed to power, but nobody was killed in that one.

I hurried to the house, twisting my ankle a couple of times because of the gravel. In the sitting room, I turned on the radio and the martial music that Patience had hummed was playing. I tried Tunde's number again, finally getting through to him, only to find out he had been trying to reach me.

"I've been calling the shop," he said.

"I was on my way home."

"Have you heard?"

"Yes."

"Can you believe it?"

"No."

We had expected a coup, but not a bloody one. What was the point of killing General Muhammed? I wondered. Was he too popular? Too powerful? Were his policies too radical for the army?

"We'd better not speak on the phone," Tunde said. "I'll be home soon."

He had forgotten he was in the private sector. When he worked for the government, we were more careful about our telephone conversations.

"Take it easy."

"Don't worry. Just stay where you are. I was supposed to have a meeting with Ibrahim this morning, but that has been canceled."

He came home safely about an hour later, by which time I was worried about how our children were faring in school. We were meant to visit Rolari on Sunday. Would it still be possible? I could see her waking up and expecting Friday the 13th to bring bad luck, and hearing the news about the coup would only confirm her superstitions. I wanted her and her brother at home. The previous coup had taken place during their summer holidays, but I hadn't had such a strong feeling that the country was about to erupt.

The radio was still playing martial music when Tunde settled into his chair in the sitting room.

"Good," he said, rolling up his sleeves. "Keep it on."

"Did you hear the announcement?" I asked.

"No."

"What was it like on the mainland?"

"Traffic everywhere."

"Any army trucks?"

"No."

On my way home from the shopping center it had seemed like an ordinary day. Street hawkers were selling their wares, and watchmen were guarding houses.

"You think they will send the children home?" I asked.

"I doubt it," he said. "The best thing is to keep them where they are."

Tunde stood up and looked around the sitting room. Instinctively I knew he was looking for his phone book. I retrieved it from the bookshelf and handed it to him.

He slipped on his reading glasses. "Thanks."

"What have you heard?" I asked.

"They ambushed Muhammed on his way to work."

"Who?"

"I'm not sure, but a man called Dimka made the announcement. Give me a moment, please."

He called Muyiwa Kasumu, of all people. He had not spoken to Muyiwa in months, but perhaps he thought an ambassador on hiatus would have more information. I listened to him after they greeted each other.

"By the Federal Secretariat? I heard it happened on Second Avenue. Yes, they wanted him dead. Yes, they've been planning it all along. It was a question of time. But who is this Dimka fellow? What is his rank? Lieutenant Colonel? Where is he now? No one knows. The story of Nigeria. How did he get past the police? Of course. That is Nigeria for you. No security."

It was comforting to hear his voice. He beckoned at me to speak to Biola, but I was in no mood and had not yet forgiven her. He, apparently, was now at peace with both Kasumus because he mouthed, "What?" as he handed the phone to me.

Biola sounded hoarse. "Remi, they killed him! They killed Murtala!"

Her desolation caught me off guard. I immediately abandoned my grudge and became tearful. Tunde reached for me, but I turned away. Who told him I wanted to have a telephone conversation at a time like this? He stood by as I listened to Biola, who was sobbing.

"I hear his wife is out of the country! She may not even know!"

I remembered General Muhammed's daughter, who was in Rolari's year. She looked exactly like her father and couldn't be more than twelve years old.

My nose began to dribble. "Why did they have to kill him?"

"I don't know," Biola said. "All I know is that he was loved. That much I know. I have to go. This is too much for me."

I passed the phone back to Tunde and sniffed as I stood next to him. After he was through speaking to Muyiwa, he told me the coup plotters had abducted the governor of his home state. Unable to bear more bad news, I went to the toilet and blew my nose so forcefully my head hurt. What a useless country, I thought. What a thoroughly useless country Nigeria was.

The radio kept playing martial music throughout the day. Unfortunately for our neighbor, the Austrian ambassador, we were still waiting for news on the coup when he came to our house in the late afternoon. Our watchman told Patience he was at our gate, and Patience came indoors to tell us.

"Please tell him we're not home," I said.

"What is he coming here for?" Tunde shouted. "Tell him to go back to his house or else I will get my gun."

Patience blinked as if he had to be crazy to expect her to talk to an *oyinbo* like that, then she hurried back to the kitchen.

He didn't even own a gun. I wondered why he was being so defensive, until I remembered his preoccupation with foreign espionage.

"Do you think a foreign country is behind this?" I asked.

"Why?" he said. "Are you thinking of your American friend?"

Frances was the last person on my mind.

"No."

"Didn't you say she was going to Ghana?" he asked.

"She said she was."

"I wouldn't worry about her. She's probably back in America now. If I were her, I would get myself inoculated as quickly as possible, to reduce the risk of rabies."

I was grateful he was trying to cheer me up, but his past accusations now seemed within reason. I thought about all the information I'd shared with Frances and all the people she had met through me.

"Do you think the Americans are behind this?" I asked.

"I don't know," Tunde said. "We'll just have to wait and see."

We never heard the coup announcement that day. We turned the radio off when we got tired of listening to martial music. In the evening, when it was time for the television to come on, the same music played until we had another power cut.

February 14

On the day the Supreme Military Council announced General Muhammed's assassination, we had twenty-four hours of electricity. The Nigerian Broadcasting Corporation stopped playing martial music on the radio and television, and instead played Chopin's "Funeral March." Like the facts of the Civil War, the details of the coup were ambiguous and disputed. Between hearsay, *Daily Times*, other newspapers and our new head of state's national address, we were able to ascertain that General Muhammed had had no security with him except for his aide-de-camp when he was ambushed; that they were both shot to death and his official car, a black Benz, was riddled with bullets; that he was rushed to the military hospital in Ikoyi, where he was pronounced dead, and within twenty-four hours, was flown out of Lagos and buried in Kano up north.

General Muhammed had been known to travel around Lagos in an unofficial car. I'd heard he lived in his house, not at the head of state's residence, Dodan Barracks. The coup plotters had planned to kill the chief of army staff as well, but that didn't pan out. They had also intended to assassinate our new head of state, General Obasanjo, who had been second-in-command, but they had inadvertently ended up shooting another officer. They were so inept and amateurish that their radio announcement had stated the curfew would be from six a.m. to six p.m.

General Obasanjo was a Yoruba man, and, like General Muhammed, a Civil War veteran. In his address, he claimed several arrests had been made, and one of the detainees was a Lieutenant Colonel Buka Suka Dimka. He promised that the Supreme Military Council would set up a board of inquiry and that all General Muhammed's policies would continue, as would government ministries. He then declared a seven-day period of mourning, designating February 20th as a one-off public holiday for prayers.

Tunde called Maurice that evening—Maurice Onyia, the judge. He had finally left Lagos and was now in his hometown, Asaba, but the phone lines were so busy it took a while for trunk calls to get through.

I'd closed my shop earlier in the day. Boniface was the only one who showed up for work anyway, and I sent him home with money for his bus fare. Now, I was pottering around the house and tidying up wherever I could. I went to the guest room and considered sorting out the knick-knacks I'd hoarded there, but I walked in, saw the boxes and was overwhelmed. I actually locked the door to stop myself from carrying out another pointless task.

I returned downstairs after Tunde had finished his phone conversation with Maurice. He sat at the head of the dining table, writing on a notepad with a silver pen I'd bought him for Christmas.

"'Reschedule meeting with Ibrahim,'" I said, reading his notes aloud.

"I have to write down everything these days," he said.

"Me, too," I said, rubbing his shoulder. "Old age is approaching. How is Maurice doing?"

"He's fine. He's farming now."

"Really?"

"Yes. He has all that arable land there. He might as well."

I couldn't imagine Maurice getting involved in farming. He was hardly the sort. He was the bookish son. His elder brother had inherited the land, which had belonged to their father, but his brother had subsequently died and the land passed to him.

Maurice had hired people from his town to farm the land, Tunde said. He had been made a chief. I was surprised to hear that because after he graduated from Cambridge, his towns-people expected him to start his legal career there, but Maurice said he didn't go to Cambridge to learn how to settle disputes over goats. Naturally, they were upset when he decided to settle in Lagos instead. Now, he was back with a tarnished reputation, and perhaps they were willing to pardon him because he had built his house using local labor. His farm would only bring more money to the town.

"How are they reacting to the news over there?" I asked.

At work, I'd called my brother Deji in Ibadan, expecting to hear that the city had burned down. He said students from the university had set a few cars on fire while protesting the coup, but that was all.

Tunde put his pen down. "Maurice says everyone is nervous. It looks like there's going to be a mass exodus out of Lagos."

"Why?"

"Igbos are already moving back to the East. They say Muhammed wanted to turn Nigeria into an Islamic state. Meanwhile, up north, they're calling it a Christian coup."

"Come on," I said, sitting in Rolari's chair.

"That's what he said. The atmosphere is almost as bad as it was after the coup of '66."

"Which one?"

"The January one."

"But the plotters of this coup are inexperienced officers."

Tunde shrugged. "We don't know who is involved yet and you can't argue with perception. Nigeria is a big country. Everything does not revolve around Lagos. Muhammed may have been popular here, but you drive to another state and the general opinion may be different. Don't forget what happened in Asaba during the war."

"So Maurice sees this coup as justice for what happened in Asaba?"

"I doubt it. One man's life for all the people that were killed there?"

"Oh, come on," I said. "This coup has nothing to do with religion or tribalism. Since when did Maurice start claiming he's Igbo, anyway?"

"What is this?" Tunde asked. "What do you have against him?"

He said Maurice had never denied he was Igbo and had only maintained that the Midwest should not be part of Biafra. There was nothing wrong with that.

Apart from his Middle Belt affiliations, Tunde had a dubious affinity with men who had that "back to the country" mentality. Men who, as far as I knew, had never picked up a hoe in their lives, but the moment they got into trouble in Lagos, they returned to their hometowns to farm.

"What else did Maurice say?" I asked.

"He thinks General Gowon might be behind the coup."

"Gowon's in England."

The last I'd heard, he was a student at Warwick University.

"He still has supporters here and they don't like Muhammed."

"Enough to kill him?"

Tunde shook his head. "I don't think Gowon is behind this, but listen, this matter is complex and it's only been a day. Let us just wait and see."

It was still awkward to talk about General Muhammed, but I admired his courage as a Nigerian leader. I had seen courageous men during the nationalist movement. There was Herbert Macaulay, who founded the first Nigerian political party. There was Anthony Enahoro, who was so young when he called for self-governance. There were brave women, too. Fela's mother, Funmilayo Ransome-Kuti, was one. She put up a good fight for suffrage rights. But for a postindependence leader of Nigeria to face up to America—*the* United States of America—in the way General Muhammed had, was unprecedented.

Tunde called me Joseph the Dreamer because every time I'd lost a relative, they had appeared to me in a dream, bearing a gift. My father had given me a Bible, my mother, a gold pendant, and my brother Akin, his reading glasses. That night I had a discomforting dream about General Muhammed. He appeared as I'd last seen him on television and then morphed into a grotesque creature. He was the leader of his pack and the rest decided he had to be eliminated, so they tore him apart, limb by limb, and devoured him.

February 15

It was not strange for a country to have a character after all, to possess a national psyche, as it were. Argumentativeness, unscrupulousness and lateness were just some of our flaws. On the plus side, we were tenacious, resilient and resourceful. But how those traits had developed was inconceivable to me.

On Sunday morning, Tunde and I went to church. It was the right thing to do. He would have preferred to play golf, but I would not have let him. The golf club was not safe territory, on account of its military members.

Our church was Anglican and our children had been baptized there. Tunde had attended a Baptist missionary school when he was a boy, but he didn't mind where he worshipped. He could just as easily have gone to a mosque, instead.

That day, Lagos was somber—even given an allowance for my own disposition. It manifested in the faces of the people I saw, in their muted voices, the harmattan mist over the marina, and the sky, which had turned an uncertain shade of gray. As we approached the church gates, Ashake Dada arrived with a female companion. If she were not with her husband, Debayo, she had to have a maid-in-waiting, usually a younger, poorer relative who looked up to her. She wore a white lace *iro* and *buba* and green head tie, with a matching *coccodrillo* bag and platform sandals. She could well have been attending a society wedding.

"You never sent your nephew to collect the money," she said.

"He'll come when things are calmer," I said, hugging her.

"Lady of the manor," Tunde said. "Where is the lord?"

"Ah," Ashake said, shaking her head. "He's in hiding. All General Gowon's friends are."

She was again in her own fantasy world. She hurried past people in the church courtyard, as if she was in danger of being mobbed by admirers. Heads turned as she and her companion walked down the center aisle and headed straight for the front pew.

Our priest gave a sermon about forgiveness, which went on for so long he only succeeded in stirring up resentment. He was an example of the duplicity I poked fun at in secular circles, but would never dare to in church, out of respect. Besides, his situation was not amusing. He was an Englishman married to an Englishwoman, yet was rumored to be in a relationship with a Nigerian clergyman. Our church was not alone in that regard. Down the road was another Anglican church and their priest was Nigerian, married to a Nigerian, but he allegedly had several children out of wedlock.

During the service, I couldn't sing the hymn "Dear Lord and Father of Mankind." It was my mother's favorite and I would have broken down and cried. Afterward, everyone we stopped to greet in the courtyard talked about the coup. If my mother were alive, she would be saying, "Don't bring it up," hoping the coup would go away. I felt the same. How many times could a person hear that General Muhammed had had no security when he was ambushed, and that there were this or that number of bullet holes in his car?

Nigeria was a morbid nation. I discovered this as a girl. The first time I saw a dead body was at the wake of a kind old

Trinidadian doctor who sometimes gave me and my brothers shiny new ha'pennies. He was one of a few West Indian émigrés who adopted Yoruba as their culture. He was lying in repose when my family arrived, and I was horrified to find him in his coat and trousers—as suits were then called. He had his spectacles on, and his pocket-watch chain hung from his waistcoat. I thought, What does he need to tell the time for? The worst part was that he had cotton wool stuffed up his nose. I turned my face away as my brothers craned their necks to see if it were true that his eyelids were stitched down.

As I grew older, I saw more dead bodies at other wakes and funerals I attended, and began to observe how hypocritical Nigerians were at such events. It didn't matter who had died. The deceased could be a despicable person and he or she would still be venerated. Another old man, Senhor Something-or-another, from Bode Hernandes' end of town, died when I was in my early teens. I knew better than to take gifts from him. He had, according to my mother, "interfered" with girls in my neighborhood and bribed them with sweets, so they wouldn't tell their parents. She had warned me that if I ever saw him in the vicinity, I was to cross the street and start running. I lived in fear of the man. My father wouldn't even talk to him. Yet, the moment he died, my parents were off to his house to pay their respects. Three weeks later, they were at his wake-keeping, singing church hymns and drinking *mingau*. The day after, they attended his funeral and returned with a poster, in the center of which was a portrait photograph of him, and at the top of which were the words "*Sun re o.*" Sleep well.

Over the years, *Sun re o* showed up not only in funeral programs and obituaries, but also on handkerchiefs, T-shirts and plastic commemorative cups as the business of bereavement became an industry in Lagos. For me, *Sun re o* became emblematic of the attitude Nigerians had toward death. Death was just a long sleep and they wished the dead peace, whether or not the dead deserved it. They didn't seem to see the indignity of death, the only state in which anyone could dress you up exactly as they pleased, clog your nose with cotton wool, stick you in a box and shovel dirt over you.

Later in the afternoon we visited Rolari at school, and she said someone in her class had told her General Muhammed had foreseen his fate in a dream, and despite being advised not to go to work that morning, he went anyway, because he had left his life in Allah's hands.

"How would she know that?" I asked.

"Her uncle knew General Muhammed," Rolari said.

We were in the Quiet Zone again, and as usual the three of us sat on the wooden bench Rolari had brought from the assembly hall beforehand. She was in her Sunday dress and beret.

"You shouldn't listen to rumors," I said.

"It's not a rumor, Mummy. Why would she make it up?"

Tunde signaled to me that I should let that pass, but I felt she was feeding her anxiety.

"To get attention," I said.

I was thinking of Ashake Dada, but if I had a kobo for every story I'd heard about an elder declaring, "I'm going on a long journey" the night before he or she died, I would be the richest woman in Nigeria. A person couldn't even die in Lagos without someone else saying, "No wonder I couldn't sleep last night." Nigerians were possessive about death ordinarily, let alone when the death involved a head of state. They would readily claim false connections to General Muhammed.

"What about his daughter?" Tunde asked Rolari, attempting to distract her.

"She's at home," Rolari said. "If I were her, I would just kill myself."

"You would do no such thing," I said.

Tunde signaled to me one more time, but again I ignored him.

"I'm sorry," I said, "but she's not allowed to say that."

"She didn't mean it," he said.

"Yes, I did," Rolari said.

Like us, our children rarely talked about General Muhammed, but Rolari was initially excited after the coup that brought him to power and couldn't wait for his television addresses. She would watch the news with us and repeat his catchphrases: "We are all together" and "With immediate effect."

"I know you're upset," I said, "but you can't dwell on the coup."

"I'm not," she said, raising her voice.

"What, then? Are you unhappy in school?"

"No."

"So try and cheer up."

She had lost weight. She was a fussy eater and would never touch the sardine-and-corned-beef sandwiches Rotimi ate. We had brought her provisions she wanted—Kellogg's cereal variety pack, Nido instant milk and Cadbury Bournvita. Boarders apparently mixed Nido powder and Bournvita granules to make a snack, which they ate out of cups with spoons. They ingenuously called the snack "Mixture." Rolari lived on Mixture. She didn't eat much at mealtimes, except on Sundays when boarders had jollof rice and chicken for lunch.

"Do you want to come home at the end of the month?" I asked her.

"Yes," she said, without hesitation.

We had an understanding, which her father mistook for hostility. He may not have realized she couldn't express her grief about General Muhammed out of loyalty to him.

"I will send your housemistress a letter. You and your brother will come home."

She frowned. "You'd better make me chicken stew."

"Dob, dob, dob," I said, giving a Scout salute.

I was a Scout when I was a girl, and annoyingly keen. Rolari was a Girl Guide but seemed more interested in their camping trips and annual bazaar than in doing her best for God and country. She had just earned herself another badge and the award ceremony was the following Saturday, so we decided she would come home the Saturday after.

Visiting hours ended before the curfew and there was no sign of unrest on the mainland, but we passed an army truck as we drove into the island, which again reminded me of the coup. The soldiers looked no better than a herd of cattle, yet, with their rifles, they were formidable.

We arrived home to find the evening papers had been delivered, and amidst the tributes to General Muhammed, I read an editorial warning the federal government to try the detainees as soon as possible to prevent the kind of instability that had led to the massacre of Igbos up north in 1966. I found that unnecessarily incendiary. It was too soon to think of justice. The country was still in a state of shock.

February 16

The curfew ended when Tunde and I woke up, so getting to work on time shouldn't have been a problem for him, except that his office driver, who lived some distance away, was unable to pick him up as early as seven in the morning. On Monday, Jimoh drove him to work and I went to the shopping center in my van. I arrived without incident, and had I been a stranger in Lagos, I would never have guessed there had been a coup over the weekend. There was no indication in the bottleneck at the entrance, or the gathering of drivers under the flame-of-the-forest tree, though one of them was wearing a black armband. They were listening to a radio and presumably following news about the coup.

I found Festus and Boniface in subdued moods when I reached the shop. They greeted me and from then on lowered their voices whenever they spoke. A customer came in shortly afterward, and they attended to her with such morose expressions we might as well have been in a funeral parlor.

Business was slow that morning, so I left earlier than normal for lunch. Patience brought my food to the dining room with a slightly stooped posture, which got me thinking about national moods. I'd long forgotten that it was possible for a country to be depressed.

I'd finished eating when she returned to tell me someone was at the gate to see me.

"Who is it?" I asked.

"The watchman say one *oyinbo* man."

I assumed it was the Austrian ambassador. Perhaps he hadn't gone to work. Perhaps he had even been waiting for my return. I kept a noticeable routine. What did he want to see me for? I wondered. Surely he couldn't be so naïve as to think I would discuss the coup with him?

This time, I decided to go outside anyway, for the sake of being neighborly, and was pleased to find that the gate was locked. At least the watchman was following orders. It wouldn't be unusual for him to break the rules for an *oyinbo*. Between the iron bars of the gate I saw a Peugeot with a diplomatic license plate. It was the Millers' car, and Frances emerged from a back door. She wore trousers and a cap, which was probably why the watchman had mistaken her for a man. I said to myself, Not today of all days.

The watchman stepped out of his cement cubicle to unlock the gate, and I signaled to him that it wasn't necessary.

"I went to the mall to look for you," she said. "They told me you were at home."

She had a bruise on one side of her face, the sight of which made my eyes water. We were both frowning, but that could have been due to the sun.

"That looks bad," I said.

"It's not as bad as it looks."

"I called you," I said. "Several times."

"You did?"

"Over the weekend."

She gestured at the gate. "May I?"

Duchess, who had wandered away from her spot on the veranda, now hovered beside me looking dejected, in her usual bid to be saved. Regardless, I was not going to let Frances in.

"I'm sorry, but this is a terrible day for me. I have an appointment and I'm running late."

I resented having to lie, but there was such a thing as showing loyalty to a country, and it was as real and unreasonable as wanting your children tucked in their beds, and being soothed by the sound of your husband's voice.

"I was hoping you could help me," she said. "Ade called. His wife got on the phone and said I shouldn't attempt to leave the country because she was going to hand my name over to the airport authorities."

For the first time I was put off by her American accent and mannerisms, and her American presumptuousness. Why was she here on a national day of mourning?

"I don't think the airport authorities are keeping track of anyone but the coup suspects right now."

She rambled on. "I know, but I can't take a chance. She was very angry. Well, you saw. But you warned me. I should have listened to you. I had no idea things were that bad between them. I met Ade the Thursday before our golf game, at Federal Palace Hotel. I didn't think...I didn't think I should mention it to you. It was...well, a disaster. I suppose I was worried you might think I was difficult to get along with, after what happened at the Bagatelle, so I decided to keep my word and partner with him. He hates to lose. He hates to lose any game. He lost at the casino, which was why he gambled again and lost his wife's clubs to me. I can only imagine what he's done in the course of their divorce if he hates to lose so much. Not that I care. But I want...I have to leave Lagos, and I was hoping you might speak to her. I don't know if the airports are monitoring anyone. All I know is that this is the worst possible time for anything like this to happen. Everyone is focused on the coup. No one will help if I'm stopped."

It now seemed unlikely she had spent the night with Ade, which only reinforced my suspicions. What questions had she asked him? Hadn't Moji accused her of spying? Why didn't she bring that up?

"Can't your embassy help?" I asked.

She was a smart woman. She ought to know what to do.

"It's impossible to get anything done right now."

"That is to be expected after a coup."

"I was hoping you would at least try and talk her out of it. It's a first step, isn't it?"

"Why would she want to stop you from leaving the country, Frances?" I asked.

"I don't know. She has this idea—"

"Where are your beads?"

"My beads?"

"You talk about them, but I've never actually seen them before."

"I don't…carry them around."

"Didn't you say you were going to Ghana?"

"I'd planned to, but under the circumstances…"

Maybe she was the adventurous woman I'd initially thought she was. Maybe she just got caught up in the Baloguns' marital drama, but I could not take a chance.

"I'm sorry," I said. "There's nothing I can do for you."

She nodded. "It was just a thought."

"I know your embassy will help, if you're prepared to wait a little longer."

"Have I upset you in any way, Remi?" she asked.

"It's a terrible day for me, Frances. For the whole country."

"I understand," she said. "For what it's worth, I may have had a hard time adjusting here, but I'm glad we met."

Of course I was remorseful, but I was still annoyed she had come to my house on a national day of mourning, and that warped into a sanctimonious assurance that I owed her nothing and had treated her appropriately. How polite she was, I thought. How extraordinarily polite. She had to be guilty.

I came home from work that evening and my own guilt was so heavy I lay on the sofa. How did I even know Frances had been traveling? What if she were busy relaying the information I'd shared with her? What if she'd been in Lagos all along, at the United States embassy, typing reports and calling Washington to tell someone she'd met a Nigerian woman who had given her insights into what Lagosians thought about General Muhammed?

I tried to recall our conversation on the beach, word for word. Then I considered the worst scenario, which was that I'd befriended someone who was in the enemy camp, someone who wanted General Muhammed dead, and someone who might even have known about the coup beforehand. Had I spoken about him fairly? Had my judgment been clouded by Tunde's retirement? What conclusion could Frances possibly have drawn from the little I'd said about him? Perhaps all she needed was a confirmation.

Rather than face such a prospect, I calmed myself with mundane sounds—Patience clanking pots in the kitchen, the Austrian girls laughing in the backyard and their mother calling them in for dinner. "Nadia? Nina?"

Tunde came home and found me lying in the dark. I had not bothered to switch on the lights.

"What's the matter?" he asked.

"I'm tired," I said.

He walked to the stereo. "Get up, my friend. I have good news for you."

"What good news?"

He switched on the lights and I shielded my eyes as "Stairway to the Stars" played. Today, the lyrics seemed trite, and much as I enjoyed Ella Fitzgerald's version, I preferred Sarah Vaughan's.

He reached for my hand. "*Oya.*"

"You must be joking," I said.

The only news that could make me dance was that he had won a million naira.

"Will you get up?" he said.

I protested. "I'm not in the mood. Just tell me the news and it had better be good."

He laughed. "That is the trouble with you African women. When one is being romantic, you become antagonistic."

"Go on, what is it?"

"We've got our house."

I was pleased, but my body ached as I stood up and allowed him to lead.

"How did that happen?"

"I met with Ibrahim this evening, and he told me."

"How come they have a vacancy?"

"I don't know. All I know is our house will be ready for us by the end of June."

I rested my chin on his shoulder. His jacket smelled of cigarettes. Could my courtesy call to Habiba Ibrahim have worked?

"You know what happened to me today?" I said.

"What?"

"Frances came here."

He pulled away. "I thought she'd gone to Ghana."

"It's all right. I sent her away."

"What did she come here for?"

"Calm down."

"If I ever see that woman…"

"Listen, just listen."

As we danced I told him about our conversation.

"You know the problem with you?" he said. "You don't know how to separate. You've never known how. You didn't know how to separate from the children. You don't know how to separate from your shop. You want to solve everyone's problems."

"I'm not like that," I said.

"You are," he said. "A friend comes to you to say, 'Talk to my husband,' and you're there, until they drag you into their fight. You meet a foreigner at a hotel, you introduce her to everybody, until she gets herself bitten. You handled it well, though. Now it's all over, learn to separate."

"Do you still suspect her?"

"It makes no difference, so long as she doesn't come to my house again. You can't take back the fact that you befriended her. You've always been friendly. Anyone who meets you can see that, and she obviously did."

"I'm no socialite, though."

"Hm."

We stopped dancing, and he turned off the stereo. I felt redundant as a Nigerian citizen. That was partly what my guilt was about and why I felt so weighed down. But with the threat of men with guns, what was one to do? Protest in the streets? Write a letter to a newspaper? Why even bother to discuss political ideas in a country like ours? You reached a point where all you could do was make sure your children were raised well and educated well, your family life and friendships were intact, and your source of income was secure. The rest you left to God.

"Who could be behind Muhammed's assassination?" I asked.

Tunde shrugged. "No one knows. Today, they're talking about foreign backers. Tomorrow it might be someone else."

"They're talking about foreign backers?"

"Well, the panel says they have traced the coup to foreign backers."

"They actually mentioned foreign backers?"

He walked over to his chair and kicked off his shoes. "General Muhammed was assassinated, Remi. You're not responsible for that."

"Aren't you sad? I mean for Nigeria?"

He shrugged again. "You can't allow Nigeria's problems to get you down. I come home, and I just want to relax. Where is Patience, for heaven's sake?"

"What is it you want?"

"Water, please."

"I'll get it for you."

I headed for the kitchen. It was one way to shake off the heaviness. At the kitchen door, I turned around.

"Why do you give me so much trouble?"

He gave me the look. "What trouble?"

"Don't you want me to be a cash madam?"

He laughed. "The day you become a cash madam, I will retire."

I smiled. "I'm thinking of selling gift hampers. I need all your contacts."

He nodded. "You can have them."

"Can I talk to anyone I want, as well?"

"So long as you stay away from the golf club."

I knew I had another reason for holding a grudge against him, then I remembered.

"If I ever hear Oyinda has called you at the office again, you will answer to me."

"Remi," he said, loosening his tie, "I'm not the one who had an affair with my wife's friend."

I had a nightmare about him that night. He was in our front yard, getting out of his office car, when soldiers arrived at our gate. They piled out of their truck, positioned themselves between the gate's iron bars and took aim. I was in the house, looking out of the window. He was not aware of the soldiers. I wanted to warn him that they were about to shoot, but couldn't move or speak.

February 20

That week, we had so many power cuts at home my fridge leaked and flooded the kitchen floor. Then my freezer defrosted, so I had to throw away the raw meat I'd stored there.

On Friday, the national day of prayer, I got a letter from Rolari saying her school had held a memorial service for General Muhammed, which his daughter had attended. They'd sung "Abide with Me" and "I Vow to Thee, My Country." I replied telling her the latter hymn was one of my favorites. My father deemed it colonial, though, which annoyed me at the time because I didn't know why he had to see everything in political terms, to the extent that he would ruin a perfectly good hymn for me. We never sang it in his church, but I did at school, without giving much thought to its patriotic underpinnings. We would sing the first and last verses only, and the last, to my mind, was the most poignant.

> *And there's another country, I've heard of long ago,*
> *Most dear to them that love her, most great to them that know;*
> *We may not count her armies, we may not see her King;*
> *Her fortress is a faithful heart, her pride is suffering;*
> *And soul by soul and silently her shining bounds increase,*
> *And her ways are ways of gentleness and all her paths are peace.*

I had no idea it referred to heaven. I thought it was about the ideal country.

Tunde and I visited the Kasumus later that day and found that Biola was recovering from a bout of malaria. She had developed a headache and temperature after the coup, and had been vomiting most of the week. Her symptoms had since subsided, but she was still taking Nivaquine tablets in case they recurred.

I went upstairs with her, and left Muyiwa and Tunde downstairs. The wall of their staircase was newly painted, as were the walls of their landing, which led to their daughters' rooms. There was a basket of clothes by their bathroom door, awaiting their washerman. Biola had not yet found a houseboy to replace the one she had sacked for stealing food. Her cook was doing her cleaning in the meantime.

She lay on her bed as I sat by her dressing table. She had several bottles of perfume, and traces of their fragrances merged pleasantly. She pointed out stains on the ceiling from leaks during the rainy season, and the air conditioner, which was as temperamental as the one downstairs.

"You don't know how lucky you are that Tunde is no longer working for the government," she said.

We could hear our husbands talking in the sitting room. Tunde had mentioned our Community Bank housing to Muyiwa, and as Muyiwa had warmly congratulated us, Biola responded with a subdued, "That's nice."

"Think of Spain," I said to encourage her.

"Spain?" she said. "All postings have been put on hold until further notice."

"I thought government ministries were continuing as usual."

She sighed. "Things are always different for us in External Affairs."

Muyiwa was convinced the CIA had backed the coup. He had never been able to trust Americans or their salads, he'd said. He actually believed their diplomats spiked salads with marijuana to loosen their guests' tongues. That had me crying out in amusement. Muyiwa was made for a career in External Affairs. He loved the pomp and circumstance, and enjoyed his wines and cigars. I found him attentive for a Nigerian husband. So attentive, it was easy to forget he had another family. He'd actually looked after Biola while she was sick. I would have to be dying for Tunde to look after me.

"Do you believe the Americans are behind the coup?" I asked Biola.

"They had it in for Muhammed after his OAU speech," she said. "You know what they say. In politics, there are no permanent friends or enemies, only permanent interests. And let's face it, they got rid of Allende. Why not Muhammed?"

She could have been repeating Muyiwa's opinions again, but she was right. Britain and the Soviets were supposedly our friends during the Civil War. France, apparently, was our enemy. The United States took an ambivalent position, on the one hand secretly assisting us, and on the other calling for humanitarianism on behalf of Biafra. None of their positions made sense without their interests in oil.

"I've never heard that saying before," I said.

I was still struggling with Tunde's advice about separating myself from recent events. Since Biola was homebound, she would not have heard about the incident at the golf club. I could imagine how smug she would be when she found out.

"Dimka is just a small boy," she said. "There is no way he could have done this on his own. You know they haven't found him yet?"

"Didn't they announce his arrest?"

"He's still at large."

"Why would they lie?"

"To hide their incompetence. You must have heard that they've arrested Bisalla."

"No."

"He's in custody now."

I wasn't especially surprised that Bisalla, the Defense commissioner, had been implicated in the coup, but was more intrigued by the fact that he and Dimka were Northerners. Why would they turn on General Muhammed?

"Aren't Northerners supposed to be more united?" I asked.

Biola lowered her voice as she did whenever she was sharing inside information.

"Bisalla and Dimka are Gowon's boys."

"You think?"

"Of course. Gowon had full knowledge of this coup. They say Dimka went to the British High Commission afterward to call him in England."

The conspiracy theories were out of hand.

"The British are implicated as well?"

"You know how much they approved of Gowon. As for the Americans, the minute Muhammed announced his support for Neto, he became a Marxist to them."

"And Bisalla?"

"Bisalla was just bitter because he was not promoted to the rank he wanted and Dimka wanted Gowon back in power, finish."

Her gossip was firsthand, if nothing else, but I still couldn't see why the United States had any reason to fear the spread of Marxism beyond academic circles. I couldn't even remember the definition of Marxism. I certainly didn't need America to tell me it spelled trouble for me.

"I hear they're calling Muhammed an Islamist in the East," I said.

I wasn't sure what "Islamist" meant, either. Weren't all Muslims by definition Islamists?

Biola eyed me. "What are those ones complaining about this time?"

"Tunde called Maurice. Maurice Onyia, the former judge. He said the Igbos have already started heading to the East, in case Northerners accuse them of killing Muhammed."

"Who might accuse them of that?"

"They have not forgiven Muhammed for what happened during the Civil War. That could make them suspects."

Her voice rose. "Who cares? Who cares whether the Igbos have forgiven him or not? Isn't that the nature of war? One side has to win and people have to die. What did they expect? Did they send their troops to the battlefront to shake hands with ours? Them and their Biafra. Biafra at all costs. Truth is the first casualty of war. At least you've heard that saying before, haven't you?"

"I have."

"So let's face the facts here. Ojukwu practically forced Gowon's hand. He made Gowon look like a fool, acting as if he was a law unto himself. He manipulated those people and deceived them while they were being killed. Then he fled the country to save his own life when his army was defeated. So who should the Igbos forgive? No, Remi. I don't want to hear it. The Igbos wanted a war, and they got one."

I was raising my hand. "How do we know what they wanted?"

"What do you mean?"

"They didn't vote to go to war. None of us did."

The idea that an individual or a group of individuals could speak for and act on behalf of an ethnic group, let alone an entire nation, was a fallacy that had gained ground with the January Boys' coup. The truth about the war, yet to be acknowledged, was that the majority of Nigerians were dumb witnesses to the spectacle of it.

"Who votes to go to war?" Biola asked. "Even in the United States they leave it up to Congress. Was Vietnam popular? No, but you follow your leaders blindly and you get what you deserve. Look, let the governor of Texas, or wherever they have oil in America, decide he wants to secede today, and take up arms against their federal government, and you will see what will happen to him and anyone who supports him. They will level Texas. There will be no Texas to speak of, and we're still sitting here talking about Biafra."

"A million of them were killed."

She hissed. "Now it's a million. Before, it was half a million. Very soon it will be ten million. Please, Remi, don't tell me anything about the Igbos. They don't know how lucky they are they still have the East to speak of. If they like they can stay there. Murtala was loved. He was loved here. Everyone is crying in the streets. You should see the women in the marketplaces, weeping publicly."

Even victors need to forgive, I thought. I was not talking about truth or facts and figures. When had any of that ever precipitated forgiveness? I was talking about compassion, but if our national memory and sense of justice were selective, so was our empathy for our fellow Nigerians.

Maurice had once said, in a moment that approached forgiveness, that trust was the first casualty of war. During the

Civil War the federal soldiers couldn't trust their leaders, sub-ordinates or allies. Anyone could be an enemy. They were often trudging around the bush hungry. Why wouldn't they end up behaving like animals? They were young men who had to fight for their lives. How could we expect them to do that with honor?

"How are the girls?" I asked, to change the subject.

Biola sat up. "We're visiting them next week."

"Are they staying in Ibadan after you leave Lagos?"

She shrugged. "What else can we do?"

"Don't worry. They will be fine."

"It's not them I'm worried about. It's what will happen in the country. I'm praying to leave now."

It didn't make sense that she was praying to leave her daughters, but perhaps she was worried Muyiwa would have more time to spend with his other family if his posting were further delayed. Knowing Biola, she would never admit that to me. For a moment I wondered if she was pretending to be sick with malaria to make sure Muyiwa stayed at home.

Downstairs our husbands were laughing. It was easier to continue to talk about the coup than to have a personal conversation with her.

"Do you think Obasanjo is capable of heading the country?" I asked.

"That one? They practically had to force him to take over."

"I hope whoever killed Muhammed doesn't end up killing him as well."

From where I sat I could see the casuarina trees in their backyard. It was a tranquil afternoon and deceptively peaceful. I questioned the value of a national day of prayer. We needed more than prayer to change the course we were on.

February 21

On Saturday morning I went to Hilda's salon to get my hair done. She had only one customer besides me, which was to be expected in the aftermath of the coup, and she insisted on shampooing my hair herself, after which she applied her homemade conditioning treatment as one of her girls made me a cup of tea.

I had made some effort to dress up for Hilda, in a brocade *boubou* with gold embroidery I would not normally wear to work. She was in a brown patterned *ankara* up-and-down that hugged her waist, and she hitched up the skirt and sat in the chair next to mine. Her legs were considerably pale. We talked to our reflections in the mirror, our voices vying with Tom Jones' "Delilah."

"How is business?" she asked.

"We're trying," I said. "Next time you visit, you might not even recognize the place."

"The coup has slowed things down for us."

"Us, too. Sometimes I wonder if we're paying for our past sins with this never-ending cycle."

"Every country has sins in its past, Remi."

She looked sad, and Hilda was rarely sad. Not even a coup could subdue her.

"What's the matter?" I asked.

"You know I don't like to spread rumors. You know I keep my mouth shut, but there's something I must ask you."

"Yes?"

"I spoke to Fran—"

"No, Hilda. I didn't come here to talk about Frances."

"Hear word."

"I said no! What is this? I came here to relax. If you won't let me relax, I will leave."

She laughed. "To go where, with your hair like this?"

"Wash it out, and dry me up!"

Her conditioning treatment was made with shea butter and coconut oil. She called it German Juju. For what it was worth, it did make my hair grow.

"Hear word, my friend," she said. "She came the day after the coup. She said the Balogun woman…" She slapped the air.

"I was there."

"She said so. I said, 'Remi Lawal?' She said, 'Yes,' then she said the Balogun woman…" She bit the air. "I said, 'That is news to me.' I asked Philip at home, 'How come I've never heard of this custom before?' Philip said illiterate women do that when they fight. Then he said Frances would need a course of antibiotics and a tetanus injection."

I managed to smile. "Tunde said she might need one for rabies."

How long would I have to keep clarifying what happened? I was disappointed that all people seemed to take away from the incident was that Moji had behaved in a manner that was beneath her.

Hilda and I resumed talking to our reflections.

"Those Baloguns," she said. "I feel as if I know them personally, after everything I've heard about them. One day I hear she is going to kill her husband, the next I hear she is going to kill herself."

"She won't do that."

"But she fights."

"She fights, all right," I said.

"Frances said Moji accused her of being her husband's mistress."

"Their fight wasn't about that."

"What was it about?"

"She wanted to embarrass him. Anyway, why would I knowingly sit with Ade and his mistress?"

"You think he and Frances…?"

"I don't know, and it's probably better I don't."

"She said Moji called her a spy."

"She wasn't the first to."

"No?"

"Tunde, too, thought she was spying."

Hilda clapped. "Heh! I done enter trouble!"

"Did she ever ask you any strange questions?"

"No."

"Nothing about what is happening in the country?"

"Never. She only asked how I adjusted here, things like that. I told her I had no problem with Nigerians, only with expatriates. But how can she be a spy?"

"Every American here is, apparently. I'm sure she told you what happened when she came to my house."

"Small, small."

"I advised her to seek help from her embassy."

"So you won't talk to Moji about it?"

"Absolutely not."

"Why not?"

"You heard what she did. How can I reason with someone like that?"

"But you're not convinced."

"About?"

Hilda gestured. "Remi, there are no secrets in Nigeria. The coup was no secret. Who needs to send a spy to Nigeria when any visa officer here can be one?"

"I honestly don't know what to think anymore."

I had doubts yet again. What if Frances were innocent? What if I had turned my back on someone who was liable to get detained for no reason?

Hilda stroked the back of her hand.

"Is that all?" I asked.

Her voice trembled. "Oh, don't mind me. My job is to listen to my customers' problems. Even before they tell me, I know. I can see it in their hair. All their palaver…"

She began to cry, so I rubbed her back. "Take it easy."

"Sorry."

"It's all right. You listen to everyone."

"Pam is sick."

"Pam Ogedengbe?"

"Cancer."

"Goodness."

"Breast."

"Heavens. But I saw her…"

Hilda reached for a box of tissues on the table and blew her nose.

"She's gone back to Dublin for treatment. Her children are staying with us. That foolish man went with her. You've heard about his other children?"

"Niyi? I heard about the child on the side."

"She was holding too much inside. That's what causes cancer, you know. Did you hear about the twins in Ghana?"

"What twins in Ghana?"

"Remi, don't let me start. That man is a very foolish man indeed. You and I married good men."

"Are things this bad with expatriates?"

"They go loony. Maybe it's the sun or something. I know one…with the housegirl."

"Goodness."

"Another one, every time her husband travels, he flies through Amsterdam. Things like that. But the difference is, with a Nigerian husband, if you talk, even your relatives will ask, 'So what?'"

I shook my head. "Pam. Always cheerful."

"My first thought was, Why her? Why not him?"

"We had dinner just the other night. I saw her at the trade fair."

"She found out last week. As soon as she told me, I said to myself, 'I will never forgive that man.' But I saw him crying. He was crying like a baby. I asked myself, 'What are his tears for?' But see, we talk to each other now. He gives me news about her, and I tell him about their children. Between us, we're preparing them, just in case, because you never know." She grabbed more tissues and wiped her eyes. "I'm not going to tell you what to do, Remi. People are wicked. Friends can be very wicked. You remember what happened to me with Kamal?"

"Yes."

"It's always the ones who are closest to you. They are the first. The first to bury you. I lost my womb, then I lost my customers, and not one of those women said sorry to me."

She blew her nose again, and her face turned redder. Why did anyone bother to talk about forgiveness? I'd not encountered one person who was able to forgive. Even my father had trouble forgiving. He never forgave the British.

I didn't have the nerve to ask more questions about Pam, but the possibility of her not surviving made the Baloguns' scandal seem petty in comparison. I prattled on, partly out of distress and partly to soothe Hilda.

"Maybe I will talk to Moji. I have her clubs in my van. It's about time I returned them. I have to go to Victoria Island today anyway. My dog's vet is there. I can't find flea medicine anywhere in the shopping center, and you know how it is with outside pets."

"Thank you, Rem-Rem."

"It's no problem. I don't want the Baloguns bringing my name up in this mess. They have no discretion, those two. I'm glad you alerted me."

I would tell Moji I wasn't aware of any relationship between Ade and Frances. I owed her that, at least. From then on, she could continue to ruin her reputation, and his, if she pleased.

Hilda called out to her girls, who had been sneaking peeks at us. "Hey, you! Face your front over there! This is a private conversation!"

"Sorry, madam," they said in unison.

"Every day I have to shout," she muttered. "Now, they think I have no heart."

I left her salon just after eleven, by which time I was her only customer. I was lucky to have had an uninterrupted appointment that morning. I was in no mood to be sociable after hearing about Pam.

On the bridge to Victoria Island I passed an army truck heading in the direction of Bonny Cantonment. As I took the road to Moji's flat, I asked myself, What will you achieve? I'd seen what Moji was capable of. I just hoped she would not end up attacking me with her wretched clubs.

Her watchmen recognized me, but they still went through their logbook routine. One of them asked how to spell my name, as if he were not accustomed to Nigerian names. I was still in a foul mood so I asked, "Don't you know how to spell simple 'Lawal'?"

"No, madam," he said.

"Spell it however you want," I said. "Just open the gate for me."

He took a while to write down my details, and his partner unlocked the gate just as slowly. It was bloody-minded of me, but I turned down their offer to help and lugged the golf bag up the stairs of the block on my own.

Moji didn't answer her door. After my second ring, I imagined she was waiting for her housegirl to get the door. After my third, I decided to leave. I picked up the golf bag and carried it down to the next landing, where I had another image of Moji. What if she had killed herself? What if no one knew she was dead? None of her neighbors would notice her absence.

Of course this was all due to anxiety, probably heightened by what I'd learned about Plath, but I mistook it for instinct and returned to Moji's floor, where I dropped the golf bag by her door. I knocked and listened, but there wasn't a sound. The watchmen would have told me if Moji had gone out. They would have been only too happy to. I knocked one more time and was contemplating going back downstairs when I heard footsteps behind the door.

Moji opened the door and her eyes widened when she saw me. "Remi!"

I was just as startled. "I thought you were out. I was just about to leave."

315

She stood in the doorway, so I had a limited view of her and an even narrower view of her flat through the door hinge. She was in an Efuru caftan, and her face was bare. I had never seen Moji without makeup before.

"I wasn't expecting anyone," she said.

What was she talking about? No one *expected* anyone; we just dropped by.

"You might need some help with this," I said, making an effort to be polite.

"I'll get my housegirl to carry it. It must have hurt your arm."

We were both watching the bag now, with its muddy, grass-stained clubs. I thought to myself, This is retribution. I really had to learn to separate. If I swore I wasn't a busybody, no one would believe me. I couldn't tell if Moji was embarrassed or being rude, but I abandoned my intentions. She didn't want me around.

"Well," I said. "I was just on my way to the vet. I thought I should return them."

"Thank you," she said. "I would have called you, but Ade said he'd already called."

Through the door hinge I caught sight of a hand frantically waving at her and instantly knew it was his. It was ridiculous to pretend I was unaware, and my expression gave me away.

"He's here?" I said. "Greet him for me."

I walked down the stairs shaking my head. The Baloguns were back together. I would have been better prepared had Moji attempted to club me senseless. When I reached the ground floor I thought, Of course they were. Conflict was normal for them. They would thrive on escalations.

I heard Ade call my name and his voice, though re-strained, echoed in the stairwell. I was just glad he didn't call me Queen Bee, as I would have immediately told him to shut up.

He caught up with me in the car park as I was putting on my sunglasses. He looked as if he'd put his shirt on in a hurry, and I could tell he didn't want to draw attention from the watchmen. My van offered us some protection.

"Remi, I'm so sorry about that. We were not expecting anyone."

"No, no. It's perfectly okay for you to have private time with your wife."

"I know what you're thinking, and I don't blame you."

He had scratches on his forearm. I remembered seeing welts on his arm from thrashings his mother had given him. Women had always beaten him up, first his mother and now his wife. It was so much easier to make him feel guilty.

"I'm not here to tell you what is right or wrong."

"Look, Remi, it's my son. I caught him smoking in his room again. It wasn't cigarettes. You understand? I confront-ed him and he started crying. I called his mother and she came over. The things he said to us. But Moji apologized to him and I had to admit that I'd failed to see the signs."

"What signs?"

"He was sleeping a lot and not doing well in school. The company he was keeping. I've decided he will be a day stu-dent from now on, but I can't keep an eye on him while I'm at work and sending him to school overseas is no solution. I'm desperate. I don't know what else to do, and you know how much I love my children."

I deliberately hesitated. "I know."

He smiled. "I'm glad you came. I'd been thinking about contacting you. I talked to Moji about Frances. She can leave the country, now. No one will stop her."

That threw me. "Don't you suspect her anymore?"

"She's a woman and no woman wants to be detained in a place like this. Not now, when everyone is upset about General Muhammed. You heard what happened to Arthur Ashe?"

"No. What?"

"He and some other tennis players were around at the time of the coup, and they got into trouble during their semifinal match. They've left the country now. So has Pelé."

"Pelé was here as well?"

"Yes, on a Pepsi-Cola tour. Arthur Ashe came for the Lagos Tennis Classic tournament. Tunde would know. Didn't he tell you?"

"We don't talk about sports and he's only going to work right now."

"Well, I was there at Lagos Lawn Tennis Club. I witnessed the whole thing."

"I take it you're not upset about General Muhammed, then."

"I had no loyalty to his regime. He was a soldier. You live by the sword…"

He couldn't finish his statement. He had made the right decision regarding Frances, though.

I switched to Yoruba. "Was Moji serious about reporting Frances?"

"You don't know the lengths to which Moji will go. But how will I tell your friend if no one is answering her phone? Do you have an address? Somewhere I could leave a note for her?"

My apprehension came out as a sigh. If a phone number could end in such calamity, what would an address do?

Ade laughed. "Let me have it, Remi. Maybe that way I can get you to like me again."

"That won't happen in a hurry."

"We've known each other too long."

"You insulted me, and you insulted my husband."

"You insulted me and my wife."

"You deserved it."

He smiled. "I refuse to allow you to quarrel with me. I've done wrong, I know. I don't deny it, but I'm not the only one at fault, and I'm trying to make amends. All I'm asking is that you give me a chance. I assure you, I will not embarrass you."

He was good at apologizing, Moji once said. He knew how to beg.

"My father's spirit will haunt you, otherwise," I said.

"The good reverend? We wouldn't want that. Where are you going, all dressed up?"

"I'm on my way to the vet. Why are you asking?"

"Don't look at me like that. You must know I've always been sweet on you."

"I've never found you appealing. That must be the attraction."

He thought I was joking. I gave him the Millers' address and told him I was dissociating myself from the entire affair, and finally meant it.

I stopped at the vet and then took the same road back to the shopping center. As I approached the diplomatic section of Victoria Island, I saw what looked like a mob advancing. They were young men, waving tree branches and chanting. I could barely hear what they were saying and wasn't about to roll down my window to find out. One rapped on my windscreen and I braked. I could easily have knocked him over. They were civilians, for sure, though they jogged in time as soldiers did. The traffic came to a halt because of them, by which time my heartbeat was racing. They turned off the main road, and when the last one disappeared, I asked a passer-by what the disturbance was about. She wore a white headscarf and carried a Bible.

"They're university students, madam," she said.

Another rap made me jump. This one came from the back of my van. A lone young man passed my window, waving a tree branch.

When I got to the shop, I immediately called Tunde to tell him what I'd seen. He said there had been newspaper reports that Lieutenant Colonel Dimka had gone to the British High Commission to contact General Gowon in England after the coup, so perhaps the students were protesting about that.

"What did you think it was?" Tunde asked, laughing. "A social revolution?"

"I thought it was the beginning of the end," I said.

"What were you doing on Victoria Island, anyway?"

"Duchess," I said. "I was looking for her flea medication."

"You had to go all that way to find some?"

"I couldn't find any at the shopping center."

I felt guilty about deceiving him. I only told him about the Ogedengbes, and he took the news of Pam's cancer badly. He and Niyi had been quite close when they were students in Dublin. Pam would sometimes invite him over for supper. Her Irish friends called her a tart when they learned she was going out with a Nigerian. Her family disowned her, yet she continued to see Niyi and support him. They came back to Nigeria and his friends and family said she was low class, and not good enough for him. Then his infidelities began. The twins in Ghana were a surprise. I still couldn't understand why any woman would love a man to her detriment, but I hoped Pam believed her marriage to Niyi was worth the sacrifice in the end.

February 22

The curfew hours were reduced on Sunday, and news of
Bisalla's arrest was all over the headlines. Our journalists, with
their usual flair, called him by every conceivable traitor's name,
biblical and literary: Brutus, Cassius, Lucifer, Judas Iscariot.
Their articles were overwrought, and they dubbed General
Muhammed's OAU address at Addis Ababa his "Africa has
come of age" speech.

There were several reports about the attack on the British
High Commission. The students I'd come across had hurled
sticks and stones at windows, and caused considerable damage.
There were also a few editorials about a colonel who was
protesting his innocence, following his arrest in connection
with the coup. The list of detainees was getting longer, and I
feared there might be a rush to judgment as the drumbeat for
vengeance grew louder.

Tunde went to play golf that morning, and I listened to
Mahalia Jackson until he returned. He said the Woods had been
at the clubhouse, asking questions about the coup, which didn't
surprise me.

"I'm beginning to suspect those two are working for MI6,"
he said.

"Everyone is a spy to you, Lawal," I said.

He left his golf shoes on the veranda and walked to his
chair in his socks.

"They knew better than to approach me."

"That Dave fellow was so rude to me."

"He was? When?"

"That day at the club. He practically shooed me away. He and that wife of his."

"They're bush people. Why do you think they're called the Woods?"

He was in a good mood if he was making jokes about names. It seemed like an opportune moment to tell him about the events of the day before, and predictably he was more receptive than he would otherwise have been. Timing was everything to him.

"You should have abandoned the clubs at her door," he said.

"I was worried something might happen to them."

"In a place like that? I doubt it."

"She says her neighbors are ruffians."

"She will fit in well with them, then."

"I thought you were on her side."

"I am, but let's face it, fighting over a man like Ade. Marrying a man like him in the first place. She's not very smart."

He was inconsistent. Muyiwa Kasumu had another family because he needed a male heir, Abubakar Ibrahim's polygamous marriage was religious conservatism, and Niyi Ogedengbe was exempt from criticism because Pam was ill. Yet, had I found Moji Balogun dead in her flat, he might have suggested laying her coffin right at Ade's feet. Perhaps the problem was that Ade had no qualms about having affairs with married women. That would intimidate most men.

"You think I did the right thing by giving him Frances' address?" I asked.

"No one asked my opinion before," he said. "I'm just grateful you've told me about it."

"How many years did it take you to tell me about the Kasumus?"

"The Kasumus did not drag the United States of America into their marital ordeals."

I cried out in delight. "Lawal! Don't kill me!"

"Ade Balogun," he said, shaking his head. "You have to admire the man. He sent his wife packing after having an affair, and she's still attending to him on a Saturday morning. Meanwhile, what do I get from my own wife? 'I'm too tired.' Too tired even to dance. I don't know what you're going to her place for. She should be coming here to advise you."

"You're not well."

"Lazy woman."

"I'll show you who is lazy tonight."

"Please don't make empty threats."

Humor was everything to me. He knew that. He could get away with anything so long as he made me laugh.

We were late to visit Rotimi in school that afternoon, and of course I was back to feeling like a bad mother for not giving him priority yet again. We found out the colonel who was protesting his innocence had a son there. Rotimi knew the boy, but they were not in the same year. The boy's mother was *oyinbo*, he said, but he wasn't sure where she was from. I was again reminded of the Civil War, when it was hard to define the enemy. I asked Rotimi not to participate in any gossip about the colonel.

"We don't know if he is guilty or not," I said.

"Fair is foul, and foul is fair," he mumbled.

At first, I thought he was speaking school slang. Then I realized it was a quote from *Macbeth*, which he was studying in his English literature class. Everyone was in a dramatic frame of mind.

February 23

Naomi showed up at my shop on Monday afternoon in a Fulani cape no Nigerian woman I knew would wear. She had just returned from her medical expedition in the North. She'd stopped at Quintessence beforehand to buy a greeting card, which she carried in a logo shopping bag. Quintessence was owned by a Swedish woman who sold Nigerian arts and crafts.

"Harris-Mensah," I said. "Are you patronizing my competition?"

"Now, don't get upset," she said. "All you have here are imported cards, and you know I don't buy anything imported if I can help it."

We went to my office and she showed me the card, which was handmade with a watercolor of a Fulani milkmaid on the front. We were just teasing each other. I was friendly with the owner of Quintessence, and Naomi had once advised me to buy Afrocentric greeting cards from Harlem. I handed the card back to her, pleased to see her in one piece.

"So once again you've survived vaccinating unwilling villagers," I said.

"Since you put it that way."

She seemed relaxed, but then, she'd been in Lagos for only a week. The coup had cut her medical expedition short. She had not heard that Northerners considered it a Christian coup, but confirmed that there had been an exodus from North to South, and vice versa.

"I thought, Lord, please don't let us have another civil war on our hands," she said.

"I was worried, too, at first," I said. "But now, I doubt it will happen."

"Why?"

"The army's exhausted."

"They managed to arrange a coup."

"How many of them were involved? *Bo*, my sister, don't worry. Let's take it one day at a time."

"It's hard to. Every time I pick up a paper, there's news about the coup. I'm sure the government will soon execute the coup plotters. I just hope they won't do it on Bar Beach."

Bar Beach, apart from being a Sunday picnic spot, was also a venue for public executions.

I lowered my voice. "Hilda told me about Pam. How is she?"

"That's the worst news this year," Naomi said. "But…she's getting good care."

"And her children?"

"They're now staying with us. Kwesi has been through this before and has been parenting longer than I have, but the way I see it, I'm sure they just want to be back home with their mother. So let's keep praying for Pam."

"I will."

"They caught it early, so her chances are pretty good. We can't afford to think otherwise. If anything happens to her, you know me—I'll take those children in."

"Please, let's talk about something else."

Naomi was usually surrounded by medical academics, so she may not have realized I was afraid to talk about Pam's treatment.

She stretched. "Honestly, Remi, it's one coup after another. If this carries on, Nigeria will never be liberated."

"But we *are* liberated," I said.

"Not if you can't vote," she said. "I'm telling you, I just don't understand why people won't rise up and take a stand against military rule."

This was a departure for Naomi and me. She and Kwesi often argued about their experiences of living in each other's countries. Kwesi would point out American racism and say black Americans didn't always embrace him. Naomi would counter that Nigerians ostracized her and point out our tribalism. To me, they were no different from Tunde and me taking jabs at each other's clans. Naturally, I would side with Naomi and sometimes defuse tension by reminding Kwesi he wasn't even a bona fide Nigerian, on account of his Ghanaian ancestry.

"We just want good leaders," I said. "We don't care how they come about."

"Nigeria is a republic, though. You can't keep calling it one if it doesn't function as one."

What was it about hearing your flaws from outsiders? No matter how much you agreed with them, their criticism was hard to take. Perhaps that was the real test of whether you considered someone an insider or not. I was reluctant to make negative statements about the United States to Naomi, but their Civil Rights Movement wasn't that long ago and Kennedy's assassination had all the makings of an African coup.

I would never be as free in the United States as I was in Nigeria under military rule. You didn't have to achieve or own much in Nigeria to feel as privileged and powerful as a Kennedy or a Rockefeller. From the moment I got up in the mornings to the time I went to bed it was "Yes, madam, no madam, three bags full, madam." Where else in the world would I be entitled to that? How many Americans made use of their freedoms, anyway? How many could? How many actually bothered to vote? Certainly, the daily impositions in communist countries would be hard to take, but so would any sort of imposition. How could a government impose freedom, of all ideals, on other countries? Freedom as defined by them, for that matter. Was it acceptable to invade another country, kill innocent citizens, and depose and eliminate their leaders in the name of freedom?

Yes, the United States sometimes had a duty to intervene, and yes, we had terrible leaders in Africa, God-awful leaders we would be happy to be rid of. But everyone knew the United States picked and chose which countries to meddle with, so they had no right to lay claim to moral superiority. As for us in Nigeria, we could forget our history if all we did was exploit it to justify or glorify ourselves. We could also forget about our precious cultures and traditions, if they were unfair. It didn't matter what political systems we had because, until we valued and respected ourselves and each other, progress would continue to elude us.

"I'm hopeful about Nigeria," I said. "I'm sure you're hopeful about America."

"I'm not sure."

"No?"

"We have a long way to go, there."

"So do we."

Change would come, I thought. I didn't know when, but I was sure it would, if not in my children's lifetime, their children's. Maybe it would come with Africa's children striving together after all.

"Whatever happened to that Cooke woman, by the way?"

Naomi asked. "Has she gone back to the States?"

"Frances? I'm not sure, to be honest."

"I'm sorry, Remi, but I found her so rude. As for the business about the beads, I mean, it's one thing to say they are historically significant, but it's entirely another to try and downplay their history. I mean, who did she think she was talking to? She was so patronizing."

I was about to ask who Frances was to patronize us, but had to admit that if she were indeed spying, she would have had the upper hand. Naomi obviously hadn't heard about the melee at the golf club yet.

"You must have heard about the CIA allegations," I said.

"No."

"People thought she was spying."

"People said the same about me, remember?"

"What do you think?"

"How would anyone know if she was?"

I shrugged. Perhaps the allegations were a reflection of the extent to which Nigerians regarded Americans as strangers.

"I never asked where she stood on Angola."

"Oh, I knew where she stood, not that it mattered to me. We didn't have to have the same political opinions, but I was just upset she was so rude to Pam. In fact, I was kind of surprised she would go that far."

"That was uncalled for," I agreed.

"She doesn't know any better. People like her are not used to having their sense of superiority challenged. They think the world revolves around them, and they can't understand that other people might feel the same way. We were gracious to her, we really were. And you know what? If the tables were turned?"

"Not a chance?"

"Are you kidding me? She would never have reached out."

"You think I was wrong to?"

"No, that's who you are, Remi. You were the first woman in Lagos to befriend me. In fact, you were the only Nigerian woman I was friendly with for a while."

She was frank, and the Nigerian women she'd initially encountered didn't always appreciate that. I'd had to explain that what she thought was snobbery on their part was social laziness. An unwillingness to get to know anyone who looked, sounded or acted differently. Snobbery required some effort. Naomi would go on about black unity and they would roll their eyes. They considered that kind of talk too heavy for polite company. Malcolm X came to Nigeria in the sixties, and they welcomed him as a celebrity rather than a revolutionary. Martin Luther King was assassinated and they mourned him as they would a statesman. Miriam Makeba married Stokely Carmichael and they read about it in *Drum* magazine as though it were a society wedding covered in *Jet* magazine. They were barely unified as Nigerians. The idea of African unity was new to them. The idea of black unity was beyond them.

"Tunde thinks I shouldn't have bothered with her," I said.

Naomi smiled. "Well, husbands are always trying to reel us in. Whenever I go to the North, Kwesi acts as if I'm going on a crusade."

I wondered if she was being kind. Frances was a reminder of my public humiliation, the adult version of *chook-chook* plopping out of my pants. Naomi would be in a better position to assess Frances' political opinions. I'd assumed they were liberal on account of her views on marriage, but perhaps she valued freedom so much she was prepared to help her government enforce it somewhere else.

"Are you glad to be back?" I asked.

"You know how it is," she said. "You come home and it's bad news."

"Poor Pam."

"I'm telling you. Whenever I travel to the North, I try and convince people to put their faith in science. Then something like this happens and you realize science is not enough."

"People die from chemotherapy, don't they?"

"It's not always the cancer that kills you," she confirmed. "But you know what Pam said? She said it's the inconvenience that bothers her most. Before, she was talking about her children and all the things she could be doing for them. Now, she's talking about herself more, and all the things she could be doing. It makes you think. It makes you value your health and life more."

I thought about my father, who'd only had morphine to help him through his cancer. I never prayed he would survive because I knew he wouldn't. I actually prayed for him to die so he would be free of pain.

"Remember when a prayer was enough to make you feel safe?" I asked.

"Do I ever," Naomi said.

I was not doing well in my bid to be hopeful, and it was tempting to imagine living in a country like the United States. A country that could convince me it was possible to make the world safer for me.

February 25

I ran out of cooked food that week, so I bought meat from Sandgrouse Market—beef, mostly, and some chicken. Patience and I cut them in pieces and I left her to wash and bag them for the freezer. I was lamenting the spate of power cuts that had spoiled my last batch of frozen meat when she suggested I should have given it to her, instead of throwing it away. She would have boiled the meat to get rid of the germs, she said. I told her I wouldn't even feed spoiled meat to Duchess.

"Duchess is enjoying, ma," she said, laughing. "See where she's sleeping. See how she relax every day on de veranda. No work to do."

Now she was competing with Duchess. She'd never enjoyed our meat-cleaning days, which normally fell on Saturdays. She was just trying to make me feel guilty for giving her extra work to do during the week, but her suggestion did make me think. I remembered a time before freezers and fridges, when fresh meat was boiled, fried and then stewed. Meat kept in those days, and if it didn't, you ate it anyway.

On Wednesday evening, Tunde and I had just had dinner when Biola Kasumu called. Tunde answered the phone, and I found it strange that she immediately asked to speak to me. Normally, she would speak to him for a short while. I took the receiver from him thinking, What now?

"Are you at home tonight?" she asked, after we greeted each other.

"Yes," I said.

"Good. I'm coming over."

That was all she had to say. I wanted to ask why, but that would have been rude, so after I replaced the phone I questioned Tunde.

"How come you didn't speak to her?"

"She asked to speak to you."

"Why would she call before coming here?"

"I don't know."

"She sounded funny. She doesn't even have a car. How can she come here at this time of the night without a car?"

"Why not ask her when she comes?" he said.

We waited, and at about ten o'clock Biola arrived, carrying an overnight bag. She said she had come by taxi. She wore an *adire boubou*. No head tie. She had beautiful natural hair, which she wore in a single plait. She got it pressed at Hilda's salon every couple of weeks.

"What happened?" I asked, as she sat in Tunde's chair and he went upstairs.

"Can I stay here tonight?" she asked.

"Of course you can. But why?"

"I don't want Muyiwa to know where I am."

"You left home?"

I couldn't say she had left him. Why couldn't I say she had left him?

"He has gone to that woman's house again," she said. "This time, when he comes home, he won't find me waiting."

I wasn't prepared to get involved in another marital quarrel, that was why, and I would have appreciated an explanation for her past behavior, as well as an apology.

"I, Biola," she said, patting her chest, "I gave him three daughters, three lovely girls, and what does he do? He goes outside. Every time we are in Lagos he sees that woman and her son. I sent my girls to school in Ibadan so they wouldn't have to suffer what I suffer. Now he thinks it gives him license, so he goes for one day, two days. This time he went for three, at a time like this, after a coup, when I've just recovered from malaria. I cursed him. Yes, I did, and I cursed that woman and her son. He said I should leave his house, and I said, 'I'm not going anywhere.'"

I tried to imagine Muyiwa acting that way, but couldn't.

Biola continued. "He said I disrespected him. I asked him, 'What have you shown me all these years?' He couldn't answer. No, this time he went too far, so I told myself that for one night—one night, at least—I would disappear as he does, and he would not know where I was."

One night only? I thought.

She read my expression. "Where can I go with three children?"

I could have suggested she find herself a job, but she might take offense.

"Come," I said.

We went upstairs and I saw the strip of light below our bedroom door, which meant that Tunde was probably awake.

As we made the bed in the guest room, I apologized for the boxes there.

"I have to get rid of all this mess soon."

"I'm used to living with boxes," she said.

"I'll give them away when we move."

"When are you moving?"

337

"End of June."

We sat on the bed when we finished making it. I never had Biola's support during the Kuramo Fiasco. She treated me as if I were a shrew, telling me that Tunde was a strong man to put up with my behavior. I'd never understood women like her, who were tough enough to withstand the strains of their marriages, yet too weak to walk away. They were hostile to other women, yet they couldn't face up to their men.

"I can't wait to leave Lagos," she said.

"Won't things be worse in Spain?" I asked. "I mean, with no one to turn to."

"She's not there, and I don't want people here discussing my marriage."

"Trust me, there are many marriages to discuss before yours."

She faced me. "I hear there was some incident at the golf club involving you. Moji Balogun went there to beat up Ade's American girlfriend or something."

"Is that the story now?"

"Isn't it true?"

"It's true that I was there."

There was nothing I could do short of taking out a newspaper ad to declare my innocence.

"That woman is something," Biola said, shaking her head. "I wish I could disgrace Muyiwa like that."

"Are you sure you want to go to Spain with him?"

"I can't let her win."

Win what? I thought.

"How can you forgive him?" I asked.

"I'm not an angel."

"Neither is he."

That was as far as I would go about Muyiwa. Despite her

one-night rebellion and claim to behavior untoward, Biola was deferential to him.

"Tell Tunde I'm sorry for putting him in this position," she said.

"There's nothing to be sorry for."

"You're lucky to have a husband like him."

I could have said that Tunde was the lucky one, but that didn't seem appropriate, so I gave her a hug and went back downstairs to lock up.

Tunde was asleep when I returned to our bedroom. I shook his shoulder to wake him and told him what had happened.

"She can't stay here," he said.

I motioned to him to keep his voice down and whispered, "Why not?"

"Muyiwa is my friend."

"So what am I supposed to do? Send her home?"

"I'm sorry. I can't harbor another man's wife in my house."

"Tunde."

"What?"

"She's not a fugitive."

He threw his hands up. "It's not right. I can't do that to Muyiwa."

"That's good," I said. "Your friend has behaved badly, and all you can think of is defending him."

"I wouldn't want him to do that to me. Though, right now, I wish he would."

"His wife thinks you're nice. Everyone does. 'Oh, your husband is so wonderful.' 'Oh, you're so lucky to have him.' What lucky? What nice?"

For a moment, I actually wished he would do something dreadful, so people would stop insinuating I didn't deserve him.

Predictably, he sat up. "What do you want me to do?"

"Put yourself in her position."

"I would never be in that position."

"Exactly."

"Even if I were a woman."

"How would you know?"

"Because I have sense in my head."

"Okay, how would you feel if someone treated your daughter that way?"

"My daughter is twelve years old. Nobody is treating her that way."

"Is Biola not someone's daughter?"

"What do you want me to do?" he asked again. "Go to their house and speak to Muyiwa?"

"Are you mad? What will happen when they reconcile?"

"Remi, you have not told me what to do, and I'm losing patience."

I nodded. "You know what? It's all right. I don't even know why I bothered to wake you up. Go back to sleep."

"You were the one who said she was sneaky and conniving!"

His voice was so loud I was sure Biola could hear him, even with our air conditioning on.

"Keep. Your. Voice down."

"You said it! I didn't!"

"Will you keep your voice down?"

"No! I'm tired of this! What is wrong with all these people? Can't they control themselves?"

"Shush," I said, waving desperately. "It's only for one night."

He pointed. "One night only. That's all. After which, you send her home."

It was easy to forgive him. I didn't expect more from him.

I left our room and stood in the corridor for a moment, laughing silently. It wasn't just the people we knew; our whole country was out of control.

When I returned to the guest room, Biola was in bed in a pastel-pink nightgown.

"I hope Tunde isn't annoyed with me," she said, causing my heart to jump.

"Why would he be?"

"Men always stick together."

I smiled. "Then so should we."

In the morning, Tunde left home earlier than usual, before Biola woke up. Perhaps if he didn't see her, she'd never stayed in our house. I had breakfast with her. Oddly, I was more self-conscious than she was, fidgeting with the butter dish and knife. We talked about our children. Mine were coming home on Saturday. She was going to see her girls at school on Sunday. Their school was on the campus of the University of Ibadan and founded by the university and the Ford Foundation. Their curriculum followed the British system, but Biola wanted her girls to go to American universities. Tertiary education was more advanced in America at the master's level, she said. Again I wondered if that was Muyiwa's opinion, but it was convenient talk.

"That American lady," she asked. "How did you meet her?"

"At Oyinda's exhibition."

"Oyinda invited her?"

"She just showed up."

"And you became friends like that?"

"We went out a few times."

From where I sat, I could see Sylvia Plath's *Ariel* on my bookshelf, its spine upside down.

Biola shook her head. "You have time for strange women."

For a diplomat's wife, she was lazy about socializing. If people didn't fit a certain profile, they weren't worth her while. I was still disappointed in her. I couldn't even trust her, but she had my sympathy and loyalty. She continued to act as if nothing had happened the night before, so I behaved the same way, listening, talking and pouring cups of tea.

February 27

Ade called me at my shop on Friday morning. I hoped he was about to tell me that Frances had finally left town. Instead he said, "Last-minute talks between Nigeria and the United States have broken down."

"Why?" I asked, resignedly.

"Your friend says she can't trust my motives. She believes Moji and I are setting her up. I told her I have no reason to. Moji isn't even aware I'm in touch with her."

He thought it was better to keep Moji out of the matter. I could understand his reasoning, but not Frances'.

"Isn't she eager to get out of here?"

"She actually wants to leave tonight, but only on her terms, she says."

Why couldn't she go to the airport with the Millers? I wondered. Or were the Millers reluctant to get involved?

"So where do I come in?"

"You could take her to the airport, since she can't trust me."

"She doesn't trust me, either."

"She trusts you more than she trusts me."

"Well, I don't trust her."

"Why not make sure she leaves, then? If she's innocent, you'll be doing her a favor. If she's not, you'll be doing your country a favor."

His return to patriotism didn't surprise me. Nothing did anymore.

"That's fair," I said, after a moment's consideration.

"Should I tell her you'll accompany her?"

"Yes, but…she must come to my house. Alone."

I wasn't going to the Millers' flat, and they were certainly not welcome in my home.

"Thank you," Ade said. "I'll inform the United States about your position."

I called Tunde, expecting him to say I'd lost my mind, but hiding this latest development from him was out of the question.

"I don't see why not," he said. "In fact, I'll come with you to the airport."

"You will?"

"Yes. I personally want to make sure she leaves Nigeria."

It was the easiest agreement we had reached in a while. I wouldn't go as far as to call it an act of citizenship, but Frances' wouldn't be the first community-sanctioned expulsion from Lagos we'd heard about that involved the golf club. A year before, an Englishwoman had come to teach for a couple of years. She would probably have been called a spinster in England. In Nigeria, she was passed around from one military member of the club to another, until they all decided, for reasons unknown to us civilian members, that she was a threat to national security. They sent her packing before the end of her teaching term. Then there was the Swiss man who had several Nigerian business partners at the club. He was the target of jokes about Swiss banks' confidentiality until he offended people with his lack of discretion. He and his wife were eventually run out of town when someone threatened to expose their business dealings to the government.

Ade later called back to say Frances had agreed to go to the airport with me. Tunde and I arranged to come home earlier than normal to avoid the traffic on the mainland. I imagined Frances would do the same, so I asked Tunde to hurry up and change out of his work clothes when he got home. In his usual bid for privacy, he insisted on driving to the airport himself, so Jimoh wouldn't be around to witness should a problem arise with Frances.

He was upstairs when Jimoh came to the front door to say she had arrived. I asked Jimoh to transfer her luggage to the Volvo. She walked in carrying an old brown satchel and a navy jacket. The bruise on her eye had faded somewhat and she was back to being calm and composed, which was a relief, as our meeting was awkward enough.

"Nice to see you again," I said.

"Sorry I'm so early."

"Not a problem."

"The traffic on the bridge wasn't as slow as I expected."

"It gets slow round about..." I checked my watch. "About now, actually. It's better to leave early on a Friday, especially if you're going to the airport. How many suitcases do you have?"

"Just one."

"I'm sure you're ready to go home now," I said.

She nodded. "I am. The Millers are ready for me to go as well."

I didn't blame them, and any regrets I had about meeting her would eventually pass.

I was about to invite her to sit when Tunde cleared his throat. He stood at the top of the stairs, his French suit giving him an official air. He then walked down looking like Francisco Scaramanga, the dandy villain in *The Man with the Golden Gun*.

"Good evening," he said.

"Hello there," Frances said, casually.

"Every time I turn around you seem to have my wife's ear."

She gave him a puzzled look and his was the summation of every suspicion he'd had.

"He's driving us to the airport," I explained to Frances, as Tunde reached the foot of the stairs.

"I hope it's not too much trouble for you," she said.

"Not at all," he said.

Despite his theatrics, I wanted him to come with us. I preferred that he did the talking on the way. He led us out as he told her we called traffic "go slow" in Lagos. I sat in the passenger seat of his Volvo and Frances sat behind him. She might have been more receptive to him had he not prepared a long list of art-related trivia questions to try and catch her out. He asked about Benin bronzes and Osogbo artists. She gave just enough answers to substantiate her claims to having visited those places, yet Tunde repeatedly asked, "Really?"

He didn't stop until we reached the mainland, by which time it was dusk, and bearing in mind the trouble he had with his vision, I asked him to stop talking and pay attention to the road. We approached a checkpoint guarded by two armed officers, who waved us to a halt. Tunde and I rolled down our windows.

"It's better he handles them," I said to Frances.

I wasn't unduly worried about the checkpoint. The officers had a cavalier attitude, anyway.

"*Oga, sah*," the officer on Tunde's side of the car said. "To where?"

"The airport," Tunde said, politely.

"National or international?"

"International," Tunde said.

The officer saluted Frances. "*Oyinbo, una* welcome o!"

She may have realized he wanted money, but she took my advice and said nothing.

"*Wetin* do your eye?" he asked her, jovially. "*Abi*, you get Apollo?"

Conjunctivitis was common in the harmattan season, but the first major outbreak in Lagos had coincided with the Apollo moon landing.

The officer on my side laughed. "*Oyinbo* no fit get Apollo o!"

"We're taking madam to the airport," Tunde said.

He was irritated. He had to be to call Frances "madam."

"Sorry, *oga*," the officer by my window said, more seriously. "We have to check everybody during curfew hours."

In fact, we were outside the curfew hours, but Tunde complied as the first officer asked for his license, after which he pointed at Frances' satchel on the back seat.

"*Wetin dey* inside that bag?"

"Madam's particulars," Tunde said.

Predictably, the officer decided to waste our time.

"Make I see *am*," he said.

Frances handed her satchel to Tunde, who gave it to the officer. The officer pulled out her passport, opened it and returned it to her satchel. Then he pulled out her black journal. I got nervous as he opened that. What if it contained incriminating evidence? She could be detained. We could be detained for aiding and abetting her.

"My friend, we're in a hurry," Tunde said.

The officer returned the journal to Frances' satchel and handed the satchel back to her.

"*Oya*," he said, gesturing. "Begin go."

"Stupid man," Tunde said as he drove off.

"I'm surprised he could read," I said.

Frances put her satchel on the floor. "He was holding my journal upside down."

Luckily we were waved through the next checkpoint. At the airport, Tunde pulled up at the departure terminal, and Frances and I got out. A group of young men circled us. My first time at the airport with a foreigner and I hadn't anticipated their aggressiveness. Two of them got into a fight over who would carry Frances' suitcase.

"I beg, leave *am*!"

"You *dey* craze?"

"Come on, clear out of here!"

They jostled each other. Tunde stepped out of his car and retrieved the suitcase as their fight escalated. He chose the least belligerent of the bunch to carry it and fended off the rest as Frances and I hurried into the terminal.

While Tunde parked his car, Frances joined the Pan Am check-in queue and I stood by watching. Directly ahead of her was an elderly American man with the same stoic expression other foreigners had. The Nigerians appeared weary from being pushed and ordered around, except for a few first-class passengers who were not subjected to harassment. The departure terminal was stuffy because the air conditioning was not working.

Frances lost patience with a woman who tried to jump the queue by stepping in front of her.

"You can't do that, ma'am," she said.

"Mothers with children have priority," the woman said.

"Not until we board the flight," Frances said.

To be fair to her, the woman was traveling with her two

sons and a baby girl. One of her sons ran the baby's pram over Frances' foot, and the baby began to cry.

Frances recovered her calm demeanor until a luggage handler slammed her suitcase on the scales.

"Sir," she shouted. "There are breakable items in there."

"Easy, madam," he said.

"Your passport and ticket, please," the agent behind the desk said, lazily.

"He can't treat my belongings that way," Frances said to her. "If anything happened to the contents, you'll be hearing from me."

I couldn't wait for her to leave. She attracted trouble. You couldn't always insist on your rights in a country like Nigeria. It didn't matter where you were from. You had to recognize your limits.

She checked in and we headed for the departure hall, at the entrance of which Tunde was waiting.

"Are we set?" he asked.

Frances fanned her face with her boarding card. "You know, I've passed through a lot of airports, but this has been an experience."

"We like it that way," Tunde said, with a smile. "It discourages rogue visitors from coming back."

I was embarrassed. To me, the chaos at the terminal was a sign that we were slipping back under the new regime. It was hard to discern passengers from loiterers as they brushed past us. We said goodbye to Frances and watched her pass through the various airport checks. She presented her passport and boarding card to a couple of officers. One of them returned her passport and she joined the queue for security. When it was her turn, a female officer patted her down. That over, she picked up her satchel and navy jacket and headed for the departure gate.

"She doesn't have much to say for herself," Tunde said, once she was out of sight.

February 28

That year was a leap year, and Sunday the 29th was the last day of February. Rolari and Rotimi came home on Saturday morning. Rolari needed a new mosquito net because hers had a hole. She could easily patch up the hole, but after Rotimi's bout of malaria, I was taking no chances, so I gave in to that. She also wanted to get a low cut at Hilda's salon. I said she wasn't allowed. She said low cuts were in. I said I didn't care if they were in or out. The moment she got her hair cut, she would want it long again. She said her hair would be easier to maintain if it were short. I ignored her until she said she might have head lice.

"My hair is scratching me," she claimed. "I have to get it cut for hygienic reasons."

"We could always douse it with methylated spirits," I suggested.

"Yes," Rotimi said, "and set her whole head on fire."

All he wanted to do was eat and sleep. I asked if he'd had too many late nights in school and he answered, "Not really," like a guilty so-and-so.

"Do boarders sneak out at night?" I asked.

They called it "jumping fence," but I would get no information from him if I used school slang.

"I don't know," he said.

"Some must."

He shrugged. "Maybe."

"Like who?" I asked. "The seniors? Where do they go? Plaza Cinema? Fela's Shrine?"

"Mummy, I said I don't know."

Rolari interrupted. "Seniors don't break bounds in my school. They'd get suspended."

Rotimi eyed her. "Who asked you?"

If he were not doing well in school, I would have strip-searched him for drugs. He was sleeping again when Rolari called a couple of her classmates and arranged to meet them at the Ice Cream Pavilion. She came to the shopping center with me in her new platform mules, and this time she didn't trip. She looked so proud of herself, walking around in them. I hoped her confidence would carry her through her teens.

Festus asked about her studies, and for the first time I learned that she was not looking forward to taking physics, chemistry and biology in her third year. I told her to concentrate on arts subjects so she could become a lawyer, like my brother. She said she didn't want to be a lawyer, she wanted to be a judge. It occurred to me that I would have been a terrible ambassador. I didn't have enough patience. I wasn't even diplomatic. I could barely anticipate people's behavior, let alone understand their motives. I was an educator at heart. All I did was instruct people. I advised Festus to go back to university to get a master's degree in English and promised to sponsor him. He said he would consider applying the next academic year.

He had been to Ashake Dada's house that morning, and she had finally paid for the cards she'd ordered for her wedding anniversary. He had also left a package in my office. He didn't know who it was from, but Boniface had accepted it. I went to my office to check and the package turned out to be a cardboard box so small it could only accommodate a pendant. I opened it to find a single blue bead with red and white patterns. It was accompanied by a gift card with a handwritten message saying, "A thousand flowers."

I picked up the bead as Rolari walked in.

"Ooh, what is that?" she asked.

"A millefiori bead," I said.

"Ooh, who from?"

"A woman called Frances Cooke."

"Your American friend?"

I frowned. "Who told you she was my friend?"

She babbled on, slipping in and out of school slang and twitching. "Remember the girl I fought with? She's such an *irriti*. She's trying to be my friend now because nobody will talk to her. She follows me everywhere. I wish she would just leave me alone. She's so *despi*. I can't be your friend once you've betrayed me, so it's *pax Romana* to her."

Her father must have told her what happened. I wanted to say grown women didn't fight, but that wouldn't have been true.

"So Daddy's been complaining about me," I said.

"Of course," she said, as if he were entitled to. "Is America behind the coup?"

"I have no idea, dearest."

Once in a while I was surprised by my wisdom, but not in this instance, and I didn't want her to worry. Rolari was a chronic worrier. During the Civil War she worried our house would be bombed. Before that, she worried that Nigeria would be obliterated should the Soviet Union and the United States engage in a nuclear war.

I gave her five naira to spend at the Ice Cream Pavilion. After she left, I put the bead in my bag thinking how much it resembled Frances, single and unattached.

Later that afternoon, Tunde and I took Rolari and Rotimi back to school. On our way to Queen's we stopped at Sabo Market to buy Rolari a new mosquito net, and I used the opportunity to buy groundnut oil and palm oil.

In the evening, when our house had fallen silent, I showed Tunde the bead. We were in the sitting room, having had dinner. He was in his chair and I sat on his armrest as he inspected it.

"Does this mean she might still be in Nigeria?" he asked.

"Of course not," I said. "She probably asked the Millers to deliver it to me."

"I bet it's fake."

I grabbed it from him before he could bite it.

"To think Africans sold each other for that," he said.

"Obviously we valued glass more than we valued each other."

"Africans. We're so stupid. We're always selling ourselves short."

He suggested I throw the bead away because it was an insult to humanity. I thought it deserved to be in the guest room with the rest of my knick-knacks. Poor man. It wasn't that I didn't value his opinions; I just didn't believe that his mattered more than mine. My love for him was constant, a given. My will, on the other hand, I could not vouch for.

MARCH

March in Lagos, and the harmattan season is over. In the mornings and evenings the air is less brisk, and the haze of dust from the north begins to subside. The dry heat of the afternoons takes on a mugginess that lasts most of the year. So it was in 1976, and like the transient weather, we had some clarity, but the matter of who was behind General Muhammed's assassination still remained.

If the attack on the British High Commission was anything to go by, then the British were instrumental, not the Americans. The British High Commissioner issued a press statement about the damage to his property, which only caused a public furor. He was subsequently recalled to London. The new regime requested that Britain extradite General Gowon, who was still in exile, but Britain refused to. General Gowon denied any hand in the coup, and Lieutenant Colonel Dimka was apprehended within Nigeria before he was able to escape. He was one of the thirty-odd coup plotters who were later executed, some at Kirikiri Prison and others on Bar Beach.

I read about the executions on Bar Beach the day after they took place. Photos of the dead men were all over the newspapers. They were given the last rites, Christian and Muslim, and faced a firing squad as crowds of spectators watched. Some doubt lingered as to whether the colonel with a son at King's College was guilty. Sadly, his wife committed suicide after his execution. The story I heard was that she was so bereft she drove her car into an oncoming truck.

By then the exodus to the East had stopped, according to the Onyias. I would have liked to find out from the Ibrahims if people up north really thought the coup was a Christian one, or if that was just another rumor. For us in Lagos, our knowledge of the events surrounding the coup had come down to public speculation. We talked about the people involved as if we knew them personally because they were friends, neighbors and colleagues of people we did know.

Aunty Eugenia died on the day of the coup. Yes, she died in her sleep less than a week after her soirée. I didn't hear about her death until March. Her obituary got lost in those for General Muhammed. There was a wake for her, and she was buried in Ikoyi Cemetery. I was miserable the day I found out. It was as if an era had passed. I went to see her sister-in-law Aunty Regina, to give my condolences, and from then on developed a friendship with her I couldn't explain, except that it was consistent with my affinity for strange women. She praised her late brother Antonio "of blessed memory" and pronounced Aunty Eugenia a snob. "I miss her," she said, "and one shouldn't speak ill of the dead, but there it is."

She was in such a sorry state. Fatimoh, who wasn't a relative, had run away. Bode's wife was trying to get her evicted from the house, and Bode was apparently too much of a gentleman to intervene. His wife had given Aunty Regina notice, after which she would remove, in her words, "all the rubbish in that house" and cart it off to the nearest dump. She was referring to the crockery.

I found Aunty Regina a new housegirl and spoke to Ade about her eviction notice. Ade was disgusted with Bode. "That man never had balls," he said. He called Bode and threatened to sully his reputation more than his wife already had, and Aunty Regina was spared.

After this, I could do no wrong in her eyes. She still couldn't remember my parents, but she would tell me they had raised me well. Whenever I was traveling to London, I would call to ask if she needed any provisions, and she would religiously ask for tinned apricots. Tunde, amused by my friendship with her, referred to her as Aunty Tally-ha, Aunty Tilly-ho, anything but her correct nickname. One day I said, "Actually, the correct term is 'tally-ho,'" and he said, "Sorry, but English is not my mother tongue."

I saw his girlfriend Oyinda about a month after the coup. She was at a photography exhibition at the Kuramo Hotel, a black-and-white collage of different views of Lagos. The photographer was a Nigerian journalist, and not surprisingly most of the guests were expatriates. Oyinda was with the Frenchman who had accompanied her to the fashion show in January.

"Have you met Pascal?" she asked.

"Not yet," I said.

He had dark-brown eyes and tobacco-stained teeth. He frowned as I shook hands with him. What was it about the French? I thought. Why couldn't they just fake a smile? Even when they were polite, you got the impression their aim was to show you lacked manners.

"He thinks we're on the brink of another civil war," Oyinda said. "But of course we're not. No need to fret, eh, Pascal? Everything is just fine."

He shrugged. "*Bien sur.*"

He was impatient with her, as a son might be about his mother's undue attention.

"How is Tunde?" she asked.

"Perfect," I said.

She winked. "He's a hard man to pin down. You must remind him to fund me."

Oyinda was not interested in Nigerian men. She certainly wasn't confrontational enough to challenge Nigerian women. She had qualities that few of us possessed: an ability to accept her circumstances and an absence of judgment I found admirable. She also had more money and time on her hands than most of us, but there was something fine about spending that on artists and celebrating their works. Her exhibition had been postponed until further notice. I promised her I would remind Tunde to make sure Community Bank provided funding for future Cultural Society events.

I traveled to London in mid-March that year. The international airport in Lagos had been renamed after General Muhammed, and Harold Wilson had recently resigned as prime minister of Britain. I stayed at St. Ermin's Hotel in Westminster and made my usual pilgrimage to Oxford Street. There, I got Tunde his new glasses, bought ties for him from Selfridges and greeting cards from John Lewis and Dickins & Jones. I asked around for records our children wanted. For Rolari, the single "Shake Your Booty" and for Rotimi, the album *Rastaman Vibration*. Neither record had been released yet, and they were both disappointed when I returned to Lagos, despite the other gifts I brought them.

Easter drew close, and they came home from school. We visited my brother Deji and his family in Ibadan, after which I began to clear out the guest room in preparation for our move to the new house. I donated the contents of my boxes to the orphanage, and that was when I remembered Frances' bead. I was still not sure whether she was involved in any espionage while in Nigeria, but I doubted that any intelligence she might have collected would enlighten her country. I had always thought Americans had access to all the information in the world, yet remained uninformed about the rest of the world, that they were confident as well as insecure. Foreigners in general were quick to call Nigerians arrogant, but what I observed in Lagos was a shocking lack of confidence. We had a history that was largely undocumented until it was interrupted after all, and no clue as to how to govern ourselves. Our society was backed by new currency; men had to learn to play by foreign rules; and women were in two minds about which traditions to follow. Yet, despite our disagreements, rivalries and betrayals, we resorted to one another. The Baloguns were together again, so were the Kasumus, who finally got their posting to Spain.

I, too, had come to the end of an interim stay of sorts, since Tunde and I had reached an agreement. He accepted that I could no longer be limited to running our home, because I would never be content to. I accepted that I would never be able to meet my own mother's standards while managing a business. In retrospect, perhaps I'd hoped to attain my father's by distancing myself from the people on whom my business depended, but I was neither my father's daughter nor my mother's in the end.

I had a card shop in a shopping center that resembled one in a residential neighborhood overseas. What had Frances called it? A mall? I sold mostly imported goods. I was not out of place in Lagos; I was of the place and could not separate myself from it, as much as I tried, and I had tried. Was it possible for a stranger with questionable intentions to come here, meet me, see that as a weakness and take advantage?

Yes, it was, but she had introduced herself as a bead collector, and in my less partial moments that was how I chose to remember her. I only wished I'd had a chance to confess that I was no different from the people I'd told her about.

Acknowledgements

Much gratitude and thanks to everyone who contributed to the publication of this book: Markeda Wade, Tade Ipadeola, Sarah Seewoester Cain, Hilary Plum, Sue Tyley, John Fiscella, Pam Fontes-May, Whitney Sanderson, Cassie Sanderell, and Michel Moushabeck. Thanks also to my husband Gboyega Ransome-Kuti and our daughter Temi for their love and companionship.